Praise for the Kitty Norville Series

"Vaughn's deft touch at characterization and plot development has made this series hugely entertaining and not to be missed!" —*RT Book Reviews*

"The open nature of Kitty's character and the way Vaughn makes her such a likable character make this the only urban fantasy world where I want to read every book of the series." —*The Denver Post*

"With the Kitty series, Vaughn has demonstrated a knack for believable characters (even if they are werewolves) and mile-a-minute plotting."
—*Sunday Camera* (Boulder, CO)

"A great series for fans of the recent werewolf-vampire craze who want to move beyond Stephenie Meyer or Charlaine Harris."
—*The Daily News* (Galveston County, TX)

"Vaughn's a skilled writer and has provided a well-paced, breezy outing. . . . An entertaining action story." —*Realms of Fantasy* on
Kitty's Big Trouble

"Kitty is an empathetic character and smart as can be in this fast-moving urban fantasy."
—*Booklist* on *Kitty Goes to War*

"Suspenseful and interesting."
—*The Denver Post* on
Kitty's House of Horrors

Kitty
Rocks the House

CARRIE VAUGHN

TOR®

A TOM DOHERTY ASSOCIATES BOOK
NEW YORK

KITTY ROCKS THE HOUSE

Copyright © 2013 by Carrie Vaughn, LLC

A Tor Book
Published by Tom Doherty Associates, LLC
175 Fifth Avenue
New York, NY 10010

www.tor-forge.com

Tor® is a registered trademark of Tom Doherty Associates, LLC.

ISBN 978-0-7653-6867-6

Tor books may be purchased for educational, business, or promotional use. For information on bulk purchases, please contact Macmillan Corporate and Premium Sales Department at 1-800-221-7945 extension 5442 or write specialmarkets@macmillan.com.

First Edition: April 2013

Printed in the United States of America

0 9 8 7 6 5 4 3 2 1

For Emery Anne Vaughn

The Playlist

Sister Sledge, "We Are Family"

Jefferson Airplane, "My Best Friend"

Buddy Holly, "(You're So Square) Baby, I Don't Care"

Fanny, "You're the One"

The Ditty Bops, "Walk or Ride"

They Might Be Giants, "Older"

The Cure, "A Strange Day"

Creedence Clearwater Revival, "I Put a Spell on You"

Rasputina, "You Don't Own Me"

Erasure, "Hideaway"

Pentangle, "The Time Has Come"

La Santa Cecilia, "La Negra"

Chapter 1

F OR ALL the death I'd seen, I'd been to very few funerals.

This one was fraught, and I couldn't sort out my feelings, or what I was supposed to be feeling. Grandma Norville had fallen and broken her hip three months ago, but the pneumonia she caught after had been the final culprit. I kept thinking I should have been there. I could have come to visit one more time if I hadn't been so busy, if I'd just made the effort. But I thought she'd hang on longer. I thought she'd always be here. How selfish was it, to feel guilty at someone's funeral, as if her passing were somehow my fault, or a personal inconvenience? I was sad, nostalgic, tired, shell-shocked.

Mostly, I was worried about my father. He seemed tall and stoic enough, his chin up, eyes dry. Mom held her arm wrapped around his and kept a tissue close to her eyes. He didn't seem to be looking at anything, though. Not the flower-drenched casket, not the dark-suited minister, not the sky or grassy lawn with its rows of modern, polished headstones. I couldn't tell what he was thinking. I couldn't ask.

The service was graveside, the springtime Arizona weather was reasonable—sunny, but windy. I kept squinting against dust in the air. The crowd gathered was small, incongruously young. All of Grandma's friends, siblings, and her husband had gone before her. All that was left were her three kids, their families, and a couple of staff from her retirement home. It had been a quiet ceremony.

My husband Ben and I had driven all night to get here. We stood a little apart from the others. Not so much as to be noticeable, but enough to be comfortable for us. Werewolves didn't do so well in groups, even ones as small as this. Especially when we were off balance. We stood side by side, our hands entwined. Ben had never even met Grandma. He was here to look out for me. A rock to stand next to. He'd pulled out polish, combing the scruff out of his light brown hair and wearing his best courtroom lawyer suit with a muted navy tie. I'd had a terrible time packing, convinced that all my clothes were inappropriate for the situation. I'd settled on a black skirt and tailored cream blouse for the service, and pinned my blond hair up in a twist. I looked like a waitress.

The rest of the family had flown ahead of us. My sister Cheryl's husband, Mark, had stayed home with their two kids. Standing next to Mom, hugging herself, Cheryl seemed small in her dress suit, which she probably hadn't worn since before she was pregnant with Nicky, eight years ago now. She was staring at the flowers with a wrinkled, worried frown.

The minister, a nondenominational chaplain from the retirement home, spoke in a calm, inoffensive voice. He'd started with a Bible verse, the one about walking in the valley of shadows and not fearing evil, and dispensed comforting words of wisdom that might have come from the lyrics of a sixties folk song.

What would the guy say if I told him that I'd had proof that people existed in some form after death? He'd probably say, of course. He was a minister, after all. I had proof of life after death. But I couldn't say I believed in heaven or hell. I still didn't know what exactly happened to us after we died. What had happened to my grandmother.

When people at the funeral told me that my grandmother had gone to a better place, did I believe them? I believed that part of her lived on. But I couldn't say where she was. Was she here, watching us mourn for her? I resisted an urge to call out loud to her, just in case. Was the cemetery filled with the shadows of the dead, all of them watching?

I'd met beings who claimed to be gods. Were they, or were they just powerful people who had existed for thousands of years and so built up a tangle of stories around them, and in those stories they became gods?

When the minister called on his own God, did he really know who he was praying to?

In matters of faith, I couldn't believe in much of anything anymore. I had my family who loved me, my friends I could count on, and that was about it. Everything else—I saw the signs, but I didn't know what they meant. All I could do was focus on the road in front of me.

The chaplain said his amens, the rest of us echoed him, he closed his book, and that was that. I decided Grandma would have been disappointed with the whole thing. She'd have wanted something big and grand in a cathedral, with organ music. But this wasn't for her, it was for the rest of us. Funny how we all seemed so anxious. I wasn't sure having a chance to say good-bye at a funeral was any better than not having a chance to say good-bye, when the people you loved were snatched away in front of you without ceremony.

We filed back to the cars parked along the curb,

leaving the flowers and casket behind. The earth that would fill in the grave had been discreetly hidden away during the ceremony, and would be brought back after we'd all left. I spotted the cemetery employees who would do the deed lurking behind a well-groomed hedge, waiting.

I squeezed Ben's hand before letting go and trotted forward to catch up to my dad.

"Dad? You okay?"

He smiled a sad smile, putting his arm around my shoulders and pulling me close to give me a kiss on the top of my head. Without a word, he let me go and kept walking on with my mother.

So what did that mean?

My aunt, Dad's younger sister, was hosting a lunch—catered, I found out after discretely poking among my cousins, which was a relief. Friends had been bringing over mountains of food as well. I didn't want to find out anyone had been cooking for everybody, but no one had. A little less guilt there. I slipped my cousins some money to help with the cost. Wasn't much else I could do. Ben got directions to their house; I'd never been there. I was close to my immediate family, but I didn't see the extended family that often. Weddings and funerals, and that was it. Another cliché in a day filled with them.

Before we reached the car, I took a last look over the cemetery's green slope, toward the row of folding chairs and the mountain of flowers that marked Grandma's grave. Said a farewell, just in case she was hanging around, and just in case she could hear.

Ben had stopped a few yards away from me and gazed off to a stand of bordering trees. Two figures, a man and a woman, were standing there.

"You see that?" he said, nodding toward them.

"Yeah. They just keeping an eye on us or do they want to make trouble?"

"You want to find out?"

"I kind of do," I said, and we started toward them.

They'd put themselves upwind so we'd be sure to catch their scents: musky, odd. Werewolves and foreign—not part of our pack. He was a big, burly Latino; she was young and motherly, her dark hair in a ponytail, a gray cardigan over her jeans and blouse. When we approached within speaking distance, they lowered their gazes. She started fidgeting, shuffling her feet—pacing, almost.

"You must be Andy and Michelle," I said.

She blushed and smiled; he nodded, only raising his gaze to us for brief moments. The werewolf pair had gone submissive, which was a little unnerving—they were the alphas of the Phoenix pack, strong and dominant. I'd been able to send a message ahead to warn them we were coming, that we had no intentions of invading, and could we please have permission to stay in their territory for as long as we needed for the funeral? They'd sent a welcoming message back. I wasn't sure we'd even meet them while we were here, or if they'd keep their distance.

"Thanks," Ben said. "For letting us pass through. I hope it hasn't caused any trouble."

"Oh, no," Andy said. "I hope *you* haven't had any trouble. You haven't, have you? You have everything you need? Is there anything else we can do for you? A place to run, maybe?"

"No," Ben said. "Full moon's not for another week, fortunately."

"Ah, good," Michelle said. "I mean, not good—I'm really sorry about your grandmother."

My polite smile was feeling awfully stiff. "Thanks. We'd probably better get back to it. We'll let you know if we need anything. Really." I started backing away slowly.

"It's nice meeting you," Michelle said. She was so earnest I could almost see her tail wagging. "I mean—you're not really what we expected."

"What did you expect?" I said.

She ducked her gaze. "Well, you both look so friendly. I guess we expected you to be . . ."

"Tougher. Tougher *looking*," Andy finished. His smile appeared as strained as my own felt. "Given some of the stories we've heard."

"Ah," I said. "I think some of those stories exaggerate."

"Even so. It's still pretty impressive."

I shuddered to think. Exactly what did I look like from the outside, anyway? I was just a talk radio host. A werewolf talk radio host who'd publically declared war on a shadowy vampire conspiracy. Alrighty, then.

"Thanks again," Ben said. "We'll be out of your territory in a couple of days."

Their smiles suddenly seemed relieved. Ben and I waved good-bye and walked back to the cars.

I frowned. "They've been keeping an eye on us the whole time we've been here, haven't they? Just to make sure we wouldn't start a fight."

"Seems likely." His smile was amused, his hands shoved in the pockets of his suit jacket. I was a little offended that he wasn't more worried, or at least insulted.

"They acted like I might try to eat them. When did I become such a badass?"

"Your reputation precedes you," Ben said.

"I don't even know what reputation that is anymore. I don't even recognize myself, the way they were looking at me."

"Don't let it go to your head."

"On the contrary, I think I'd rather ignore it completely." I wouldn't know how to act like the badass tough they'd expected.

Cheryl was watching our approach from the edge of the groups of relatives still lingering and talking.

There was one person who'd never see her little sister as a badass.

"Do you know them?" she asked. Andy and Michelle were walking away, into a different section of the cemetery.

"Not really," I said, and left it at that.

"You're kinda weird, you know that?"

"I'm a *werewolf*," I said, glaring. "Trust me, Cheryl, you don't want to know."

She rolled her eyes at me.

It wasn't until the reception was almost over, after Mom, Dad, and Cheryl had already left for their hotel room, after I'd said good-bye to all the relatives without knowing when I was going to see any of them again—we made noises about a family reunion, or maybe a big wedding anniversary celebration, or something—and Ben and I were walking out to our car, parked at the curb a block down the street, that I started crying. The tears burst, all at once, without warning, soaking my cheeks. I choked on a blubbering breath I couldn't quite seem to catch.

Stopping, I squeezed my eyes shut and held my nose in an effort to stop the stinging.

"Kitty?" Ben had gone on a few more steps before looking back.

I took a deep, stuttering breath that staved off the waterworks. "I'm fine. It just got me for a second."

He took my hand and leaned close, not to kiss me,

but to let his breath play over my neck. His touch, the scent of him, calmed me. I was safe, I was protected. We stood like that for a moment, taking comfort in each other's presence.

"I'll drive, okay?" he said finally.

"Okay."

I slouched in the passenger seat, watching the suburban tract housing pass by as we drove away. I turned over the thought that had pushed me over the edge, had triggered the grief I'd kept at bay for the last few days. Grandma had always called me Katherine, refusing any less dignified nickname. Never mind that I hadn't displayed a lot of dignity as a kid. To her, I was Katherine.

Then it hit me: now, the only people in the world who'd call me Katherine were vampires with an overdeveloped sense of decorum. It was enough to make anyone cry.

Chapter 2

SOON AFTER returning to Denver, I had a meeting in the basement of a downtown art and antiques gallery. The gallery, Obsidian, was a front, disguising the vampire hideout of the Master of Denver. In a room that looked way too much like an average suburban living room to be part of a vampire hideout, I sat on a sofa with Rick, looking over the coffee table at our visitor.

The vampire sitting in the armchair across from us defied classification. Nasser was Master of Tripoli. He appeared to be in his midthirties, and had an imposing presence—long face, serious frown, and dark, simmering eyes. His dark hair and beard were perfectly trimmed, aristocratic. He looked like he should have been riding camels with Peter O'Toole. But instead of flowing white robes, he wore a charcoal gray three-piece suit with a white shirt and conservative burgundy tie. The style of it should have dated him, making him seem more at home in the 1950s than the modern era. Instead, Nasser was timeless. He'd be at home anytime, anyplace, and pinning an age to him became impossible. Rick thought he was at least a thousand years old. That he'd come to Denver himself instead of sending a minion said something about how important this was to him. I was flattered, and wary. He'd brought an entourage of sorts, a trio of male vampire bodyguards who looked the part, with linebacker physiques and dark suits. They waited outside, sizing up Rick's own entourage, the vampires of his Family.

Rick's apparent age was thirty or so. He had refined features and an elegant bearing; he made his dark silk shirt and tailored trousers look good. Though he was some five hundred years old, he'd held the position of Master for only a few years, which made him a newcomer compared to someone like Nasser. But the visitor regarded him as an equal, without a bit of condescension in his voice.

He drew a pendant from an inner jacket pocket and set it on the coffee table before Rick and me. "I'm given to understand that you've seen one of these before?" His accent was crisp.

The pendant was a bronze coin about the size of a nickel, worn and darkened with age. Whatever image had once appeared on it was mangled beyond recognition, smashed flat and scored in furious crosshatches.

I nodded. "Several, actually."

His lips pressed thoughtfully, he glanced at Rick for confirmation.

"They're Dux Bellorum's marks of . . . ownership, I suppose you'd say," Rick said. "His followers wear them. They bind them to him. Where did you find yours?"

"It belonged to one of my predecessors. A group of us mounted a coup against him, oh, quite some time ago now."

I leaned forward. "How long ago? I mean for you, exactly how long ago is that?"

"She's very concerned with precision of timekeeping, isn't she?" Nasser said to Rick.

"It's an obsession with her," he said, shrugging with his hands, and I scowled at them both.

I had four of the mangled coins sealed in a jar and locked in the safe at New Moon, the downtown restaurant Ben and I owned. The place was the spiritual, if not actual, center of our territory, and we'd had some evidence that vampires couldn't cross the threshold without permission. Roman—Dux Bellorum—shouldn't be able to track them there. Destroying the image was supposed to break the spells attached to them. But you could never be too careful about this sort of thing.

Maybe we should have just thrown the things away, or melted them down. But I was keeping them as if they were some kind of perverse forensic evidence that we didn't yet have the means to understand. They might be able to tell us more about their creator someday, and I couldn't throw away a tool like that.

That Nasser had kept his encouraged me that I'd made the right decision.

I said, "I keep thinking there must be a way to use the magic in these against him."

Nasser shook his head. "I've searched for a wizard or magician who could do such a thing, and haven't found one. I think such a thing is impossible."

"No, I don't believe that. I've got a couple of leads," I said.

I had my own networks, my own resources to tap when a supernatural problem presented itself. Tina McCannon, resident psychic for the TV show *Paradox PI,* hadn't known anything about the coins off-hand, but offered to scry for information. She'd handle the coins herself the next time she was in Denver. Odysseus Grant, a magician hiding in plain sight with his own Vegas stage show, knew about the Long Game and what it meant. He offered to research the coins as well, but hadn't found anything yet. Then there was Cormac, right here in Denver.

Nasser furrowed a skeptical brow, and who could blame him? If a thousand-year-old vampire couldn't find a powerful wizard, could a loudmouth nearly-thirty werewolf do it?

"Even if we can't find a way to use them," Nasser said, "they are proof that Roman can be defeated. His followers can be defeated. There are many more like us, who do not wish to trade our autonomy for power, to sacrifice ourselves to some arcane war. No matter what great reward was promised to us."

"What great reward is that?" I asked.

"Dominion over humanity," he said matter-of-factly. "We emerge from the shadows, not to live as equals among the mortals, but to rule over them as a shepherd does his flock."

I'd heard vague gossip along those lines for years. The rumors were easy to dismiss because they sounded like something out of a bad thriller. But having met Roman, having fought him and his followers, I could well believe that this was their goal.

It would be easy to sit back and scoff that this could never happen, that vampires would never accomplish such an outrageous objective. Mortal humans outnumbered them. But Roman's vampires had a plan. They were slowly coming into the public eye. Broadway star Mercedes Cook had publicly declared herself a vampire—she was one of Roman's. A respected historian had published a book of interviews with vampires giving their eyewitness accounts of great events in history—the defeat of the Spanish

Armada, the Battle of Agincourt, the army of Genghis Khan. That one infuriated me—I'd have given any of those vampires an interview slot on my show. But I had a feeling they were all followers of Roman, which meant they'd never talk to me. They were building public trust—promoting themselves, promoting vampires in general. Getting on the good side of public opinion, inserting themselves into pop culture— probably exerting influence over the politicians of a dozen countries as well. If . . . when . . . if vampires managed to take over, they'd probably convince us it was humanity's idea to let them do so all along.

If they succeeded, vampires like Roman and his followers would make werewolves their slaves, their enforcers in this new world order. I couldn't let that happen; I had a pack to protect.

So we gathered allies of our own. As Nasser said, many vampires didn't want to trade their autonomy for some future, nebulous power. They didn't want to be in Roman's debt, or wear his coins.

"Can it really happen?" I asked. "How close is it to happening?"

"I don't know," Nasser said, which wasn't comforting. "He has been traveling across Europe, Asia, the Middle East, and North Africa for two thousand years. The Americas and Australia, he does not have such a firm hold on. He's sent followers and has come here himself only recently. Only a few cities in South

America have Families—I hesitate to guess how many of them owe their allegiance to Dux Bellorum. I'm also not certain of Australia. As far as I know, no vampires live in Antarctica."

"I'd have thought the long winter nights would be just the thing for you guys," I said.

"Perhaps. But the food supply is a bit wanting."

I didn't want to think about that too hard.

Nasser went on, "For centuries, the few of us who knew of him, who knew of his plans, have worked in secret. We couldn't investigate him and his followers, or we'd risk retribution. Roman is ruthless, and he strikes from afar, sending his followers. But now—I hardly know what to think. We are moving into the open. We have some initiative. We have you to thank for that."

"Don't thank me," I said. "I may have just blown our cover. Given them a target."

His smile was thin. "Oh no. They have chosen to battle in the arena of public discourse, that is where we will face them."

"Organized resistance exists, then," Rick said. "What can we do to help?"

"For now, we need aid and support for those of us who travel, who move from city to city in an effort to identify his followers. Often, we can inspire the followers of a city's Master to rebel, to free their Family from Dux Bellorum's influence."

"Anastasia worked on this," I said.

"Yes. There are a few others, like her. Have you heard from her? I haven't had word of her in years."

Now, that was a story. "She's . . . not with us anymore."

"That's . . . that's terrible news. How was she destroyed?"

"She wasn't. I mean, she's not dead. *Dead* dead. She . . . there was this goddess, see, and . . . and I prefer to think of her as battling evil in another dimension." I blinked hopefully; he regarded me blankly, nonplussed. "Never mind. I'm sorry, I know that doesn't make a whole lot of sense. She's fine, really. She's just not *here*."

The perplexed lilt to his brow indicated that my explanation hadn't helped at all.

"That's unfortunate," he said. "She was a good ally."

"I think she still is." We just didn't know where she was, or how to contact her, or what she could do . . .

Rick said, "How do we proceed, then?"

Nasser said, "If those we must persuade to our cause believe that we're the stronger side, we have a chance. Kitty, you may be the most important ally of all—you can do this more easily than any of us, through your show and in your writings."

I was afraid he was going to say that. "I'm getting in a little bit of trouble for that."

"I'm sure you'll find a way to persevere."

If we didn't come up with a specific plan of action, we at least had an agenda. A mission, of sorts. If enough of us out there were holding the line, maybe we could stop Roman.

Rick and Nasser started trading gossip about acquaintances, more centuries-old beings and shadow histories. I had the feeling of being a fly on the wall, listening to two immortals speak of years as if they were hours. I couldn't comprehend. But I tried.

Then Nasser turned to me. "Did Marid really call you a Regina Luporum?"

Rick raised an eyebrow, waiting for my answer, and I blushed. Regina Luporum, queen of the wolves. Marid—a twenty-eight-hundred-year-old vampire who I'd met in London, easily the oldest vampire I'd ever encountered—suggested the idea originated with the wolf who'd fostered Romulus and Remus, and who'd helped found Rome. He said he'd called me that because I stood up for werewolves when few others did. It wasn't an official title, it didn't mean I was queen of anything. It was more like . . . a hope. I was still trying to decide how I felt about the label.

"Maybe," I said, noncommittal. "Not that it means anything."

"I think it means I shouldn't underestimate you." He smiled like it was a joke, which was a bit how I'd regarded it when Marid called me it the first time.

Nasser turned back to Rick. "You meet with who, next? Mistress of Buenos Aires, yes?"

"Her representative, I think," Rick said. "You're the only one bold enough to leave your city in the hands of your followers."

"Ironic, as I'm the one advocating rebellion among others. But I trust my Family. As do you, I'm sure, Ricardo? As Kitty trusts her pack."

I looked at Rick, interested, because I didn't know his answer to the question. He'd taken over this Family by force. Did any of the previous Master's followers resent him?

"I believe my Family is satisfied with the current management," Rick said.

Nasser laughed. "Spoken like an American! You truly are of this country and not of the old Families." Rick tipped his head in agreement. "She will be a good ally, I think. Her city has not been home to vampires for long—she has been its only Mistress. She'll not want to give up her place to Roman. I must confess that I worry about the two of you. You have made targets of yourselves, and you're both so young. I could send you help—extra foot soldiers, perhaps. Guardians to keep watch over you and yours."

I had a hard time thinking of Rick as young. To Nasser, everyone must seem young. He meant well, I was sure, but I bristled. I didn't appreciate the suggestion that I was weak. I'd worked so hard not to appear so.

"Thanks, but we've done okay so far."

"Your offer is generous," Rick added, more politely. "But I think we'll be all right."

Sometime after midnight, we stood from the sofa and chairs, made our farewells, as if this were an ordinary dinner party in an ordinary house.

"How long will you be staying in Denver?" I asked Nasser.

"Tomorrow night I leave for Washington, D.C., to visit with Alette. But tonight, Rick has offered me the hospitality of Denver." The two vampires shared a sly smile between old friends.

I decided I didn't want to know. Rick had his ways and means, and as long as they didn't involve dead bodies, I wasn't going to ask.

"Well then. I suppose I'll leave you to it."

"It was very good to meet you, Katherine," Nasser said.

My throat tightened, thinking of my grandmother. But the moment passed. "Nice to meet you, too. Keep in touch."

"Assuredly."

Nasser went ahead to speak with his entourage, and I hung back with Rick.

"You have an opinion," he said.

I shrugged. "He seems to know a lot. I definitely like the idea of getting more information, of organizing. I just . . ."

"Seems a bit like putting your finger in the hole in the dike and hoping."

"Yeah," I said.

BEN WAS working when I got home. His briefcase was open on the floor beside him, papers spread out on his desk in the corner of the living room. He was a law firm of one, a criminal defense attorney, and a few of his clients were prone to calling him from jail late at night.

"Well?" Ben said, turning away from his desk when I shut the door behind me.

"That was interesting," I said. He raised a brow. I supposed I could have been a little more specific. "I like Nasser. He's creepy, but he seems sensible. For a vampire."

"I suppose that's encouraging," Ben said, his tone neutral.

"You could have gone to meet him."

He nodded at the briefcase. "I think I'd rather spend all night springing clients from the drunk tank. So, is there a plan? Does this guy have a way of getting at Roman?"

"I wouldn't call it a plan. But he has his network,

we have ours, and the more allies we have the stronger we are. At least that's the theory."

"It certainly can't hurt. By any chance did he call you Regina Luporum?"

"I'm never going to live that down," I said.

"I think you should embrace it. It has a nice ring to it." He was grinning.

"In fact, Nasser implied that I was too young and inexperienced to get much of anything done. He offered to send bodyguards. Of course, he implied the same about Rick so I'm thinking he treats everyone like that."

"And that's another reason it's a good thing I didn't go." He reached out a hand, and I moved forward to take it, letting him pull me close, wrapping his arms around me. His warmth, the pressure of his embrace, chased away some of the night's tension. Better to leave Nasser, Roman, the Long Game, Regina Luporum, and all of it, outside.

"Please tell me you're done working for the night," I said, leaning in to kiss his scalp.

"I am now," he said.

"Good."

Chapter 3

FRIDAY NIGHT saw me where most Friday nights saw me: at the KNOB main studio, in front of the monitor and microphone, watching for the next entertaining morsel.

"Welcome back to *The Midnight Hour*. I'm going to take the next call, now. Diane from Eugene, you're on the air."

She came on breathless, exhausted. "Hi, Kitty, thanks so much for taking my call, you have no idea how much it means."

"You're welcome, Diane. What's your problem?"

"It's my husband. I think—I think he's a zombie."

I smiled. "Believe it or not, I get this one a lot. Can you describe his behavior? Why do you think he's a zombie?"

She huffed. "He doesn't *do* anything! He sits on the sofa all day watching TV and that's it."

Leaning into the mike, I said, "I'm not sure that makes him a zombie. *Lazy,* but not zombie, you know?"

"But he doesn't even get up for meals. If I put a sandwich in his hand he'll eat it. He shuffles to the bathroom a couple of times a day. But ask him to come to the table? Take out the trash? Wash the car? It's like I'm not even here."

Oh, to have a secret video feed into her world. Radio was a challenge, because the only information I had to go on was what she told me and the tone and quality of her voice. She sounded desperate, and the details could have meant anything. I had to dig.

"How long has this been going on? Did you notice anything strange about him around the time it started? Did he have contact with anyone you don't know?"

"He works in construction. Or he used to. He could have been in contact with anyone. He just came home one day, sat down on the sofa, and that was it. That was a month ago. He's lost his job, and I can't go on like this."

"What *exactly* are his symptoms? Can he move? Do his eyes focus? Does he say anything or just make noises, or nothing at all?"

"His skin's kind of clammy. He smells kind of

rank. And he doesn't *do* anything. That's why I figured he must be a zombie."

"Or he hasn't taken a shower in a month. The reason I'm asking all this is because I encountered a zombie once, and it's . . . well, it's a form of poisoning, may be the best way to describe it. It damages neurological function. If he really is a zombie, I think it would be more obvious."

"What do you mean *if*?"

"Because zombies don't just sit there. They're enslaved to someone, and they're compelled to follow that person, or search for the supernatural element that binds them to their captor. So I'm thinking something else is going on—not that it's not a problem, mind you. But this may be more . . . how do I put this? Psychological rather than supernatural." I tried to find a way to soften how this sounded. "Has your husband ever been diagnosed with depression? Have you considered that he may need help? I mean, more help than a late-night radio talk show can offer."

"Wait a minute—you think he may just be *depressed*?"

I winced. "I don't think there's any *just* about it. I tell you what—either way, this is a medical issue. You should really call a doctor." I didn't wait for her response, because I wasn't qualified to diagnose a case of depression over the radio or anywhere else, and I didn't want her trying to argue with me about whether or not he needed real help. I hoped she listened to me. Really, though, all I could do was switch to a different line. "Next caller, you're on the air."

Ozzie, station manager and producer of the show, sat in a corner of the studio beaming at me. He was an aging hippy, complete with thin gray ponytail and a lot of attitude. I tried to ignore him, forcing the frown off my face. He'd decided to sit in on the show tonight, to "observe" as he'd put it. He'd done that a lot over the last few months, in an effort to keep me in line. Making sure I didn't climb on any conspiracy soapbox regarding vampires taking over the world. I'd tried that, and had lost some credibility—and market share. Ozzie wanted that market share back. Stick to what I knew, he insisted: human interest, fluffy features, sensationalist advice. "That's always been the meat of your show. Your bread and butter," he'd say. I'd tell him to stop mixing metaphors because it was giving me a headache.

But he was right. My ratings stopped falling when I stopped talking about vampire conspiracies. So much for getting the word out.

"Hi, Kitty. Thanks for taking my call. I have a really serious question." He was male, soft-spoken, grim.

"They're all serious, as far as I'm concerned." You wouldn't necessarily know that by listening to me.

"Yes, but, this is *really* serious."

"Okay, lay it on me."

"Do you believe in interspecies dating?"

I'd even gotten this one before, though maybe not in such blunt terms. "What, you mean dogs and cats, living together?"

"I mean do you think a relationship between, oh, like a vampire and a werewolf, or a were-lion and a normal human could ever work?"

"You call that interspecies dating, do you?"

"Well, yeah."

I double-checked the name on the monitor. "Well, Ted, I believe we're all human beings. A relationship between any of them has about as much chance of working out as a relationship between any other combination of people. Nothing interspecies about it."

"You know what I mean."

I decided to be difficult. "No, I'm afraid I don't know what you mean. Care to explain it to me?"

"They may have started out human, but they're nothing alike. How are they supposed to have relationships when they have nothing in common?"

"Except that they're all human, at the core," I said, insistent.

"I think you're wrong."

"Did you call in to argue with me about it?"

"No, I just wanted to ask, and I think you're wrong. It's been proven over and over again."

This was where I was supposed to say, *Some of my best friends are vampires . . .* "Proven by whom?"

I said instead, and didn't give him a chance to answer. "While I do think it's difficult for an uninfected human being or mortal lycanthrope and a vampire to carry on a relationship, because they age and the vampire doesn't, I know it can work because I've seen it happen. As cliché as it sounds there really are cases where love conquers . . . if not all, then a lot."

"You still believe that? After how many years of people calling you with all their problems? If you were right, you wouldn't have a show."

"The very fact that people call in with their problems gives me hope that those problems can be solved, and that people want to succeed. I mean, sticking two people who are human together doesn't guarantee a successful relationship, does it?"

"Well, no . . ."

"Word of advice—never attribute to supernatural malice what just may be human nature. Next caller, lay it on me." I hit the line.

"Um, hi. Yeah. Um, thanks for taking my call. I think."

Okay, this guy was more nervous than even my more anxiety-prone callers. He sounded hushed, like he had laryngitis. Or like he was trying to disguise his voice. This ought to be good.

"You have a problem you want to talk about?"

"Yeah, um, I do." He took a breath, gathering himself for the coming ordeal. "I'm a werewolf. And I'm okay with that, most of the time. That is, I think I'm pretty well-adjusted. But I've met this girl. Woman. My girlfriend. And she's great." A wistful tone entered his voice. "She's more than great. I—I really want to ask her to marry me."

"But—" I prompted. There was always a but.

"She doesn't know I'm a werewolf. And I don't know how to tell her. On top of that I want to introduce her to my pack, but I don't know where to even start with that. I have a pretty good pack, they're good people . . ."

"But—"

"I shouldn't complain, my alpha pair are really laid back, as long as we don't run around killing anything they let us do pretty much what we want. They *encourage* us to do what we want. But sometimes I could use, you know, a little guidance."

"They sound like the parents who provide the beer at their teenagers' parties."

"Funny you should mention beer. I mean, um, what I really want is some advice about how to tell my girlfriend what I am. I shouldn't ask her to marry me until she knows that."

His voice had become clearer, more confident. And familiar. It was the line about the beer that did it. His alpha pair, providing the beer for the parties.

"I'm sorry," I said. "Where are you calling from?"

The monitor said "Bob from Westminster." Westminster, the suburb of Denver. Right. I knew him.

"Um . . ." he said, the anxiety back in his voice.

"Listen, caller from Westminster, could you stay on the line just a second? Thanks. And now I'm going to break for station ID. I'll be back in a couple of howls." I made a desperate waving motion at the window, and my engineer Matt cued up station ID and PSAs, and the ON AIR sign dimmed. Then I took my caller off hold and talked through the headset.

Bob? I didn't think so. "Trey, is that you? Tell me that's not you."

"It's me." The man sighed, his secret revealed at last.

"What are you doing calling me on the show? On the air? You can talk to me anytime you want. Why didn't you just call my regular number?"

"You're not exactly the easiest person to pin down. If you're not working, you're traveling, or you're wrapped up in some plot. It never seems like the right time to sit down and talk, or you're too busy, and, well. I figured this was the one time I'd get you where you'd be ready to listen."

Hearing this from Trey didn't quite feel like getting kicked in the gut, but it was close. I leaned my head on my hands, glad he couldn't see me slouching, tail between my legs.

"Wow. Okay. Message received. I'm really sorry, Trey. I hadn't realized I'd been so . . . so . . ." I couldn't think of a word for what I'd been. I didn't even know he had a girlfriend he was this serious about. "I'm sorry. But your girlfriend. That's great. I'd really like to meet her."

"If you think you can pencil me into your schedule."

"Fine. I get it. I'm a bad den mother."

"Kitty, I didn't say that. I just . . ."

I waited for him to finish the thought, but he didn't. "Look," I said. "Name a time. We'll get together—"

Matt's voice cut in through my headset. "You have a minute, Kitty."

Of course I only had a minute. I closed my eyes and sighed.

"Trey, I'm not sure if this is irony or just a stupid joke, but I have to get back to the show now. I'll call you."

"Sure. I'll take my answer off the air." I could hear the smirk in his voice. At least he waited for me to hang up first.

I watched Matt count down to the next segment and the ON AIR sign lit. "All right, thanks for waiting. The question we have is how to tell your significant other that you've been keeping a pretty big secret. The answer: very carefully. How you tell depends a lot on your significant other, how well you know them, and how well they're likely to take something like this. But I'll stand by the answer I always give in cases like this: if this person really loves you, she'll stick by you and be willing to work it out. Normal human beings really can carry on relationships with lycanthropes and others. I'm not saying it's easy. But nothing that's really worthwhile is, is it?" Stupid platitudes. Would that be enough for Trey? Probably not. I wanted to meet his girlfriend, and for his sake I really hoped she could handle it. "Next caller, you're on the air."

"Oh my gosh, I'm *such* a big fan," the guy gushed. "I'm, like, your biggest fan."

"Well, thank you very much," I said, trying to be gracious. "Did you have a question?"

"Oh, yeah. I was just so excited about finally getting through . . ."

"What's your question, then?"

"I really just want to know . . . what do you think about prosthetic fangs? I mean, I know you really discourage people from wanting to become vampires, but if they wanted to *pretend* . . ."

Yeah, well. It's a living.

ABOUT A week later, Ben and I were at New Moon. One of our packmates, Shaun, ran the place for us, and he'd brought a funky hipster vibe to what otherwise would have been just another downtown bar with brick walls, exposed ductwork in the ceiling, and a lot of pretension. New Moon had good bar food, no TVs, a casual atmosphere, and late hours. It did okay as a business, but it worked splendidly as a central home for the pack. And the menu specialized in steaks and ribs. On any given night, a few werewolves were here, having a beer or grabbing a bite to eat. They felt safe here, and for me that was a victory.

Cormac had joined us tonight at our usual table in back, and I'd taken the jar of Roman's coins out of the safe so he could study them. Cormac, or Amelia. I'd been having trouble telling the difference lately.

Ben's cousin Cormac had been a bounty hunter specializing in supernatural targets. He'd spent two years in prison for manslaughter, and while there met the ghost of a Victorian wizard. Lady Amelia Parker died over a hundred years ago, wrongfully executed for murder. When Cormac was released, she came with him. He assured me it wasn't possession, that she wasn't hurting him. But sometimes, she was in charge, the one speaking or doing. When Cormac worked magic, it was really Amelia the magician. The two had formed a partnership—she got to leave the prison walls she'd been haunting for over a century, he got access to a different kind of power than he was used to using, since as a convicted felon he could no longer legally carry firearms. However odd it appeared, the system seemed to work.

The man sitting across from me and Ben at a back table at New Moon looked and smelled like Cormac, with his rugged thirtysomething build, lined face and almost permanent frown under a trimmed moustache, and his scent of worn leather jacket and male musk. He usually acted and sounded like Cormac. But sometimes, every once in a while, Amelia came through. I would get a sense of displacement, watching Cormac doing something odd, or say something profoundly out of character. Sometimes, he even smelled different, a taste of burning candle and old books. She had crept into his life that extensively.

Sometimes, I felt as if our territory had been invaded. At the same time, I suspected that Amelia was helping to keep Cormac in line and out of another prison sentence. He had incentive to stay straight now, whereas I wasn't sure he did before. I was grateful for that.

He held what looked like a jeweler's loupe, a lens set in an aged brass housing, and examined each of the coins through it.

"Nasser isn't convinced we can use these against Roman," I said. "But is there any chance they still carry some of his magic?"

Cormac shrugged. "It's like I said back in San Francisco, they're inert. No magical activity that I can see."

"Just chunks of old bronze, now," I said.

"I wouldn't say that," he said. "They carry traces

of what they were. But unless we wake them up, re-charge them, I can't guess what they might do."

"How do we wake them up?" Ben asked. We all looked at him.

"I'm not sure that's such a good idea," I said.

"I agree. But we can do some more research," Cormac said. "Mind if I take one?"

"If you promise you can keep it safe."

"Sure I can. Probably."

Probably. What a great word. I gave one to him—the one that had once belonged to Anastasia. He wrapped it in a white handkerchief and put it in his pocket.

"Consider this a job," I said. "Standard rate."

He looked away, surly, like I knew he would. "You don't have to pay me anything—"

Ben grinned at him. "We're going to force you into business whether you like it or not."

Cormac just scowled, because while he might argue with me, he wouldn't argue with his cousin.

Supernatural PI: Cormac was particularly suited to the job, if he would only admit it. We were working on him, slowly.

I put the other three coins back in the jar and went to the restaurant's back office to lock the jar back in the safe. When I came back to the table, Cormac was gone.

"What, he just left?" I said to Ben.

"Said he wanted to get started."

"It's past midnight, the library's closed."

He made an exaggerated shrug, indicating his cousin didn't make any more sense to him than he did to me.

"I can't decide if I want him to find a way to use them or not," I said.

"I think I'd just as soon have the coins turn out to be harmless."

"But then we don't have *anything* we can use." I fidgeted, tapping my feet. I'd gotten to where I half-expected Roman to show up anywhere, anytime; I always felt like he was looking over my shoulder. Ben regarded me with an amused hazel gaze, the lines around his eyes crinkled. His hair was shaggy, always two weeks overdue for a cut. I reached up and brushed it. He caught my hand and kissed it. Warmth passed between us, and once again I felt a tingle—he was my *husband*. The fact often amazed me.

He pulled away, turned to his briefcase, and drew out a stack of papers—way too many real estate listings. "To get your mind off conspiracies, you want to start making some decisions?"

I called for a round of beers.

We were supposed to be looking for a house. Ben had been doing most of the work, narrowing down choices, checking out neighborhoods. I kept dragging my feet. It wasn't that I didn't want to move into a house—preferably one on the edge of civilization, with access to forest and places to run. The condo we shared had gotten a little cramped over the last couple of years. But I was having a hard time taking that first step. If I was really honest, I was afraid of change, of moving into a situation that resembled far too closely that of the previous alpha pair who'd led the Denver pack. Having a house in the wilderness where the pack could gather would make us look a little too much like them, and they had been abusive and evil and incompetent.

Maybe I just didn't want to admit that even after being in the position for years, Ben and I really were the alphas of the Denver pack. People kept coming to us for answers. I would never get used to it.

"Kitty—" Ben must have sensed my consternation.

"I know, I know. What have we got?"

He shuffled the pages in front of me. "These are all the ranch-style houses on at least one acre of land between Castle Rock and Boulder."

"Closer to Denver would be better."

"Agreed. We have Golden, Evergreen, Georgetown, Idaho Springs, Brighton—"

"I'd rather be in the mountains than out east, if we can swing it." Frankly, the listings had all started to look the same to me. They all said the same things: lovely, sunny, big yard. Lots of character, which I'd come to believe was the real-estate version of "has a nice personality."

He shuffled a few more pages, pulled one out. "What about this one? It's the right size, great location, it backs up to open space—"

I pulled the page out of his hand and stared. I knew this house—the ranch design, the roof shape, the spread of the driveway, the landscape around it. I checked the address just to be sure, and my stomach flopped. I swallowed back nausea.

"No," I said, wadding up the page and shoving it back at him.

"But it's got everything we're looking for—"

"That was Carl and Meg's house." I'd had no idea it was on the market. I didn't even know what happened to it after they died. After I killed them, rather. It should have been funny, seeing it for sale. It should have been *really* funny that it had made Ben's list. Carl and Meg, former alpha pair of the Denver pack. The two werewolves I vowed I'd never be anything like. What was the saying, that you always turned into your parents whether you wanted to or not. Did that include wolf parents?

"Really?" Ben said, sounding equally unhappy. He took the lump of paper from me, smoothed it out, and studied it. "I didn't even notice. I was only there the one time. And I guess I was a little distracted."

Tortured, he meant. Beaten and bloody. I shouldn't have been surprised that he didn't remember the house. He couldn't have known. The pictures on the listing made the place look so pretty. Those back windows had a great view.

"It's the place. I spent a lot more time there than you did," I said.

"Right. Not this one." He tore the page in half, then into quarters, then into eighths. I wished we were a smoking restaurant, so I could burn the bits in an ashtray. I took Ben's hand, he squeezed it back, and kissed my hair, lingering there, letting his warm breath play on my scalp. And all was well, for that moment in time.

He threw the torn-up pieces away behind the bar. If only the memories were so easy to discard.

That tiny bit of exorcism performed, we spent the next twenty minutes narrowing down the choices until we had a dozen or so we actually wanted to look at. The idea of moving started to feel like it was really going to happen.

The restaurant had cleared out, and about ten minutes before closing, Shaun was wiping down the bar when he called, "Hey, Kitty?"

I looked, and he nodded to the front door, where a man in a black wool overcoat was knocking on the glass. He was short, round, with silver hair so close-shaven he almost appeared bald. He seemed hunched, urgent inside the coat, as if he was hiding.

The man caught my gaze through the glass of the door, and my vision swam for a moment. I couldn't have said what color his eyes were; I couldn't have said much of anything. I felt like I had walked into a room and forgotten what I came there for.

I shook my head and looked at Shaun. The moment of vertigo passed. "You haven't locked up yet, have you?"

"No," he said.

"Then why doesn't he just come in?" I said, moving to the door.

"Kitty. Careful," Ben said, tapping his nose.

I paused and took a breath, scenting around the beer and fried food, the eddies of people coming and going all night, the signature of the pack that permeated the corners and made this our territory.

The door had enough of a draft that I caught the chill from the outside, a thread far too cold for the weather outside. Which explained why he couldn't just walk in—he was a vampire, and he hadn't been invited.

I sauntered up to the door, arms crossed, donning an amused smirk. I didn't meet his gaze this time.

"Hi there," I said, full of false cheer. "What can I do for you?"

"I cannot enter here. Why not?" he said, the door muffling his voice. He had a rolling, cadenced European accent. Italian maybe, which made me wonder if he was part of some kind of vampire Mafia. That would have been too much.

"It's our home," I said.

"It's a place of business," he declared. "A public thoroughfare."

"Yeah, about that. Turns out it's enough of my pack's territory to make a difference. It's our home. I have to invite you in."

"Then invite me in."

Here was a guy used to giving orders and having them obeyed. "No, I don't think so."

The last time this had happened—a vampire showing up on the doorstep of New Moon, cranky and frustrated because he couldn't enter—it had been Roman. Dux Bellorum. Lesson: strange vampires showing up demanding to be let in could only mean trouble. All I had to do was not let him in.

He spread his arms. "I mean you no harm, believe me."

"I'm still not letting you in," I said. Ben had sidled up to the bar and leaned there, casual but wary. Shaun watched, worried.

"We would both be more comfortable if we spoke inside, where it's warmer."

Cold didn't bother vampires. Or me, much. "You're

used to werewolves doing what you tell them to, aren't you?"

The stern expression cracked into the tiniest of smiles. "You must be Kitty Norville." The name trilled with his accent. "I was told I could find you here."

"And you are?"

"I am Father Columban." He inclined his head in a bow. "Now will you please invite me into your home?"

My brow furrowed. "Father? Like a priest?" He nodded assent. I was confused. "How is that even possible?"

"Invite me in, and I will tell you."

"No. Tell me why you're here first," I said. "Did Nasser send you?" That would be just like a Master vampire, to go ahead and do what he wanted despite what we'd told him.

"Nasser of Tripoli?" He waved his hand dismissively, then took a deep breath, which was an affectation—vampires didn't need to breathe except to speak. But he could demonstrate that he was about to make a speech, and how much trouble I was causing him. "I need to speak to Ricardo, Master of this city, but I do not know where he keeps his domicile. I'm given to understand that you can reach him. I would be most grateful if you could arrange a meeting between us."

Sometimes I wished Rick would just publish his

number in whatever vampire directory existed, so people wouldn't go through me. Arranging a meeting wouldn't be hard; Rick would want to talk to this guy. A vampire priest? I had no idea.

I pulled my phone out of my pocket. "I don't need to let you in for that. Hang on just a sec."

"But—"

I turned my back on him and called Rick. The phone rang four, then five times. I didn't know what I was going to do if he didn't answer. Tell this Columban guy to come back later? Send him to Rick's secret hideout? That'd go over well.

Finally, he picked up. "Yes? I'm a little busy at the moment."

"What could you possibly be doing that you can't immediately drop to come take care of my problem?"

He hesitated a beat. "Sometimes I can't tell when you're joking."

"It's my secret pain. But I wouldn't bug you if it wasn't important. I'm at New Moon and there's a vampire here wanting to talk to you."

"That's never good."

"No. He says his name is Father Columban."

"Father—like a priest?" He sounded more startled than I had.

"That's what he said. Interested?"

"Are you sure he's for real?"

"Just a sec," I said and lowered the phone to speak

to Columban through the door. "Do you carry a coin of Dux Bellorum?"

He cocked his head, narrowed his gaze. His tone held astonishment. "How do you know about the coins?"

The answer didn't tell me anything, really. Except that he was as neck deep in this as the rest of us, one way or another. "I get around. So, do you?"

"No," he said, with such earnest simplicity that I was inclined to believe him.

Back to the phone I said, "Did you get that?"

"I did. I'm intrigued."

"Yeah, I thought you'd be. Where do you want to meet?"

"Do you mind letting him into New Moon? I'll get there as soon as I can."

I kind of did. This was our sanctum, and this made it vulnerable. I glanced back at Ben, who shrugged. Shaun didn't do anything—leaving it to the alphas.

I sighed. "Okay. Come on in." I opened the door for Columban. "Welcome to New Moon."

He gave another precise bow. "*Grazie, signora.*"

Inside, he looked over Ben and Shaun and passed them by to sit at a table in the middle of the room. Ben and I lingered by the bar.

We waited.

*   *   *

I HELPED Shaun close up the restaurant, and after the kitchen staff was done cleaning up, I sent everyone home. Ben kept his eye on the vampire, who didn't move, didn't speak. Didn't make trouble, at least. He might have been meditating.

When I got back to the front, I tried to start a conversation.

"So. How old are you?"

Columban only raised an eyebrow at me, as if asking how I could possibly be serious. I looked back expectantly. He didn't say a word. Ah well.

A tapping at the locked front door drew our attention. Rick smiled at me through the glass and glanced with interest at the other vampire. Columban stood, fingertips resting on the table. I opened the door for the Master of Denver.

Rick swept into the restaurant in a puff of cool night air, his coattails fluttering around his knees. He paused as the door closed behind him, gazing around the place. Chairs had been put upside down on tables, the floor had been swept.

"Hello," Rick said, regarding us all, his expression calm. Columban bowed his head the barest inch. Neither made a move.

We might have stood there all night, nobody saying anything. Except I wasn't going to let that happen.

"Rick, he says he's Father Columban," I started the

introductions. "And this is Rick." I figured after that, my work here was done. I could be a spectator.

Rick waited a long time for Columban to say something, but the self-proclaimed priest just stood there, studying him.

"Shall we sit?" Rick finally said, gesturing to the table.

The man looked at Ben and me, standing off to the side. "Should they remain here while we talk?"

"It's their restaurant."

"Then you allow wolves to learn your secrets?"

"Not only that, I feel better with them watching my back." Rick gave me a quick look, nodding. I straightened, pleased with the vote of confidence.

Columban's expression darkened, as if he'd discovered a part of the universe had fallen out of alignment. "Very well," he said, with a pointed sigh, as he sank back into his chair.

Rick sat across from him, and I inched over to Ben. The two of us stayed standing, where we could at least pretend like we had some dominance over the situation.

Columban continued. "I suppose I should thank you, then, for speaking with me at all." His voice held something like wonder, or maybe confusion.

"Father Columban. That's an affectation, of course," Rick answered.

"I assure you, it isn't."

"Then you were a priest before. I know priests can be turned—"

"No. I became a priest after."

"How?" Rick said, curt and disbelieving. "Surely you don't carry or wear a crucifix—"

"I carry the symbols in my heart. Before I answer your questions, may I ask a question or two about you? I have heard only a little. You are Spanish, yes? From the seventeenth century?"

Rick hesitated, looking as if he was about to lay down a hand in a game of poker. "Sixteenth."

"How long have you been in the Americas?"

"Five hundred years."

"Then you were here from the start."

"From the first wave of Spanish colonization, yes."

Columban leaned back, nodding as if impressed, and pleased. As if he had found what he was looking for. "Then you are Catholic."

Rick turned a wry smile. "It's difficult to be very religious at all in my condition."

The so-called priest's hands were on the table. He leaned forward and asked, "Yes or no. Are you Catholic?"

A long, anxious moment followed, and my heart thudded, racing on Rick's behalf. Why did this feel like an inquisition? What answer was this man looking for? I'd known Rick for years, and I didn't know what he was going to say.

Rick's voice caught before he murmured, "Yes. Still. Somehow. Whether or not God thinks so. When you haven't actually taken communion in five hundred years—"

"This isn't about God. If the pope says you're Catholic, you are, yes?"

Rick seemed taken aback at that. "If you insist on leaving God out of it—I suppose it depends on the pope."

"You're making this too complicated," Columban said. "If we are wise, we judge men by their actions. Not by the labels other people use on them."

"I'm fairly certain my drinking human blood on a semiregular basis justifies at least one of the labels used on me."

"But do you believe in one holy and apostolic Church? *Are you Catholic?*"

"Are you here to tell me that if I do, then I am? That if the pope says I am—"

"Yes," Columban said.

I couldn't keep my mouth shut. "The pope knows about vampires? Has the pope always known? Have all the popes known? What has the pope got to do with vampires?"

"Kitty, maybe you should let them talk," Ben said.

"But—" They were all looking at me now, so I shut up.

Columban turned to Rick. "You have not asked what order I belong to."

"A liberal one, obviously," Rick said.

"I belong to the Order of Saint Lazarus of the Shadows. Those who return from the dead to do God's work on earth."

"That's not the original Order of Saint Lazarus," Rick said. "The leper knights of the Crusades—"

"We were hidden among them. Now that lepers and crusades are not as common as they were, we are all that remain."

Rick stared. "An order of vampire priests? That exists with the blessing of the pope? Really? That's . . ."

"Crazy. Yes. It is, rather. Ricardo, I am here to ask you a question: Would you like to become one of us?"

Chapter 4

I HAD collected Rick's story in bits and pieces over the years. He had arrived in colonial Mexico in the early 1500s, a young Spanish nobleman seeking his fortune. Like hundreds of others, he joined Coronado's expedition to find Cibola, the City of Gold. The expedition failed, but Rick—Ricardo—remained in Mexico. Soon after, he encountered a vampire and was turned against his will. The rest, as they say, was history. He made some kind of peace with his condition and eventually found that fortune he'd been looking for. Until recently, he'd kept to himself, and his existence had been quiet. Now, he was Master of Denver and attracting the attention of people like Father Columban, who apparently was on a mission from the pope.

As a young Spanish nobleman, of course he would

have been Catholic. Could that kind of faith last for five hundred years? When most of the church's symbols were weapons against him?

If Columban had just told him he could be made human and mortal again, Rick could not have looked more astonished. I kept my mouth shut, waiting for Rick's answer. I tried to picture the calm, elegant man before me, who I'd known for years now, as a priest. Oddly, it wasn't too difficult. He'd be the kind of priest you could confess anything to, and he wouldn't even have to prompt.

"Why?" Rick said finally.

"We need more allies. When you became Master of Denver, you came to our attention. You are already fighting for our cause—think of how much more you could do as part of our order."

"And what of Denver?"

"Surely others can look after one city."

"You know of Roman? Dux Bellorum?"

"We have known of him from the beginning."

"And you couldn't stop him before now?" I blurted.

Columban gave me the kind of look he'd give a small child who'd just brought a frog into the house. Disgusted, dismissive. Obviously, I didn't know what I was talking about. So I looked to Rick for an answer.

"Roman has allies," Rick said, still regarding the other vampire. "We've always known that. Obviously, they're powerful allies, to stand against the Catholic Church."

Columban couldn't exactly admit that out loud, could he? Well then. "So what you're saying," I said to him, "is that you need all the help you can get." He didn't twitch a muscle in response.

After another long pause, Rick said softly, "This war just keeps getting bigger, doesn't it?"

"You know how much good you could do with us," the priest said.

"I always thought I was doing some good here," Rick said.

"You are," I said. The priest glared at me.

"The battle is larger than this one city." Columban rose and smoothed his coat. "Your faith is strong. It could not be otherwise, to last so long. Think about what I've said. I'll give you time," he said, and turned to the door.

Rick stood with him, raising his arm, as if he might reach out to the other vampire. "Stop. Wait. I have so many questions."

"I will answer them, in time." He glanced at me, Ben. The werewolves. He wasn't going to say anything in front of us.

"How can I reach you?" Rick said.

"Think about it. You'll know where to find me." Columban smiled, touched his forehead in a salute, and walked out.

Rick started pacing, back and forth along the length of the bar. He made three passes before I asked, carefully, "Rick?"

"I am astonished," he said, stopping, giving a short laugh. His cheeks were almost flush, whatever blood he had borrowed rushing through him. "It's been five hundred years, but when I close my eyes I can smell the incense, hear the chanting voices echoing off the stone walls." And he did so, closing his eyes, tipping his head back, his nostrils flaring as if he really could take in the scene he described—the inside of a church.

"Then you think he's telling the truth," I said.

"Who would lie about something like that?" Rick said, his tone wondering. "No one would believe it."

On the other hand, I didn't want to trust anyone who could walk in here and get Rick so agitated. This couldn't be that simple, that straightforward. I looked at Ben—what did the lawyer think?

"In any other case I'd say do a background check on the guy," he said. "But I have a feeling that isn't going to be too helpful here. You can't exactly call up the Vatican and ask for references."

If only. Rick was staring into a far distance. He looked like someone who'd just had a religious experience. Which might not have been too far off. He murmured, maybe to himself, not intending anyone to hear, "This is what I get for isolating myself for all this time. I cut myself off because it was the only way to maintain some kind of . . . of *morality*. I'd never considered an alternative. That there might be others. My God."

Was that a curse or a prayer? "I wish I could offer you a drink," I said.

"I wish I could take it." He shook his head a little, as if waking up from a dream, and strode back to the table, slumping into the seat. "I'm sorry. I suddenly have a lot on my mind."

"What are you going to do?" Ben asked.

He hesitated a long time, hands resting lightly on the table. "I don't know. Do—do you mind if I sit here, just for a little while? I need to think."

"You want us to leave you alone?"

He pursed his lips. "If you don't mind staying . . ."

He wanted company. He'd been essentially on his own for five hundred years, and now he wanted company.

I drew a pitcher of beer, brought over two glasses, and Ben and I sat at the table across from him. None of us said anything. Rick's face was lined with worry, revealing something of the older man he never would become.

Half an hour passed, then Rick stood. "Thank you," he said. "I've imposed on you enough. I should be going."

I said, "It's no imposition. Rick, if there's anything we can do—"

"I know, and I appreciate it. For now . . . I need to consider this all. Kitty, Ben, good night."

I unlocked the front door for him, and he swept out into the night. Ben came to stand beside me, and we both looked after him, though Rick had vanished almost immediately, lost in shadows.

"Should I be worried?"

"Rick can take care of himself," Ben said.

"You don't sound convinced."

"All right. I'm worried. This sounds like a scam. What are we supposed to do about it?"

I didn't have an answer to that.

THE NEXT afternoon, I called Cormac. His cell phone rang, and rang, and rang, and I waited, because I knew he'd answer eventually. I pictured him driving in his worn, veteran Jeep, calmly hooking the hands-free in his ear, keeping his gaze on the road. Stuff happened, and him hurrying wouldn't change it. I had to smile. Didn't matter what happened or how much time passed, some things never changed.

The line clicked, and he finally came on. "Yeah?" A background hum indicated that yes, he was driving.

"You busy?"

"Why do you ask?" he replied.

Nobody could ever give me a straight answer. "I have another job for you."

"Tracking down or spying?"

I wrinkled my nose. "Is there a difference?"

"I suppose not." He sounded like he was grinning, which meant he was making fun of me.

I let it go. He smiled seldom enough, let him have his fun. "There's a new vampire in town. I want to find out if he really is who he says he is."

"Is he one of your conspiracy friends?"

"I'm not even sure I know what that means. But no, he just showed up at New Moon last night without an invitation or anything. He said he's a priest."

"Vampire priest? Is that even possible?" he said.

"I'd love to find out. His name's Columban, and he said he's on a mission from the pope."

"Huh," he said, which was about as surprised-sounding as he ever got. "Why's he here?"

"He's trying to recruit Rick."

"And is Rick inclined to be recruited?"

I hesitated. I really wanted to say no, that Rick was one of us. But the look on his face last night—that he'd found a long-lost relative, or even—obviously—found religion. "I don't know."

"Where's this new guy staying?" Cormac asked.

"I don't know. He told Rick he'd know if he thought about it. Can you look for him?"

"I'll see if I can find anything. No guarantees."

"Of course not. Thanks, Cormac."

"I'll add it to the invoice."

"What? Oh . . . well, sure, now that you mention it. Maybe we should just put you on retainer. Can you have PIs on retainer? I could look it up—"

"Good-bye, Kitty." He hung up.

I kept thinking he was softening up, getting a little more friendly. Maybe even domesticated. He'd been through so much. He even had a feminine side now, in the form of Amelia. But not likely. I got the feeling Amelia had never been any more domesticated than Cormac. They made a pretty good team.

Rick didn't need me looking after him, I reassured myself. He'd been taking care of himself for five hundred years, I had absolute confidence in his ability to keep taking care of himself. Mostly.

In the meantime, I wanted to find out everything I could about Father Columban, vampire priest. Just in case.

Chapter 5

THE DAYS I wasn't doing the show, I spent preparing for the show, promoting the show—or dealing with fallout from the show. I tracked down interviews, filed hate mail, and Googled myself to see what people were saying about me. I'd end these afternoons feeling like I had a desk job. Downright respectable, even. I even had a 401(k) these days. I loved my job—that I could define my job and do exactly what I wanted to most of the time. But some days, I liked nothing better than to leave the KNOB offices and head home, to some peace and quiet and Ben. Not think about vampires, conspiracies, mysteries, or anything.

One of those days, late in the afternoon, I was halfway to my car when I caught a familiar scent, a person crossing KNOB's parking lot. Female, human, tension and tobacco smoke. Detective Jessi Hardin. Her unmarked police sedan was parked in a far corner of the lot, giving me a chance to see her coming. I had an urge to run, but as Ben was fond of saying, running from the cops never did anyone any good. Standing my ground, I tried to smile in a way that was friendly and not challenging.

"Detective, what can I do for you?" I said, sounding far from innocent. Detective Hardin headed up the Denver PD's Paranatural Unit—one of the first in the country. Mostly in spite of herself, she'd become an expert on the supernatural and crime. Mostly, she got that way by talking to me, because I knew all the dirt.

"Ms. Norville, how are you?" she said, also sounding not very innocent. She definitely hadn't just happened to be walking across the parking lot and didn't just want to say hello. She wore a white blouse, unbuttoned at the collar, and dark slacks, and her dark hair was in a short ponytail. Her badge hung on her belt, along with her semiautomatic.

"Oh, I'm fine. How are you?" This felt like theater. I wished she'd get to the point.

"I have a few questions for you," she said.

"Of course you do." The last couple of weeks had been a little crazy, but I didn't think I'd done anything wrong. I tried to remember if I'd done anything the least bit suspicious. I hadn't even staked out any haunted houses. "Whatever it was, I didn't do it."

"You seem a little jumpy. There something I should know about?"

"Standard cop reaction. I think you enjoy doing this to people."

"Can't deny it," she said. "Seriously, though, you have a couple of minutes?"

I slung my bag into the backseat of my car and leaned against the hood.

She said, "I have reports of strange vampires visiting town."

"Strange vampires—are there any other kind?"

She smirked. "You know what I mean. Foreign vampires. Powerful. You know anything about that?"

I wasn't a great liar. "Maybe Denver's tourism campaign is paying off. Maybe they're taking Warren Zevon seriously." Between "Things to Do in Denver When You're Dead" and "Werewolves of London," I had begun to wonder about Mr. Zevon.

"You're keeping secrets," she said.

"Yeah, well, not by choice," I grumbled.

"What can you tell me?"

"Can you trust me when I say that no one's causing any trouble?"

"Rick's in on this, too, isn't he? Should I talk to him?"

"If you can find him."

"I'll give him a call."

I didn't know that she had Rick's number. I wondered when that had happened.

She drew out a manila folder she'd kept tucked under her arm. "How about a more specific question. Have you seen him?" She opened the folder to show me a sketch artist's drawing of a man's face, round and stout, frowning, short-cropped pale hair. It was Columban.

Vampires couldn't make themselves invisible, precisely. But they could influence the way light did or didn't strike them. They could appear on camera, if they wanted to. Or they could hide in shadows and leave no trace of their passing—keep their reflection from appearing in mirrors, that sort of thing. Security camera footage would never catch the vampire priest. But someone had witnessed something, to get this sketch.

"You've seen this guy," Hardin said, because I couldn't hide my shock.

"Where'd you get that? What's he done?"

"Got it from my counterpart at Interpol, and he's wanted for arson and homicide in Hungary."

So many questions, I hardly knew where to start. "Homicide?"

"Two workers were killed in a fire he's suspected of setting in a warehouse."

I may have been suspicious of Columban, but he didn't strike me as being criminal; arson and homicide didn't jive very well with the serene priestly image he'd presented to us the other night. Just went to show,

I didn't know anything about him at all. Neither did Rick. I needed to call him. In light of this new information, I felt confused more than anything. Hardin had startled me on a couple of fronts.

"You have a counterpart at Interpol?" I said. "Why didn't you tell me this? Why didn't you tell me this before I went to London? Can you imagine the interview I could have gotten—"

"Wait a minute, slow down. Yes, I have a counterpart, and to be snide about it, you never asked. We were all sick of being embarrassed in our local departments, so we started talking to each other. Amazing what we're finding out."

"What? What are you finding out?"

She pointed at the sketch. "Tell me about him, first."

If I gave away anything about this guy to Hardin, Rick would never forgive me. I gave her a very bland smile. "You'll have to talk to Rick."

"Is this some kind of supernatural territory thing?" she said. "Vampire versus werewolf, not stepping on toes, all that?"

"More like a not stabbing friends in the back thing," I said. "I'm sorry. Rick really is the guy you want to talk to. He knows more than I do anyway."

"This guy's here in Denver, isn't he?" she said. "If he really did commit those crimes, aren't you worried about him pulling the same shit here?"

Which was why I wanted to get out of here so I could call Rick before Hardin did. "Yeah, actually. And I'll call you if I hear about anything that urgent. I promise."

She frowned, arching her brow. I looked back at her, wearing my best innocent face. We probably could have stared at each other like that for the rest of the afternoon. But I didn't have the time.

I gestured over my shoulder to the car. "I'm going to go now."

She slipped the picture and folder back under her arm. "I'll be in touch."

"Nice talking to you," I said, waving. Then I jumped in my car and started the engine. She watched me drive off. Pure intimidation.

After driving around the corner, I pulled over and called Rick. Half a dozen rings later, the call went to voice mail. Of course it did—the sun was still up. I'd have to wait until after dusk to talk to him. I had to comfort myself with the knowledge that Hardin wasn't getting through to him, either.

I did the only thing I could—left a message and waited for his return call.

NIGHT FELL, and Rick didn't return my call. We had a couple of weeks until our meeting with the vampire delegate from Buenos Aires, which seemed simultaneously too long to wait and too little time to prepare. And always, always, I had the sense that a timer was ticking down to something, and that some malevolence was waiting for me just around the corner.

Usually, I could trust Rick to return calls, but this time I wanted to get to him before Hardin did, and he could decide whether or not to warn—or even trust—Columban. I went looking for him.

Cormac hadn't called, either, which meant he hadn't learned anything about where the priest was staying. I had no other leads.

I parked my car behind Obsidian, but never made it to the stairs leading down to Rick's lair. The spring air was still, sharp with the last cold of winter. My nose flared, awakened by a scent, thick and intrusive, both familiar and alien. Lupine, fur and musk overlaid with human skin, civilizing soap. Male. Werewolf, but not one of ours. Another stranger. Hardin was right, too many weird people had been coming through Denver.

A strange werewolf was downtown, and he hadn't asked for permission to be here. Just showed up without any warning. He probably had a perfectly good reason for it that would elicit my sympathy, and we would become great friends as soon as I got the explanation. In the meantime, Wolf bristled. She wanted to hunt him down. One more thing to worry about. Ticked me off.

I pulled my phone out of my jeans pocket and called Ben.

He answered, "Hey."

"Hey, I'm downtown. Can you get down here?"

"What's wrong?"

"Someone's in our territory. I don't recognize the scent."

"Give me ten minutes. Meet at New Moon?"

"Yeah." We hung up.

The strange werewolf had been through here recently. Last full moon had been three weeks ago, and our territory had been safe then. He could have arrived in town anytime since then and kept to ground, or he could have just gotten here. So was he announcing his arrival, or was he too stupid to cover his trail?

I tracked him west. He was on foot, following sidewalks. Just a guy out for a stroll. He wasn't traveling in a straight line, though. His path veered north, toward Civic Center Park, then circled the block back toward the art museum. Like the guy was sightseeing or something. I checked my phone—I needed to get to New Moon to meet Ben. Oddly, the stranger's trail bent toward the same path. He'd headed to the restaurant, too, and recently.

Who was this guy? I called Ben again.

"Hey, Ben? You at New Moon yet, because I think he's headed in your direction." My voice was tense.

"Um, yeah," he said. "The guy's already here."

I started jogging. "Who is he? What's happening?"

"We're outside. We're waiting." He sounded calm. Not relaxed, but not panicked, either. Guy was there, but not threatening.

"Yeah?" I said, wanting to know more, not knowing what to ask.

"Just get over here."

I made myself slow down, so I could have the last couple of blocks to catch my breath and not be gasping when I faced the stranger. This was going to be some stupid misunderstanding. I was going to have to play self-help guru face-to-face to some adoring fan who didn't know any better, wasn't I? I ought to be grateful something like this hadn't happened before now.

Within sight of New Moon's brick façade, his scent became crystal clear. My nose gave me a picture before I actually saw him. He was a werewolf, but a civilized one, with clean clothes and washed hair, comfortable with being human. Ben caught my gaze first. He was standing at the outside edge of the sidewalk, arms loosely crossed. His shoulders were stiff, though, his back straight as a rod and his chin up in a show of dominance. After a second he turned away from me to glare again at the man leaning on the wall of the building.

He was the kind of werewolf who you could look at and imagine that he really was a werewolf, a monster, under the human skin. Muscular, with broad shoulders and powerful arms. No doubt he worked out and knew how to fight. Slouching, he was as tall as Ben, and would tower above us both if he straightened. But he was carefully keeping himself small. He was smiling, seeming way too casual for the situation he was in—facing an alpha pair whose territory he'd intruded on. He wasn't making a challenge—his gaze was downcast. But he didn't seem at all worried. So maybe everything was okay and he had a good reason for being here.

Wolf didn't like him. She stirred in my gut, sent shocks down my limbs, and I imagined her claws curling into him. No reason for it. Just something about the way he smiled, looking at Ben like he wasn't a threat. He thought he knew us, and I was pretty sure he didn't, not really.

Shaun was waiting inside the glass doorway, looking out, hands clenched at his sides. He glanced at me for a cue, and I shook my head once, telling him to wait.

I approached, hoping the pause in my stride wasn't too noticeable.

"You must be Kitty Norville," the stranger said in a steady tenor, forthcoming and friendly, just as I was opening my mouth to speak.

He'd gotten in the first word, throwing me completely off my stride. My radio DJ aversion to dead air saved me from too much of a pause. "Right," I said, putting a leash on Wolf so we could keep this as human as possible. We were all civilized here. "And who are you?"

"It's an honor to meet you, finally," he said, reaching out a hand for shaking. I did so, and he turned to Ben, who had to uncurl his arms before he could shake. "And you must be Ben. Good to meet you." Ben raised a brow at me.

I blinked the unanswered question back at the stranger.

"Oh! I'm Darren. I wanted to know—do you have room in your pack for me?"

Chapter 6

WHAT ELSE could I do but invite him inside? We sat around our usual table in back and talked. I asked Shaun to bring waters all around. Not beer, not yet.

I wanted to ask Ben what kind of vibe he was getting from the guy, but I couldn't. Doing so would make me look uncertain. Weak. Besides, Ben was playing strong and silent. He hadn't taken his gaze off the new guy, and if the stare wasn't an outright challenge, it was at least a warning. Not that Darren noticed. He was so self-assured, so unwary, even surrounded by unknown werewolves, I almost couldn't believe he was one of us, despite his stance and his scent. Even the toughest were always looking over their shoulders for the next challenge.

I wasn't here to challenge him, but to take the

measure of him. Find out his story, then figure out what to do about it. Maybe I should look at this as a job interview. *Tell me, what's been your greatest challenge as a werewolf?* Yeah, right . . .

"So. Darren," I said. "What brings you to Denver?"

"Job offer from a cousin. In construction. Couldn't say no."

"You're not on the run from something, or trying to elbow your way in?" Ben asked.

He tilted his head, questioning. "No. Does it look like I am?"

"I'm a lawyer, I assume everyone's guilty," he said. His smile showed teeth. Darren's smile slipped a bit, which felt like a small victory.

Three members of my pack were on hand: Becky— a tough woman, slim, with tousled auburn hair— moved to the bar, sitting to watch with Shaun. Tom, one of the higher-ranking wolves in the pack, stood from the table where he'd been sitting. All three had grown wary, their bodies bracing for some kind of response, fight or flight. Waiting for whatever fallout was on its way. If I told them to pounce on this guy, they'd do it right here in the restaurant. They were waiting for my signal. Their attention made me itch. I made my smile match Darren's and looked over to them.

"Guys, can you give us a few minutes?" I looked at each one of them, meeting their gazes, emphasizing the command. Tom sat and turned away. Becky hunched over her beer. Shaun gave me a raised-eyebrow, are-you-sure look, and I glared. Yes, I was sure. The manager found something to do at another part of the bar. It was nice that he wanted to help.

"They're good people," Darren said. "You should be proud of what you've done here."

Did he think I needed his approval? I suddenly wanted to growl. I hadn't had to work this hard keeping my back straight and my proverbial tail in the air in a long time. "Not that I asked or anything."

"I'm sorry, we're getting off on the wrong foot," he said, but in a way that made me think he'd known exactly what he was doing and wanted to see how I would react. He continued matching my gaze. I couldn't look away. "I'm a friend of Nasser's. He said you impressed him. Denver sounded like a place where I might fit in, so I called my cousin, and he had the job. Easy."

I didn't know if that made things better or worse. "*Nasser?* He didn't send you to keep an eye on us, did he? I told him we didn't need any backup—"

"No, really, I've just been looking for a place to settle—a pack to join. From what he told me, yours sounded good. I've been on my own for a while, moving around a lot, doing this and that. It gets old. Really, Nasser knows I'm here, but he didn't send me."

Lone wolf—that made sense. He certainly knew

how to carry himself. "Why do you want to be part of a pack now? You strike me as someone who'd do just fine on his own."

"Why do you?" he returned. "You tried being a lone wolf, didn't you? How long did you last?"

He must have listened to my show, to know a detail like that. Made me warm to him—a bit.

"Less than a year." It would have been longer, but Ben had gotten infected with lycanthropy, I'd taken care of him, and we'd fallen in bed together. Not long after that we were back in Denver, running the pack. Darren was right, I hadn't been happy on my own.

Could him coming to Denver be that simple? He just wanted a pack he could get along with?

"You see?" he said, arms open like it made perfect sense.

"Fish gotta swim, bird gotta fly, werewolf gotta have a pack?" I said wryly.

He chuckled. "I'm surprised you don't get werewolves coming here all the time, wanting to be part of *your* pack."

"Most werewolves know better, I think."

"You sound sensible," he said. "I wanted to see it firsthand. But if I flunk the audition, just let me know, and I'll leave. No hard feelings."

As if I were the one who needed to feel bad for rejecting him. I was getting to the point where I wanted to keep him around just to learn what made him tick.

He was either the most well-adjusted werewolf in history, or he was up to something.

"You could have called ahead," I said. "A little warning would have been nice."

That smile of his never dimmed. "Maybe I wanted to see how you'd react if I just walked in. That kind of thing will tell you a lot about a pack."

It would, indeed. "You're not really endearing yourself to me."

"Right. Sorry. I won't cause trouble, I promise."

Ben wasn't any more tense than he'd been when the interview started. Which meant he didn't sense any more threat than he had twenty minutes ago, when Darren first appeared. If Ben had reservations, he'd let me know. I couldn't think of a reason to say no. Besides, if he was a friend of Nasser's, that made him an ally. Theoretically.

"Okay," I said. "We'll give it a try. You just have to follow the rules: be nice, and don't be stupid."

He stared at me. "Don't be stupid? That's it?"

"That's it," I said. And it really was. Anyone who couldn't manage those two things, I probably couldn't help. "Well, and I'd like your address and phone number so we can stay in touch. If you need a place to stay we can probably find you something."

"No tithing?" he went on, and I shook my head. "No rituals of submission? No hierarchies?" He was talking about ceremonies that some packs went through—

alphas demanding demonstrations of obedience, usually involving violence and bloodshed.

I said, "As a wise alpha wolf recently told me, if you have to beat people up, you're doing it wrong. I'm not saying you won't get challenged by anyone else in the pack, because you will, but we can be relatively civil about it. I prefer to put the 'were' ahead of the 'wolf.' "

"Nasser also says you're not subservient to the local vampire Master."

"Rick? No. I mean, we're friends. But just friends." That sounded weird . . . Speaking of Rick, I still needed to talk to him about Hardin and her wanted poster.

"That's really unusual," he said. And was I pleased that he sounded impressed?

"We work together, hopefully for the good of everyone. And who's interviewing whom, here?"

He spread his arms in a show of apology. "All right, then. What else do you want to know about me?"

Ben and I looked at each other—me passing the ball to him. Because just like "How old are you?" was the obvious question I always asked vampires, werewolves had their obvious question.

"How did you become a werewolf?" Ben asked. "Did you choose it or were you attacked?"

"I was attacked," he said, without any self-consciousness. Totally straightforward.

"I'm sorry," I said.

"It happened a long time ago. I was nineteen. Still a kid, really. I was out fishing near my family's cabin, stayed out too late, the full moon was up. You probably hear stories like that a million times. The local pack took me in, helped me cope. I started making the alpha there nervous, so I left rather than cause trouble. I've been seminomadic for probably ten years now."

"And how do you know Nasser?" I asked.

"I've helped him out a time or two, whenever he needed an extra pair of arms. Or claws." His smile carefully didn't show teeth.

That made him hired muscle, for whatever shenanigans Nasser got up to. Anti-Roman shenanigans, probably, but still. Darren the mercenary.

My skepticism must have shown through, because he quickly continued. "That was only when I was on my own. Lone wolf. When I'm here, when I'm part of your pack, I answer to you, and that's it. I figure that's part of 'don't be stupid,' right?"

I smiled in spite of myself. "You're catching on."

"So, do I pass?"

I suddenly realized what was driving me crazy about this whole situation: I was being asked to decide someone's fate for the immediate future. I shouldn't have that kind of power. Most werewolves—and vampires, and probably a dozen other supernatural beings as well—would see it as completely normal. He'd asked permission to live in our territory, I could give it or not as I chose. But this wasn't just about settling down; he was asking to become part of our family—and it was up to me to say yes. When really I should be calling up everyone in the pack, talking to Shaun and Becky, and Ben of course. Maybe even Rick. Might not hurt to consult Cormac as well . . .

"You're thinking deep thoughts," Ben said.

I'd been staring into space, my lips pursed. "No deeper than usual." Darren was looking at me expectantly. "All right, you're in. Don't blow it." I offered my hand for him to shake, which he did, again. Shaking hands was a human gesture, not a wolf greeting, but he overcame his wolf instincts without hesitation. He was civilized. Housebroken, even. Deal accomplished. I still felt weird.

"Why don't I introduce you around?" I said, gesturing at the others to join us. "I imagine you'll meet the rest of the pack on the next full moon." I did the mental count in my head—eight days away. Sooner rather than later, then. We'd get to see both sides of the new kid.

Shaun approached obliquely from our side of the table, keeping a wary gaze on the newcomer. He was our lieutenant, the strongest wolf in our pack. Our backup. Becky and Tom were tough, but ranked lower than Shaun. They hung back to see how Shaun reacted.

"Everything cool?" he asked.

"Everything's cool," I said. "Darren, Shaun. And that's Becky and Tom. Darren's going to be staying with us for a while. And not causing trouble."

Shaun's lip curled. Yeah, he'd help keep Darren in line, if it came to that. I still couldn't get a good read on the guy. He seemed unconcerned, smiling and friendly.

"Right," Shaun said. "Can I get you a drink?"

"Sure, that'd be great," Darren said.

Maybe this seemed weird because I felt like we should have been doing this out in the woods, on four legs, duking it out with growls and teeth instead of sitting at a table in a restaurant. We were acting human. But our wolves were sizing each other up. Full moon was going to be interesting.

Shaun brought beers, the others sat with us, and we embarked on a perfectly normal conversation, asking about jobs and work and places we'd lived. Tom knew about an apartment for rent, and Darren seemed to think it sounded good. They agreed to meet about it tomorrow.

Well, this seemed to be going well. Swimmingly, even. The tension around us faded a few notches. My shoulders relaxed, and I didn't feel a need to keep watching Darren, waiting for him to strike. I was suddenly exhausted. I turned to Ben. "Time to go home?"

"Sounds like a plan."

"Thanks, Kitty. I really appreciate it," Darren said, beaming his calm smile at us.

Not only did he get in the first word, he had to get the last one, too. Whatever.

Shaun went back to work at the bar, but Becky and Tom stayed behind to talk to Darren. The glamour of the new.

Outside, a faint breeze brought the scent of distant mountains, of spring pines and stone, through the asphalt and fumes of the city. I filled my lungs, and the walk to the car was calm.

"Did I make the right call?" I asked Ben.

"We'll find out," he said.

"That's not comforting." I took his hand and squeezed.

"You're still wondering if you're doing this alpha thing right, aren't you?"

"I'm pushing thirty. Isn't life supposed to get easier?"

Ben laughed.

Chapter 7

RICK NEVER returned my call that night, and I worried. As I tossed and turned in bed, reaching to the nightstand to check my phone on the off chance I hadn't heard the ring, Ben kept pointing out that Rick had survived a very long time and could reasonably be expected to take care of himself for the foreseeable future.

"Besides," he added, "Columban didn't seem interested in hurting Rick."

"Then what about those arson cases in Europe? Rick doesn't know about those and I doubt Columban would tell him."

He murmured sleepily onto the back of my neck. "Kitty. Relax. Please."

I tried, honest I did. But I kept waiting for that call, as I watched dawn lighten the sky outside the bedroom window.

Somehow, I got myself to work and made a show of accomplishing something, despite all the potential interviewees who wouldn't return my calls, press releases I was supposed to be reviewing, messages I should have been answering, my second book that wasn't writing itself. The file for it glared on my monitor, displaying too much white space.

When my cell phone finally did ring, I dived for it. The prey had revealed itself at last, and I pounced. Even though in the middle of the day, in full sunlight, it couldn't possibly be Rick, who was holed away in his lair, asleep. I hoped he was.

This call came from Cormac. Maybe he had some good news. I answered, "Yeah?"

"I think I found where your vampire priest is holed up."

"You did? Where?" If we found Columban, I'd bet we'd find Rick.

"You want to go see?"

"We're not going to be sneaking up on this guy, are we?"

"It's the middle of the day, what can he do? I'll pick you up."

Twenty minutes later his Jeep was at the curb in front of KNOB. Bag and jacket in hand, I piled into the passenger seat. He drove off without a word.

We'd gone six or seven blocks before I couldn't stand the silence anymore. "So what'd you find?" I asked.

He wore a thin, wry smile. "You gotta ask yourself, if you were a priest, and a vampire, where would you go?"

"I'm not really in the mood for this," I said.

"It's pretty funny."

"Come on? Where?"

He was enjoying himself too much to give the surprise away. I crossed my arms and slouched.

We crossed the freeway into downtown, and he turned from Colfax onto the Auraria campus, a collection of university buildings on a surprisingly pastoral campus for being the middle of downtown Denver. He made a couple of turns into a warren of buildings and parked in a circular drive beside a large, pink church. It had two square, neo-Spanish colonial towers in front; a curved, graceful roofline; gray trim. It must have been almost a century old, and the rest of the city had clearly grown up around it.

"Here it is."

I pointed at the crosses at the top of the building. "It's a church."

"Yup."

"I thought vampires couldn't go into churches," I said. "Consecrated ground and all that."

"But this one's not a church anymore. The parish moved out in the seventies, and it's been used as an auditorium ever since. There's a dinosaur museum in the basement."

So, where do you go to find a vampire priest? A

deconsecrated church. Of course. I chuckled. "Well, that's cute."

He opened the door and climbed out.

"Wait, what are you doing?" I called, scrambling out of my side of the Jeep. "You can't go staking him or anything. Rick'll kill us."

He glanced at me sidelong, and I growled under my breath.

"I'm only guessing he's here," he said. "A vampire isn't going to leave a trail or reveal himself unless he wants to. Nothing's better at hiding than they are. But you've seen it before—don't look for the vampire, look for what he's using to protect himself. I made a list of likely places and started visiting them, and I found something."

We walked around to the back of the building, to a quiet space by a house connected to the church—the former rectory. A row of shrubs and a flower garden, daffodils nodding and lilacs filling the air with a heady smell, sheltered the space from the foot traffic on the sidewalk.

Cormac knelt on the ground, and I knelt with him, watching. He pulled items out of his pockets and arranged them on the lawn in front of him, which meant he was going to work a spell. Or, Amelia was. Because of her, I never knew what Cormac was going to draw from his figurative hat next. His pockets always had arcane bits and pieces in them.

He picked up a stub of a red candle, the wick already blackened; a sprig of some herb; and a piece of black twine. He wrapped the herb to the candle with the twine, then lit the candle using a cheap lighter, which seemed wrong somehow. A real wizard ought to be able to spark it out of thin air, right? But I'd hung around with enough magicians over the last few years to know the answer to that: you don't waste magic on something you can do without it. The cheap lighter ignited the candle's wick just fine.

Cormac's lips moved, mouthing words. He stepped forward, toward the church wall, holding the candle in front of him, its flame wavering with the movement. About twenty steps away, the yellow drop of fire went out. The air was still, but a stray breeze might have extinguished it. I looked around, as if expecting to find that some invisible person nearby had blown it out.

He backed up, and the candle flared to life again. He walked a little ways farther down, following the line of an invisible circle, moved toward the building— and again the flame died. He tried it two or three more times, and each time he crossed that invisible threshold, the candle went out, or relit.

"That's really weird," I said, unnecessarily.

"Yeah, Amelia saw markings, there and there." He pointed to black squiggly marks, one on a corner of the church, another on a nearby tree, and a third on the back of a NO PARKING sign near the street. I'd have figured they were random graffiti tags, if I noticed them at all. But now that he'd pointed them out, they had a pattern—pairs of stylized letters, medieval alchemical or zodiac signs maybe.

I tried to visualize what the candle told us was there in spirit. "Someone cast a protective circle here," I said. "Protecting against what?"

"That's the question, isn't it?" Cormac said. "May be nothing. May be a habit of his."

"You're sure it's Rick's vampire friend that did it?"

"Because we don't know any other vampires who are magicians, right?"

My shoulders unconsciously bunched up, an imitation of hackles rising. He was talking about Roman, who'd spent part of his two thousand years as a vampire learning how to work magic. Guy could do it all.

"Are you saying Columban is with Roman?"

"I'm just saying that vampires and magic aren't mutually exclusive. And that this guy knows how to cover his ass and doesn't seem to need any help doing it. The symbols are European, medieval—it's what I'd expect from a vampire working for the Vatican."

"So he's a vampire Catholic priest *and* a magician. I'd have assumed those would all be mutually exclusive."

"I don't think we can make any assumptions. Guy'll do what he needs to do."

Didn't really make the situation any *better*.

Cormac continued, "This is just a defense against a supernatural threat. Won't stop someone with a stake, if it comes to that."

"He may have mundane servants for that," I said. "So no, we're not staking him. This is Rick's problem." For now. I really had to let him know about Hardin's police sketch.

"We know where he's most likely staying, now. We can keep an eye on him."

That would have to be enough. I looked over the building. It probably had a basement or cellar, or at the very least a windowless utility closet, locked and protected. People moved around here all day, never knowing about the vampires lurking here.

We returned to the Jeep. I mulled possibilities. Not knowing what to expect next made planning ahead difficult. Was Columban worried about something specific? Did I need to be worried about it, too? Or was this a general precaution? I asked, "Would a protective circle like that work if the church were still consecrated? Still a church, I mean?"

"If it were still a church you wouldn't need the circle. But then, the vampire wouldn't be there."

Maybe that was why Columban did it, and for no other reason. He couldn't use a real church, but he could make a facsimile of one.

Cormac asked, "If Rick decides to go with this guy and leave Denver, what are you going to do?"

I couldn't imagine such a thing. Rick leaving Denver—Rick *was* Denver. He'd been around since before there was a Denver. He couldn't leave Denver. I almost blurted the words, unthinking. But Columban represented something Rick thought he lost centuries ago. I remembered the way he looked that night, as if the universe had rearranged itself around him.

"Try to talk him out of it?" I said. I honestly didn't know what I'd do if Rick left. Try to be happy for him.

I had a bigger question. We were supposed to be working to oppose Roman together. The only way this whole opposition thing worked is if Rick and I were in it together. If Rick left to become some kind of vampire priest, I'd be on my own. Would vampires like Nasser even listen to me, then?

"You should know," I said. "Hardin's looking for this guy, too."

"I'm not telling her about this," Cormac said, with the contempt he held for all cops.

"That's what I thought. I need to hold her off until I can get ahold of Rick."

"She won't hear it from me."

Cormac drove me back to work, waiting until we were in the parking lot at KNOB to ask, "Heard there's a new werewolf in town."

I looked at him, startled. "How do you know about him?"

"Keep my eyes open, that's all."

Cormac hadn't been at New Moon last night, I was sure of it. Had Ben told him? "Are you *spying* on us? On New Moon?"

"Like I said, just keeping my eyes open. So, how's that going?"

I slouched in the seat and growled. "It's fine, everything's fine," I said, noncommittal. He gave me a sidelong look.

"When's full moon, Saturday? He going with you?"

"What, you thinking of tagging along, just in case?"

"I could."

I glared at him. "And how exactly would you accomplish that? You think you're going to dig some of your silver bullets out of storage and sit on a hillside playing sniper?" That was exactly the kind of thing he'd have done in the old days, before his time in prison. Now, as an ex-con, handling firearms could get him thrown back into prison. Ben and I seemed to treat the threat more seriously than he did. Or he was purposefully pulling our chains. I would never know. "No. We'll be fine."

"You change your mind, call."

"We can handle it. This is normal pack stuff. Everything's fine."

"You keep saying that."

He was worried. This was his way of saying he was worried. So I didn't snap back at him. This time, instead of saying everything would be just fine, nothing to worry about, I said, "If we need you, we'll call." Which was all anybody wanted to hear from family in the end, wasn't it?

"GOOD EVENING, this is Kitty Norville and in case you didn't know, you're listening to *The Midnight Hour*. Cutting edge, controversial, and all that good stuff. I know what you tune in for, and I'm here to make sure you leave happy. Tonight I've got a couple of guests on the show, calling in from their respective offices to discuss with me a brand-new book making the rounds: *In the Blood,* a memoir by a guy named Edward Alleyn. That's Edward Alleyn, vampire, in what might be the first widely published vampire memoir ever. I should also mention that the author claims to be Edward Alleyn, the Elizabethan actor who starred in the great plays of Christopher Marlowe, which means he's been alive for some four hundred years, and he wants to tell us all about it. The book is stirring up a lot of heated discussion in some quarters. It's been called a window into the Elizabethan age, as well as the century's lamest hoax. What do you think? Have you read the book, and was it really written by a four-hundred-year-old vampire celebrity, or is it some ghost writer's shameless bid for publicity? I've found a historian and a literary scholar who've both read the book and have come to different conclusions about the author's claims. For all our edifications, I've brought them here to discuss."

Now, I knew very well that the book really was by Edward Alleyn, vampire, who really was the Elizabethan actor. These days, he was Master of London, and I'd stayed with him last year when I traveled to the city for the First International Conference on Paranatural Studies. I was the one who talked him into writing the thing, and I read an advance copy to give him a nice glowing review. Not that he needed it. He'd sparked enough publicity all on his own to hit the bestseller list in the first week of release. This was without doing any kind of promotion, public appearances, interviews, or anything. That was his condition for doing the book—that he could remain in the shadows, out of the public eye, as he'd done since his "death" in 1626. Plenty of controversy could be generated without his direct participation, though, and I had a feeling he was enjoying the show from the safety of one of his sumptuous manor houses.

"Professor Sean Eret is a historian from the University of Michigan, and he'll start us off. Welcome to the show, Dr. Eret." Eret had written articles defending the book, and I was looking forward to hearing from him.

"Thank you for inviting me. This should prove energizing."

"Lay it out for me: you believe the author of *In the Blood* is telling the truth and really is the actor Edward Alleyn turned vampire."

He had a pleasant, rumbly professor voice. Like he ought to be sitting in a big comfy chair by an old-fashioned fireplace. I chose to imagine him so. "It's not outside the realm of reason that this book is a work of fiction. But if it is, a ridiculous amount of historical research went into its creation. Alleyn has details here that most historians have never even thought to research. The names of Queen Elizabeth's hounds and falcons, for example. He's right, by the way, and I had to call in favors at the British Library to check. It's astonishing."

"So the historical accuracy was enough to convince you?" I said.

"It's impressive all on its own, but there's so much more to the book than that. It's the *personality* of it."

"You want to explain what you mean by that?"

"Facts, historical detail, no matter how obscure, can be researched. But the author of this book has managed to take on the mind-set of a person living in that time and place. The chapters dealing with his early life—they're exquisite. It's difficult for a modern author, no matter how diligent, to replicate the historical mind without some kind of judgment or commentary on that time as history. Alleyn is so comfortable with the biases and prejudices of a man from that time and place, I'm very much inclined to believe his claims."

"The gossip about Shakespeare and Marlowe doesn't hurt, either," I said.

"If the anti-Stratfordians won't take the word of Edward Alleyn that Shakespeare wrote Shakespeare's plays, I'm not sure there's any hope for them."

"I think I have to agree with you, sir," I said. "This sounds like a fine time to bring on my second guest, to offer a counterpoint. Professor Amanda McAdams, who teaches literature at the University of California at Santa Barbara and has written extensively on Elizabethan drama, thank you for joining us."

"Thank you," she said, brusque and businesslike.

"I know you have your own thoughts about *In the Blood* and its author."

"Yes, I do. Professor Eret has been fooled by a very convincing piece of fiction," she said. "All those facts, those details he praises—they can be researched and constructed. All the cross-referencing with secondary sources in the world will just tell you what the author used for source material. Even if the man himself came forward and allowed himself to be interviewed, and even if he does turn out to be a vampire, what proof do we have that he's really Edward Alleyn the actor? Birth certificate? Driver's license? I don't think so."

"What proof would convince you that this book

really was written by the Elizabethan Edward Alleyn, Professor McAdams?"

"That's just it, I don't believe this book could possibly have been written by someone from the Elizabethan era. There's no hint of historical idioms in the writing, of Elizabethan uses of language. The facts and mind-set within the writing may be historically accurate, as Dr. Eret says. But that's just a matter of research and careful characterization. The syntax of the writing itself is that of a *modern* author."

"That shouldn't be at all surprising," Eret interjected. "This isn't time travel, the book didn't land on us straight from 1620. It was written by someone living in the modern world for a modern audience. Well, perhaps 'living' isn't the right word."

I remembered something Ned said about accents. That a vampire who lived for a long time had to change his accent if he wanted to continue to blend in with the world around him. Language didn't stagnate. Rick was born in sixteenth-century Spain, but he sounded like a modern American. Ned himself cultivated a modern, dramatic voice that was probably quite different than the one he'd used on stage during his prime.

Smiling at the microphone I said, "Am I right in thinking that both of you are writing scholarly essays either refuting or defending the book?"

"My refutation has already been published online,"

Professor McAdams said. "I'll be happy to write a rebuttal of any published statement Professor Eret cares to make on the subject."

"*My* essay is appearing in *The New Yorker* next month," Professor Eret said.

I could imagine the glares they'd be exchanging if I'd had them both in the studio. I almost wished I'd been able to arrange it. I moved the conversation on. "What if I said I'd met the author and I'm absolutely certain his claims are true? He really is Edward Alleyn, the actor, and now vampire. I mean, he's got a near-mint First Folio sitting in his living room."

Professor McAdams said, "All you need to get a First Folio is a lot of money. It doesn't mean anything."

"He quoted Marlowe from memory."

"Any decent actor from the Royal Shakespeare Company can do that," she added.

Eret said, "This man you met, who claims to be Edward Alleyn—is he involved in the theater at all? I notice that this memoir deals very little with his life currently."

"He's protective of his privacy," I said. "But I believe he owns at least a couple of West End theaters."

"You see, that rings true to me. The original Edward Alleyn made his fortune in the theater and in spectacle. I have to believe that some of that impulse would still exist. But more than anything I offer this: of all the historical figures a vampire could claim to be, why on earth would anyone pick an Elizabethan actor who, apart from appearing as a secondary character in a popular film a dozen years ago, is virtually unknown to anyone outside the field? If this is a wild bid for attention, why not impersonate Walter Raleigh or Francis Drake, or even Shakespeare himself? If you're trying to be famous, impersonating a celebrity hardly anyone remembers is not the way to go about it."

When she didn't respond right away, I prompted McAdams. "Professor? What do you think about that?"

"I have to admit, you have a point there." She sounded thoughtful rather than disappointed.

Eret said, "Then you concede—I'm right, and the memoir is real."

"I wouldn't go *that* far," she said. "There's still a reputation to be made in establishing myself as the professional skeptic on the topic."

I said, "All right, level with me—that's why the Shakespeare debate's still out there, isn't it?"

"Because there are people who are professional skeptics on the topic? Of course."

"Well, I have to respect your honesty, at least."

Eret said, "Professor McAdams, would you be interested in staging a series of public debates on the subject?"

"That's a wonderful idea. Maybe we could even co-present at the next MLA conference?"

"Splendid! Each of us ought to be able to get a book or two out of this. Are you tenured yet?"

"No—I could really use a high-profile book. Maybe even for a popular audience . . ."

"Then a formal rivalry could help both our careers," Eret said cheerfully.

Are you *kidding* me? I wondered if they even remembered that I was here. "You guys do realize you're still on the air, right?" They both made polite affirmative noise. "Do I dare ask about any conclusions on the subject of *In the Blood* and its author?"

"We'll obviously never be able to come to some kind of consensus," McAdams pronounced decisively. Nay, happily even.

"Right then. Thank you both for speaking with me this evening. I'm going to wrest control of my own show back and open the line for a couple of questions. Hello, Arthur from Spokane."

"Hi, yes, I just wanted to say that you really can't be so cavalier in dismissing the argument that the front man purportedly known as William Shakespeare did *not* write those plays. The actor Edward Alleyn may not have even been aware of the cover-up, as many contemporaries were not—that's why it's called a cover-up—"

God, I really needed to check the monitor more closely. "I'm sorry, that's a little off topic tonight. Can you tell me if you think Edward Alleyn is really a vampire?"

"Well, of course he is, if he says he is."

And yet Shakespeare couldn't have written Shakespeare. I stared at the microphone. "Seriously? You're going to stick with that?"

He sounded offended. "Well, yes, and if I could get back to the question of Shakespeare—"

"No, you can't. Next caller, please, and let's stay on topic. Hello?"

"Oh, Kitty, hi! I just have a quick question—do you think maybe that *Shakespeare* is a vampire?"

I had to think about that a minute. No, I needed to think about that for several minutes. But I didn't have a few minutes. I had the threat of dead air and a sudden wish that I had done this week's show on the possibility of psychic houseplants. "No, I don't. And I think it's about time to break for station ID and go have a drink. Or three . . ."

Chapter 8

I'D DONE worse shows. I'd done better.

Shaun had a beer waiting for me at New Moon as soon as I walked in, and that was only one of the many reasons we kept him around. This late, right before closing, only a few stragglers remained. Lingering parties, successful dates. Darren was sitting at a table for two—with Becky. At the moment her smile sparkled brighter than I'd ever seen it. Oh dear . . .

"How long have they been at it?" I said to Shaun, nodding at them.

"Couple of hours. She'd been here for half an hour or so, stopping by after work, and he showed up. They've been together ever since."

"So—what do you think?"

"He hurts her I'll rip his face off," he said. I was thinking the same thing. But for the moment she seemed so gosh darned happy, I could hardly judge. But it seemed . . . odd. Darren was certainly making himself at home.

I sidled over to their table. Just checking, I told myself. Politely interested, not intruding. "Hi, guys. Sorry to bother you, but could I have a word with Darren, just for a sec?" My smile was so big it hurt.

Becky actually glowered at me, offended. I didn't glare back and made what I hoped was a comforting shrug. For his part, Darren only seemed confused as he followed me back to the bar.

"What do you need?" he said as he hopped up on the stool next to me and leaned in close—closer than I was comfortable with. But I couldn't flinch back, not a millimeter. I couldn't figure this guy out. Maybe he was a were–golden retriever? We'd find out soon enough.

"Full moon's tomorrow night, I just wanted to go over a few things. We have territory in the mountains—"

He waved a hand as if to say, *no problem.* "Becky told me all about it."

"We usually carpool. You can ride up with Ben and me if you want—"

"You don't have to go through the trouble, I'll be okay."

But he didn't even know where we were going. The dirt roads we followed were Forest Service roads, not marked on the usual maps. How was he going to get there without a guide? Oh—he was riding with Becky.

I soldiered on. "We hunt together, as a pack. We keep an eye on each other. Livestock and roads are off-limits." I assumed I didn't have to tell him that people were off-limits as well. Maybe I shouldn't make that assumption . . .

He just kept smiling. "You don't trust me, do you?"

I sighed and shook my head, as if I could shake away my misgivings. "I just want everything to go smoothly. Full moon nights are always touchy."

"Everything'll be fine."

"Get there at twilight. We run as a pack."

"Yes, ma'am."

I scowled. Now he was just being patronizing. "Oh, and if you hurt Becky we'll all rip your face off."

He blanched, just a bit, but covered it up with his winning smile. "Don't worry, I'm not crazy."

Becky watched him as he returned to their table; they hunched in close, to confer. I felt suddenly tired, but didn't dare slouch.

Shaun had politely removed himself to the other end of the room, but drifted back over after Darren left.

"It's all cool?" he asked.

"I don't know." I finally took a drink of the beer

that had been waiting faithfully for me on the bar. It had gone a bit warm. "I guess we'll find out."

Ben wasn't meeting me tonight, which meant I'd have the one drink and head home. By then, most of the buzz from the show would wear off and I'd be ready to sleep. Or if the buzz hadn't worn off, maybe I wouldn't be ready to sleep, and maybe Ben wouldn't be, either . . .

My face was buried in the mug when Shaun said, "Hey, look," and nodded at the front door.

Rick was standing there and tapped the glass when I spotted him. Rick, finally.

I opened the door and let him inside. "You've been invited. You can come in."

"Yes, but I thought I'd be polite," he said. "Since I'm here to talk and not drink." He eyed the few people at the bar and scattered at tables apprecia- tively. I was pretty sure he did it to be funny.

"And for that, I thank you," I said.

I guided him to a table in back. He sat across from me and, folding his hands before him, regarded me with a serious expression, lips pulled down. I focused on his chin instead of his eyes. He'd never used his vampiric influence on me before—that I knew of— but he looked like he might be willing to start.

"What is it?" I said.

"You and your hunter friend have been digging," he said.

Oops. My cheeks flushed to burning. "Well, I mean . . . It was broad daylight, how did you even know?"

He raised a brow at me, indicating that I should know better than to ask such a question. However he'd found out, he wasn't going to tell me. They were vampires, and that should be enough to explain anything to a mere mortal such as myself.

"You all are very invested in your reputations for omnipotence, you know that?" I said.

"As you say," he answered.

Omnipotence and inscrutability. How did I ever expect anything different? I said, "I'm just worried. About you. About that *guy*. I've been trying to call you—we need to talk. Detective Hardin's looking for him. He's wanted for arson and murder in Europe."

"That's really not your concern," he said, and I started getting angry.

"Yeah, until Hardin comes to me asking questions and I have to cover your ass."

He turned a hand in apology. "I appreciate that. But this is my business, mine alone. Hardin won't find him, even if you do help her. In the meantime, it would be better for you and Cormac if you stay out of this."

"I'd solve a lot of my problems by just staying out of things," I said. "But if Hardin is right and Columban caused that trouble in Europe, what's to say he won't cause the same trouble here?"

"He won't. Nobody's in any danger—"

"He makes me nervous," I said.

"Are you worried because he's a vampire, or because he's a Catholic priest?"

"Um, yes?"

He took a deep breath, measuring his words. "You've trusted me for years now, Kitty. Have I ever given you a reason not to?"

He never, ever had. In fact, he'd been one of the true friends, an anchor I could count on. He'd helped me more times than I could count. He was my first and strongest proof positive that being a vampire did not make someone a villain.

"No, of course not. You're right, I shouldn't be going behind your back and I shouldn't be worried about you."

"I don't know about the second of those," he said with a wry smile. "Trust me, if I need help, I'll call."

"You really should check your messages occasionally, you know. The Mistress of Buenos Aires is going to be showing up in a week. We need to plan."

"Yes, I know." He sat back and gazed around the dining room. I watched him take stock of each face, each mundane story unfolding before him. As he usually did in public crowds, he seemed amused, satisfied. He'd said it before: he liked people and being around them. It kept him human. Made it hard to see the five-hundred-year-old vampire in him.

He glanced toward the table where Darren and Becky were sitting. Darren laughed at something, she curled a short lock of hair around her finger. They may have been werewolves but those mating signals were all human. "Who's the new kid?" Rick asked.

"That's Darren. A lone wolf who wants to join the pack."

"How is that working out?"

"This is one of those times I wish this alpha gig came with an instruction manual. So far, so good." I made an expansive shrug, as if to take in the universe. "We'll find out for sure on the full moon."

"Good luck with that."

"Yeah, no doubt. But you—you're sure you're okay?"

"Never been better," he said.

I needed a moment to consider what a statement like that might really mean for a vampire.

THE FULL moon pulled at me. The sun was setting, the moon would rise soon, and Ben and I needed to be in the hills west of the city, with the rest of our pack, letting our wolves loose. But I couldn't, not yet. This happened every month, a battle in my mind, in the core of my being. Part of me could already taste the blood on my tongue. I *needed* to hunt, because nothing felt so good, so real, so *right*. My four legs and furred body would burst through this weak human skin. The feeling burned through me, stronger than the anticipation of sex. It must have been what addiction felt like.

Each of us stewed in our own roiling emotions, listening more and more to the wolves in our bellies, increasingly unable *not* to listen. We locked up the condo and headed to the car. *Soon, soon,* I whispered to my Wolf, begging her to stay calm. Just for another hour, just a little while longer.

Then my phone rang.

I flinched, and Ben jumped as if a gun had fired. His lips curled from his teeth. "Can't you shut that off?"

Caller ID said Cheryl. I probably shouldn't even have looked, but I couldn't ignore my sister. "Yeah?" I answered the call, wishing I didn't sound so brusque. I stood by Ben's car, clutching the phone to my ear, staring at nothing. Ben paced nearby, jangling the keys in his hand.

"Kitty, hi, it's me."

Why did people still say that, in this age of caller ID, when we knew who was calling before they said anything? "Hey, Cheryl." My foot started tapping. Cheryl didn't call me that often. We lived just across town from each other, but usually relayed messages through Mom, who called each of us every Sunday like clockwork. My sister only called directly when she wanted something, or if something was wrong. She didn't *sound* like something was wrong.

"So, how is everything?" she asked.

How is everything. I could give her a blithe answer, vague and cheerful, but a growl lodged in my throat. I had to swallow in order to continue.

"Fine. Busy, actually. I've had a lot on my plate this week." Ben stopped pacing and stared at me, his brows raised, asking, *Are you serious?* "In fact, I was just on my way out with Ben. Like, right this minute."

She made a thoughtful hum. "It's Saturday night, isn't it? Nice to know somebody still gets to party on the weekends." Her tone was cutting.

"Actually, it's a full moon tonight," I said, frowning.

"Wait, what? What's that got to do . . . oh."

"That's right," I said. "And I really need to get going."

"Right, okay, but I just need to talk for a second."

"Make it fast."

"I want to have a party for Mom, since her birthday's coming up and to celebrate her last scan coming back clean. But if I'm going to pull it off I really need your help."

I groaned. I didn't mean to, it just came out. It wasn't that I didn't think a party was a good idea—every day with Mom healthy was worth a celebration. She'd been diagnosed with breast cancer almost four years ago and beat it. Nothing to worry about.

Except medically speaking she wasn't out of the woods yet. She was in remission, but the cancer could always come back. She hadn't crossed that five-year mark yet, but for now, she was good.

So, party, yes. But I just couldn't take on another project right now.

"What was that for?" Cheryl shot back, annoyed.

"I'm sorry, but how much help are we talking about here? I'm kind of overbooked as it is—"

"Oh yeah, I always forget how busy you are, with all your jetting off to Europe and partying on Saturday night—"

"I wouldn't call it *partying*—"

"I've got two kids here, Jeffy's starting kindergarten this fall, I never seem to get anything done, and I thought that just for once I could count on you to help out, just a little."

The topic of this discussion had turned into something else entirely. This wasn't about a party at all, was it? In a twilit sky, the silver moon was edging over the horizon. I didn't have time for this . . . That was the trouble, wasn't it?

I took a breath and did what I could. "Cheryl, are you okay?"

"I just want to know that when I call you for help you're going to be there, you know? That's what family's supposed to do."

"Cheryl, I love you, and everything's going to be

okay. But can we talk about this tomorrow?" I winced. I wasn't trying to get rid of her. Except that I was. How did I make this not sound so bad?

Her voice turned flat. "Sure. Of course. Tomorrow. Fine," she said, taking a deep breath. Like she was trying to keep from crying. Oh God, my big sister was having a nervous breakdown, and I'd triggered it.

"We'll do the party," I assured her. "I'll help. But I can't talk about it right now. Okay?"

"Okay, okay," she said, and hung up. And that was that. I clutched the phone to my chest.

Ben watched me. "You heard all that?" I asked.

"Yeah."

"Is my sister losing it, or am I?"

"Either way, it'll pass."

"I really don't need another thing to worry about."

He squeezed my arm. "Let's get going. We'll worry about that later."

THE OTHERS would already be gathered, waiting for us. Not quite checking their watches or time on their cell phones, but watching the full moon rise and wondering where their fearless leaders were. This would take some damage control. I wasn't worried about most of the pack; we'd been stable for years, and no one was much interested in challenging our authority.

But this time we had Darren. What would he think, the alphas not taking charge on the one night when being a werewolf really meant something?

Like I had to impress him or something.

The farther out of town we got, the better I felt. We were leaving our human selves—our human anxieties—behind. The wilderness in the mountains meant freedom. At least for a night.

Tonight we were meeting at a little-used dirt service road on National Forest land. We carpooled so we'd only leave a handful of cars parked suspiciously in the middle of the woods at night. Ben turned off the main road; another ten minutes of driving brought the first of the other cars into view. I counted them, and sure enough, everyone else was already here, or should have been. He switched off his headlights and parked. We stashed our wedding bands in the glove box.

The sky above was deep blue, touched by the silver light of a rising moon. *It's time, it's time.*

Hand in hand, we walked into the woods to meet the others. I could hear a few murmuring voices, and running feet brushing through foliage. A rangy, oversized wolf came at us, ears up and tail out like a rudder, loping along with his mouth open, smiling almost.

"Wow, Tom, you a wolf or a golden retriever?"

He put his ears back and veered away from us,

snapping at air, enjoying his time. He could never be bothered to wait for the rest of us before shifting.

A few of the others had shifted as well, and they circled the spot where the rest of us waited, trotting up to Ben and me, brushing along our legs and nuzzling us in greeting, then bumping shoulders with the others. Chaos waiting to burst free.

"Hey," Shaun called. "Everything okay?" Leaning against a tree with his arms crossed, babysitting the rabble, he wore a T-shirt, jeans, and went barefoot.

"Got a late call. It's okay," I said.

"The gang's antsy."

"I expect so." Wolf kicked out, a stabbing pain under my rib cage. I winced and hugged myself against a sudden chill. *It's time . . .*

"So where's the new guy?" Shaun asked. Becky, in a tank top and yoga pants, had come up behind him. She'd been looking back and forth between us and the path behind us, as if expecting someone else to arrive.

"He's not here? He didn't get a ride with you, Becky?" I'd half-expected to see him next to Becky. I looked around, marked every face, taking in the scent of the gathered pack. In the cool night air I was able to sense every little odor; nothing smelled out of place. And that was the problem, because I should have been able to smell Darren's new, foreign scent. He'd need a couple of full moon nights of running with the rest of us, piling together as wolves and sleeping until morning, before he smelled like pack.

"I thought he'd be with you guys," she said.

"Damn. I should have called him," I said. "He said he'd be here . . ."

"Maybe he decided he didn't want to be part of the pack after all," Shaun said.

Becky worriedly bit her lip. "No, he would have told someone, he wouldn't have just left."

We all looked at her, and instead of wilting she stood up a little taller. I sighed. "We can't worry about it now."

Still frowning, Becky turned away, pulled off her top, dropped it on the ground as she shoved down her pants. Naked, her lithe form was a shadow in the moonlight. She was still walking when she started shifting, back hunching, limbs bending, fur sprouting over skin. As she dropped, she grunted once, and the Change passed over her like water. Rolling his shoulders back Shaun stripped and followed Becky. The world's focus grew sharp, narrow. Nothing else mattered but the pack and the forest.

One of the pack came toward me and Ben. Shirtless, he slouched, head bowed, slinking low and submissive. He wanted something and was afraid to ask for it. Now wasn't the best time. My lip curled, but Ben brushed his arm against mine, calming me.

Ben said, more calmly than I would have, "What is it, Trey?"

"I need to talk. About Sam."

Sam, Sam, who was Sam . . . Oh, his girlfriend. Right. I steadied myself. "What's wrong? Did you talk to her?"

"Yes. It . . . it didn't go well." Anxious lines marred his face, and not just from the stress of keeping his wolf at bay. He was worried, on the edge of shifting, trying to stay human so he could get out the words.

"I'm sorry," I said, the only thing I could think to say. "We should talk. In the morning." In moments, none of us were going to be able to say much of anything.

"Yeah. That's all I want." He nodded quickly, ducking again. He was afraid we'd be angry with him.

I brushed my hand over his hair; he leaned into the touch of comfort. "In the morning," I said. "Go now."

He spun and ran, a ripple of dark fur sprouting along his back.

Next to me, Ben pulled off his shirt, folded it distractedly, and set it on the ground. Then he stood in front of me and tugged up the hem of my T-shirt. Like a little kid, I raised my arms and let him pull it off. I wasn't wearing a bra, and the cool air brushed deliciously across my skin. Fur strained to burst through in a million pinpricks.

Ben hugged me, skin to skin, and I could have melted against him. "I love you," he said.

"I love you," I whispered.

He convulsed once in my arms, then dropped to all fours, grunting.

I stood there, staring into the trees—still resisting, until that growling voice inside me barked, *Now.*

Yeah, now.

THE NIGHTTIME forest is freedom. The hunting pack is like a storm, a wind through the trees, constant and unstoppable. A rainbow wash of scents greet her: live wood and dead leaves, air that tastes of distant rain, and prey, large and small, from mice to rabbits to deer and elk. Alive, quivering, filled with meat and blood. Her mouth waters.

Feeding the pack takes larger prey. Since they hunt together, they can be ambitious. Her mate finds a trail, nips her flank to gain her attention, urging her and the others to follow. But she snaps back. The thread of another scent has caught her attention. Foreign, alien, stabbing through their territory, this draws her far more than her hunger. This is a threat.

Circling around her, and it, her mate finds it, too. They brush shoulders, bury noses in each other's fur to reassure themselves of their familiar marks. The rest of the pack mills, uncertain. Their anxiety has spread. This invading scent is alien, but familiar. She knows this wolf, which somehow makes the intrusion worse. This is an invitation refused.

She tips her nose to the sky and lets loose a thin howl, hoping for response—for explanation.

The pack waits for a reply to travel through the silvered night, but none comes. So she puts her nose to the ground to follow the scent, and the pack follows her.

They are wide-ranging, fanned out through the forest, claiming their territory, watching for danger. Prey of every sort crisscrosses their path, and her wolves yip at her, telling her they're hungry and that food is close. Time enough for that later. She trots on, and the stranger's scent grows stronger.

They leave the forest and reach an open meadow, a rolling field of grass tucked between hills, glaring with the brightness of the moon. She hangs back, unwilling to expose the pack without more information. They pace behind her. Her mate nudges her shoulder and looks over the wide space with her.

Far ahead, there is movement in the grass. The stranger is here. She also smells blood, freshly spilled. A growl sticks deep in her throat when she realizes what has happened. At the far edge of the meadow, a wolf is eating, moving around a carcass, ripping away mouthfuls. But it's the wrong prey—a scent

*they have always avoided. Rich prey, so easy to kill,
but they have never hunted it, they can't, not if they
want to stay hidden.*

*Her hackles rise stiff as boards. She howls again,
a long note that falls away. The distant wolf, gray
and tawny in the moonlight, pauses and looks up. He
sings back, a bright tone that leaves her confused—
it's a greeting, a call to wolves who share territory.
Not an invader at all. At least he doesn't think so.*

*But he has hunted without the pack, and hunted
badly. She feels a driving need to see him cower.*

*She pushes her mate and huffs at her strongest,
her enforcer, one of those who leads the hunts. Together, they run, stretching to cross the field of
grasses in long strides. Her hope is that this wolf will
see them coming and drop to show his belly.*

*He does not. Instead, he stands on the carcass
he has killed, in victory, in dominance. She pins her
ears, lips contracting to bare her teeth at him. When
he meets her gaze—a calm, unconsidered challenge,
a rage fills her. She charges. Her mate and her second are with her, as is right. Reaching the challenger
first, she crashes into him, jaws open and claws
reaching. He rears to meet her—and falls away.
Tumbles off the bloody meat he's been picking at.
Her mate and enforcer circle. The challenger sidles
away, tail lowered. Not between his legs. Not quite
submissive. But he's dropped his gaze.*

He's larger, she can't stand over him, can only show dominance by glaring, curling her lips. Stand between him and his kill, show her anger. He circles, paces. Mostly seems confused. As if he doesn't understand what he's done wrong. As if he doesn't know the rules.

Her mate and enforcer run at him, nip at him, and together they drive him to join the pack. She follows at a stiff-legged lope, looking back once at the half-eaten carcass. Much meat is left. She's tempted to make use of it, but they've already left too much sign of their passing. The urge to flee this tainted spot overcomes her hunger.

The pack has scattered. The deer they might have hunted together has been forgotten in favor of easier, smaller prey. They hunt from desperation now, for rabbits or such, for the scant morsels they can find. Not the organized feast they could have had. For the moment, she has lost control. So she runs, and runs, kills what she can, a couple of rodents, swallows them whole. Runs again. A cry stops her. An arcing note, echoing against the night sky, stabs into her mind, and calls her back.

Her mate meets her halfway. Nips her ear. She yawns at him, rubs herself along his side, fur to fur, and finally feels right.

The pack gathers in their night's den. All of them,

even the stranger. The others give him wide berth. She snaps at him, drives him off in a run before letting him circle back. Just to show him.

She is only able to sleep when her mate curls up beside her, resting his snout against her neck.

Chapter 9

OFTEN, MORNINGS after a full moon were muddy, full of strange dreams and half-remembered images. A taste of blood lingering in the film over my teeth, with no real memory of how it got there. Only assumptions, and a hope that I hadn't done something terrible.

This morning, the night came back to me with the clarity of a photograph. Darren's solo hunting expedition. His sheer . . . *stupidity*. What did he think he was doing? He'd put us all in danger.

I propped myself on my elbows and let my nose widen, taking in scents. The pack was here, curled up together after the previous night's anxiety and chaos. A dozen and a half naked human bodies tucked up against the shelter of the rocks that formed the night's den. Gaze alert, body tensed, Shaun was awake and looking back at me. I gave my head a small shake. No need to panic. We could handle this, calmly, sensibly, like human beings.

"Where is he?" I growled.

"Hmm?" Ben murmured. He wasn't awake yet.

I shook his arm. "Come on."

"What . . . oh." He scrubbed his face, waking himself up, but I was already on my feet and stalking around the edges of the den, looking for Darren.

He'd curled up to sleep a few paces off from the others. And Becky was with him. They were naked, together, his arms around her body, her legs tangled up with his, and I didn't want to know what they'd been doing all night and into the morning. Was this how it felt to walk in on your teenage kid?

I stood in front of them and crossed my arms. I might have tapped my feet.

Darren woke first, moving arms and legs, nuzzling the back of Becky's neck. Becky started to roll over, to place herself more firmly in his arms, then stopped. Her nostrils widened, taking in my scent, and her eyes shot open, looking at me.

"Morning, sunshine," I said. She froze, ducked her gaze, and suddenly seemed trapped in the other werewolf's arms.

"Isn't it a little early?" Darren mumbled. Still hadn't opened his eyes.

"Kitty, don't you want to put some clothes on?" Becky said.

Yeah, I was naked, standing in the middle of the woods, chewing out a guy I barely knew. Didn't much matter when we were all naked.

"You should talk," I said.

She shrank, slouching and curling up. Darren leaned over her protectively. Ben, who'd come up to lean on the rocks behind me, straightened and took a step forward. This was not how I wanted my morning to go.

"You look kind of angry," Darren finally said. "I know I was supposed to meet you last night—"

"That's actually not what I'm pissed off about," I said. "Do you remember what you killed last night?"

He thought a minute, and donned a slow smile. "That was pretty sweet. You have a great territory up here. Easy pickings."

He didn't get it. Not even a little bit. I yelled, "We do not kill cattle! How are we supposed to stay under the radar if we eat someone's livelihood?"

"You're getting this worked up over a *cow*? What's the big deal? One dead cow isn't going to hurt anything."

"Have you ever seen a UFO investigator go after a cattle mutilation investigation? This is exactly the kind of thing they live for, and if they go looking for aliens and find us instead . . . sure, people know about werewolves, but if they knew exactly where to find us, and came *hunting* for us—"

"I think you're overreacting."

"I think you flunked your audition," I said.

"Whoa, wait a minute." He extricated himself from Becky's sleepy embrace, and she shuffled out of his way as he stood. If I really thought about it, I couldn't blame Becky in the least—he was a good-looking guy, with well-defined muscles and a confident stance to his body. A little too confident—chin up, shoulders back. Looming over me, and not bothering to show a bit of submission. He was taller than I was, which meant I had to figure out how to stare down at him. Fortunately, I had help. Ben stalked forward, arms crossed. Shaun joined me on the other side. Darren took a step back. Good for him.

"Okay, okay, fine," he said, glancing away, letting his shoulders slump. As if he had to consciously think about showing signs of submission the way I had to think about showing dominance. "You're right, if I want to be here I need to follow your rules. I'm sorry. I really didn't think it would be a big deal."

"If you'd shown up when and where you were supposed to and hunted with the rest of the pack, you'd have known what the rules are."

"I thought you had a reputation for being different. For being more free-spirited than other wolf packs. 'Don't be stupid' left it pretty wide open, I thought."

"Disappointed?"

"Maybe surprised. I guess I didn't really know what to expect."

"Well, now you do. We have rules, just like grade school."

He tensed for a moment, maybe getting ready with another snappy comeback. I'd have had some words for him then. Ben and Shaun probably would have had a little more.

But he lowered his gaze and said, "Okay. I understand." He slunk away, to where Becky was getting dressed near a stand of trees.

He knew what he needed to say to get me off his back, even if he wasn't entirely submissive about it. Same thing in the end, and did it matter when I got the result I wanted? This was going to take some negotiating if Darren really wanted to stick around.

And we were all still naked, like some weird low-intensity *Lord of the Flies* re-creation. I could tell my human self was slipping back into place, because my skin prickled in the breeze, and I suddenly wanted to put clothes on.

"Let's get out of here," I muttered.

The rest of the pack seemed happy to abandon the standoff. The tension in the space faded as people retrieved their clothes, spoke in low voices, and moved back toward the road. Wearing a wry smile, Ben held my shirt and jeans out to me.

"You look like you need coffee."

"I need coffee," I muttered, pulling the shirt on, not caring if it was inside out or straight or what, and hopping awkwardly to get the jeans on. Then came the epic debate that I had with myself every morning after a full moon: coffee first, or shower? Which one would make me feel more human? Which did I need more: to clear the morning fuzz, or to feel clean? Some months the coffee won, some months the shower did. I still hadn't decided what I wanted this morning.

Side by side, Ben and I turned to make our way to the road. We stopped, though, because Trey was standing there, in rumpled T-shirt and dirt-streaked jeans, his frown taut, wary.

Our talk. I'd said we could talk. I closed my eyes and turned my gaze to the sky. I was juggling. Been juggling for a while. This was what it felt like to watch balls drop to the floor in front of me with a thud. Nothing for it but to pick them up and try again.

"You up for coffee?" I asked him.

He blinked, surprised. "Sure."

"You?" I said to Ben.

"Wouldn't miss it."

"The coffee, or me trying to dig myself out of this hole?"

"Yes?" he said, smiling.

The predictability of his answer was somehow comforting.

* * *

WE HAD a favorite diner that we ended up at mornings like these, the kind of place that had coffee cups already on the table and poured without asking if you wanted some. I breathed in the scent—hot, bitter, rich—and felt my skin settle over my body a little more comfortably. Wolf curled her nose at the scent and retreated even further into the background, calm after her night out. Sleeping. Staying human would be easier for the next week or so.

Trey held his cup but didn't drink. His gaze darted, his leg bounced under the table. He was nervous. I did what I could to set him at his ease, trying not to seem too earnest and demanding. Ben was doing a better job of not looking worried, slouching back against the booth, expression bland. He'd ordered a plate of bacon. Along with coffee, bacon made everything better, right?

"So," I prompted. "Your girlfriend. Sam."

His smile was strained. "We talked. I told her." He sighed.

"And? How did she take it?"

"That's just it, I don't know. She said she had to think about it. That she wanted some time alone and she'd call me when she was ready. That's a bad sign, isn't it?"

"I don't know that I'd jump to that conclusion," I said. But he was right, this certainly didn't sound *good*. "Telling her what you are, that's a pretty big

deal. She probably really does need to think about it."
I hoped I sounded confident.

"I'm worried I'm going to mess this up," he said,
putting his head in his hands, despairing. "I think
I've already messed this up. She'll never talk to me
again."

"If she's really the one, she will. You won't mess it
up."

"But if she's really okay with it . . . with *me* . . ."
He clamped his mouth shut, looking away, struggling
for words, then said, "Wouldn't she just say so? But I
scared her off, I know I did."

"Not really," I said. "Not until she really doesn't
call you back."

"I can't wait that long. I have to call her."

"When did you talk to her?"

"Yesterday."

I grimaced. "You probably shouldn't have waited
until the day of the full moon to talk to her." We were
at our worst on days of the full moon, stressed and
irritable. He must have looked slightly mad to her eyes.

"I know," he moaned. "I just kept putting it off."

"Give her time, Trey. For real. More than a couple
of days. If she hasn't called back in a week . . ." Then
what? Give up on her? Call her back? Stalk her? "Try
giving her a call. Don't crowd her."

"That's your advice. That sounds like something
you'd say to anyone."

"Yeah, it kind of is," I said. "Why should my advice to you be different? You're both still people."

He huffed. "I'm not exactly *normal*."

"You are for us."

He seemed startled, sitting for a moment with his gaze turned inward, eyes looking blankly at the surface of his undrunk coffee. The bacon arrived, its fatty scent cutting across the coffee. Another wake-up call, a summons to humanity. Ben nibbled on a piece. Trey looked at him, maybe for confirmation, maybe for a different opinion.

"She's the expert," Ben said. Trey raised a disbelieving brow, and Ben added, "Unless of course Sam wants you to chase after her, to prove you really love her, and if you don't call she'll feel neglected—"

"Don't try to game the system," I said. "Give her a couple of days at the very least. Then call."

"Can you do it?"

"Do what?"

"Call her. Put in a good word for me."

"No! I mean, I'd love to meet her, but only when she's ready. If she's nervous now imagine what'll happen when she faces a whole room of werewolves."

"I don't want to think about it."

"Besides, imagine what she'd think if this strange woman she's never met butts into business that ought to be between you two."

He sagged again. "I guess that would look strange."

More than a little. "I know it's tough, but you can get through this. If she's as great as you say she is, she'll come around. She'll be fine." Please, let Sam be a sensible woman, let this all work out . . .

Trey was about to respond when my phone rang. Still shoved into my jeans pocket after last night. One of these days, I was going to take a hammer to the device. Justifiable technocide. I checked the caller ID.

"It's Detective Hardin," I said, as justification for taking the call. I wouldn't have, for just about anyone else, but I clicked the talk button.

"Kitty?"

"Detective Hardin?" I said, worried, but at least I didn't start declaiming about how I'd done nothing wrong and it wasn't my fault.

"I'm here at the emergency room at St. Joseph's with your buddy Cormac."

She kept talking, but I didn't hear anything. Something had gone wrong, and it didn't matter that he'd been keeping his nose clean, trying to stay out of trouble—at least as best he could. Someone from his past had found him, he'd gotten into a fight he couldn't get out of—

"Kitty?" she said. "Are you there?"

"What's wrong, what happened?" Ben had gone tense, sitting up and leaning forward, straining to hear, bacon and coffee forgotten. Even Trey responded to the anxiety, straightening, as if we faced danger right here.

"Don't worry, he'll be fine. But he asked me to call you and Ben. You should probably get down here." It couldn't have been too bad. She sounded almost amused, not at all like someone delivering bad news. In fact she may have been enjoying this. That still could have meant bad news, knowing how she felt about Cormac . . .

"What happened?" I squeaked.

"He said he'll explain it when you get here."

"Right. Okay. We're on the way." I clicked the phone off. I stared at it for a moment.

"Go," Ben said, pushing at me to let him out of the booth. "I'll drive."

"What is it?" Trey said. He hadn't been close enough to hear Hardin over the phone. "You've gone completely white."

"Ben's cousin's in the emergency room," I said starkly. I looked at him despairing. "Can we pick this up later? I'm sorry—" Wolf, curled up deep in my gut, growled a little. We were alpha, we shouldn't be apologizing. But I was human, and Trey had asked for help. I couldn't do everything.

"Yeah, sure, of course," Trey said. Ben had the presence of mind to slap a twenty on the table as we were leaving. At least we didn't stick him with the check.

Ben took my arm and pulled me toward the door. Shaken out of my shock by his urging, I hurried to keep up.

Once outside, we ran to the car and drove to the downtown hospital in silence.

Chapter 10

FINDING PARKING took forever. Of course it did, we were in a hurry. I suggested just parking right outside the big sliding doors with the red EMERGENCY sign posted over it, but Ben indicated that that would be a bad idea when the next ambulance plowed into his sedan. Never argue potential traffic violations with a lawyer.

Walking to the emergency room after finding a parking spot also seemed to take forever, as if the space between us and the doors kept expanding.

"What did she say?" Ben asked for the millionth time. "Did she say what happened?"

"You heard as much as I did. She said he'd be fine, but that was it. Said that Cormac wanted to explain it himself."

"God, if he's broken parole . . ." he muttered.

Detective Hardin's involvement did seem to suggest Cormac had done something illegal. He'd been doing so well, and he only had a couple more months on his parole. Surely this couldn't be that bad.

"We should have more faith in him," I said, as much to myself as to Ben.

"You haven't known him as long as I have. Him and trouble, they're like magnets."

"Like somebody else you know?" I said, my grin lopsided.

He huffed at that, and we were inside.

The lighting was oppressively artificial, and the mood in the waiting room was dour. A dozen people slouched in plastic chairs watching a talking heads news show with the sound off on a TV hung in the corner. A kid sleeping in his mom's lap coughed. The place smelled like illness, and bodily fluids covered over with antiseptic. My nose wrinkled.

Ben marched straight to the reception desk. "You've got a patient, Cormac Bennett? We're his family."

The nurse, a tired-looking woman whose brown hair was coming out of its clip, checked a sheet of paper and nodded. "Yes, let me take you back."

She led us around the corner to a series of exam spaces separated by curtains. Halfway down the row, she held back a curtain and gestured us in.

Cormac was sitting on the side of the bed, his legs hanging over, slouching and looking annoyed. At first glance he didn't look different; he was dressed in his usual jeans and T-shirt. His leather jacket lay over a nearby chair. But he smelled of sweat and adrenaline—of pain. His left arm was resting on a rollaway table that fit over the bed, wrapped in a bandage and covered with blue cold packs. Hardin stood a few paces away, arms crossed. She regarded us with amusement, eyes crinkled, smirking.

"What happened?" I burst. I had an urge to rush over and hug Cormac and make protective cooing noises over him, but I didn't. He wouldn't have appreciated it. I was just so relieved to see him alive, conscious, sitting up, and being himself.

Cormac's moustache curved with the strength of his frown. "I fell."

"We're waiting for the X-rays to come back," Hardin said. She was definitely smiling now. So, it wasn't parole he'd broken.

"Is he in trouble?" Ben said. "He's not under arrest or anything?"

"Nope," she said. "Just feeling kind of dumb, I bet."

Cormac made a noise like a growl.

"Okay, there's a story here," I said. "Who's going to spill?"

"She's been tailing me," Cormac said, jutting his chin at Hardin and scowling. "Can we sue her?"

"Probable cause," she said. "I'm tracking down the

same vampire you are. You're a possible witness. That vampire, he's there, isn't he?"

"I'm doing your work for you," he said.

She merely shrugged in assent. "It's a good thing I *was* following you, so I could drive you here." I tried to imagine that car ride, Cormac in the passenger seat next to Hardin, cradling a hurt arm, both of them snarling at each other. It was almost cute.

"I ought to charge you consulting fees," Cormac said.

"Not a bad idea," Ben added.

The detective brushed them off. "We can discuss that later."

"Right," Ben said, with a sigh that indicated impatience. "But what happened?"

"I fell," he repeated.

"Something knocked him down," Hardin said. "Outside St. Cajetan at Auraria. What exactly is going on over there?"

I turned to Cormac, glaring. He'd been staking out the church, Columban's hideout. I couldn't yell at him for it without revealing to Hardin that Columban was there. I couldn't say *anything* with her standing there. So, he'd found something. Something had happened. Something had attacked?

"At least you weren't staking us out last night," I muttered.

"Last night was the full moon, right?" Hardin said.

"Were you expecting trouble? Anything I need to know about?"

I didn't even want to go there. "No. Nothing at all." Back to Cormac. "You found something?"

"I fell and landed wrong. That's it." So he didn't want to talk about it in front of Hardin, either.

A woman wearing a lab coat and a professional air came around the curtain holding an oversized manila envelope. "It's definitely broken," she said, and Cormac blew out a breath.

I'd spent the last couple of years being so worried that Cormac would get himself killed or thrown back in jail or a million other things, a broken arm was almost anticlimactic. Cormac seemed embarrassed more than anything. He wouldn't look up.

A doctor and nurse bustled in, making ready with needles and bandages to set the arm. They politely herded us out. This time, I had to pull on Ben's arm. He didn't want to leave his cousin alone, but Cormac himself told us to leave. Didn't need the moral support—or didn't want witnesses to his vulnerability? Almost wolflike, not wanting to show weakness.

Hardin walked with us to the waiting room. "I know cops aren't your favorite people in the world," she said. "But we're on the same side here. I'm not out to get anyone. I just want to keep the bad guys out of Denver, same as you."

Everything she said was true. We'd worked together often enough in the past, sharing information, chasing down supernatural villains, pooling our experiences when neither one of us had enough on our own to go on. But this time, she didn't even know who the bad guys were. How far this went. She'd met Roman once, sure, when he came to Denver before to size us up and test our weaknesses. She'd had brushes with the Long Game and had been there when Rick killed his predecessor. But she didn't know anything *about* the Long Game. The details, the alliances. How it was closing in on us . . .

I didn't know how to explain it all to her now. I didn't want to without talking to Rick, first. We should explain it to her together, if at all. She either wouldn't believe us, or she'd try to take the battle out of our hands. She'd think she could oppose the Long Game via official channels. It wouldn't work.

"I'm not trying to be difficult," I said. "But this . . . I can't just tell you everything. I'm not even thinking straight right now." Ben and I were still dressed in our post–full moon finery, jeans and T-shirts, our rattiest sneakers without socks. My unbrushed hair was crammed into a wild-looking ponytail; Ben needed a shave. Surely she could see we weren't at our best.

She said to Ben, "You're the lawyer, can you talk some sense into her?"

"I agree with her," Ben said, offhand. "I think you're in over your head."

She studied us, not afraid to meet our gazes—she had enough experience with us to know it meant a challenge. "I'll be in touch," she said finally and walked out of the emergency room into the midmorning light.

Ben and I took up places in the waiting room on hard plastic chairs as far away from everyone else as we could get. I leaned on his shoulder, and he put his arm around me, and even though we were in a hospital emergency room, it was nice getting to rest for a moment. We waited until the doctors turned Cormac loose with a big orange bottle of pills and a blue ice pack. His arm was in a sling, encased in an off-white fiberglass cast that went past his elbow. I couldn't tell if he was in any pain. He had a serious, stoic expression, same as always.

Ben took the pills and ice packs from the nurse, and that Cormac didn't argue about the help told me something about his state of mind.

"Where'd you leave your Jeep?" Ben asked.

"By the church," he answered.

"Right. Kitty, if you drop me off I can pick it up before it gets towed, and meet you back at the condo."

"You can just take me home," Cormac said. "I'll be fine."

"Nope," Ben said. "I'm not leaving you alone with a broken arm and a bottle of codeine."

"I'll be fine."

But he couldn't do a thing about it. He only had one arm, and whatever they'd doped him up with to set the break left him shockingly docile as we guided him to the backseat of the sedan and strapped him in.

"Give it up," I said, smiling at him where he sprawled out in the backseat. "You've got family, might as well enjoy it."

He grumbled, but he stopped arguing. By the time we all got back to the condo, he was asleep, and we had to wake him up to get him upstairs. Once inside, he parked himself on the sofa and promptly fell asleep again.

We let him alone.

IT WAS a little like having a bear in the living room.

The following morning, I ate toast and juice at the kitchen table, watching him, waiting for something to happen. In the painkiller fog, did he remember us bringing him here? How pissed off was he going to be when he woke up?

Ben emerged from the bedroom. "He still asleep?" he whispered.

"Yup," I whispered back.

Ben joined me at the table, where we both sat staring at him.

"This is a territory thing," I observed. I joked that Cormac was part of our pack, but he wasn't wolf. He was sleeping in our *den*. He'd been to our place before, but he'd never slept over.

We watched him. He snored, faintly.

Ben said, "We really need to work on getting a house sooner rather than later."

"A house with a guest room," I said.

"Exactly." Ben stood. "I'm going to make some coffee."

"Think that'll wake him up?"

"Dunno. I just need coffee."

The smell hit the condo's open living room as soon as the brew started dripping. Not much longer after that, Cormac squirmed and groaned. He tried to sit up, but his stiff muscles didn't cooperate.

For a moment he lay still, blinked at the ceiling. Then he looked at his arm. "Fuck."

"How you feel?" Ben asked.

"Stupid," Cormac said. "Thirsty?" He sounded uncertain.

"Does it hurt? You want some of that medication?" I asked.

He thought about it. "Yeah, I'd better."

Which surprised me. I expected him to tough it out, broken bone or no. Cormac-in-pain was an entirely new phenomenon. While I fetched a glass of water and the bottle of pills, Cormac managed to haul himself off the sofa and head to the bathroom. I didn't bother offering to help; neither did Ben. He'd only snarl back. If he collapsed, *then* we could help. But he managed, somehow, and stumbled back to the sofa where he returned to horizontal and sighed.

I dragged a chair to the sofa to play nurse. Ben brought over another chair, his cup of coffee, and a second for me. With his good hand, Cormac popped the medication and took a drink from the glass I offered. We waited for him to say something; he scowled.

Finally, Ben said, "So. What happened?"

"I fell."

I would have yelled, but Ben knew him better. "Oh no, that's not going to cut it. What were you doing at the church?"

He adjusted his arm in the sling, grimacing at the awkwardness. "You know those magical protections? I wanted to see what it would take to set them off."

"You poked the hornet's nest," I said flatly.

"Guess so."

"And how did that work out for you?" Ben asked.

"Found the hornets," he answered, grinning sleepily. "Any kind of offensive magic crosses the line, *zap*. The protections retaliate with some kind of fire-based magic. Anything else, mundane attack or passive magic, nothing. This tells us something."

"That you shouldn't poke hornet's nests?" I said.

"This guy's worried about something specific. He's not worried about guys with stakes, or Girl Scouts selling cookies. He's worried about a certain kind of magical attack, something that can be stopped with fire, and that's what he's defending against. I'm guessing he's got a stalker out there who's tangled with him before."

"And that stalker is probably going to follow him to Denver," I said, heart sinking.

"If he hasn't already," Cormac said.

"I need to tell Rick about this."

Ben said, "I think we can assume that Rick knows, if he's been talking to this priest guy."

Maybe I just wanted to talk to Rick, to find out more about Columban. To find out what Columban knew about his stalker.

"I wouldn't worry too much," Cormac said. "It's between the priest and whoever he pissed off. Shouldn't bother the rest of us."

"Back to your arm," Ben said. "I'm assuming that when the magic went *zap*, that's when you fell."

Cormac gave his head a frustrated shake. "Stuck my arm out and *bam*. Hardin saw the whole thing. She's asking way too many questions—she's after the vampire, and she was following me to get to him. She could have just asked." His words were starting to slur, the medication taking effect. He sank back against the mound of pillows under his back.

"Would you really have agreed to work with her if she did?" I said.

"Hell, no."

"And what does Amelia think?"

"The word 'idiot' might have come up. Idiot, clumsy, oaf . . ."

"Easy for her to say, she doesn't have a body," Ben said.

"That's what I told her."

I said, "I meant about the magic, the boundary, the stalker?"

"Amelia's the one doing most of the work. We don't know anything about the stalker—just that the vampire's worried about *something,* something he can beat with fire."

And he was wanted for arson in Hungary, which meant he'd faced down this thing before. When he came to Denver, had he brought his enemy with him? It would be wishful thinking to say no.

"Do we need to worry?"

"Always need to worry," he said, voice fading to a mushy whisper.

Ben patted his cousin's good shoulder. "Get some rest, we'll talk more later."

Cormac was already asleep, slouched against the pillow on the sofa.

"It's weird, seeing him knocked out," Ben said.

"Yeah. But at least he's okay. He'll be okay." No matter how bad things got, it always seemed like they could be so much worse. Had to keep that in mind.

"What are the odds he'll let it go after this?"

I huffed a laugh—quietly, to not disturb our invalid. "The best we can hope is that the arm will slow him down."

"I can't believe he broke his arm. All the crap we got into as kids, everything he's done since, he's never even smashed a toe. And then he *fell*?"

I frowned. "I need to talk to Rick."

"He taking calls now?"

"He'd better be."

RICK WAS not, in fact, any more diligent in answering his phone or returning calls than he'd been the week before. Whatever was keeping him busy, Father Columban or otherwise, must have been fascinating.

I decided to track him down at Obsidian, assuming I didn't get distracted like I had last time. And who in their right mind walked into vampire lairs and knocked on the door? Me, that's who.

One of the younger vampires—young being under a hundred—answered. She had pale tan skin, which meant she'd probably started life brown, probably Latina. I'd met her once or twice—Christina.

"Hi," I said brightly. "Rick here?"

"No," she said and moved to close the door.

I stuck my foot in the way. She kept pushing, and I leaned forward to keep it open, just enough to talk. If we got into a battle of brute force, I'd lose, so I talked fast.

"Where is he, then? I really need to talk to him. We've got a meeting with that Argentine vampire set up for Friday, and we need to strategize. Not to mention some weird stuff going on out at the Auraria campus, and he's not answering his phone—"

"He's *not here*." Her expression was so neutral, so still, she might have been painted on wood.

"Is everything okay?" I said.

She gave an extra hard shove to the door, and I fell back as it slammed shut.

Okay, fine. I had another spot to check.

Some stereotypes were stereotypes because of the seed of truth at the heart of them. Psalm 23 was a vampire nightclub to its core. Filled with beautiful people in startlingly hip clothing drinking from sleek martini glasses. Tailored jackets, skintight sequined cocktail dresses, very high heels. Not a beer bottle or pitcher of margaritas in sight. I was always a tiny bit shocked to realize that former cow town Denver had— had always had, really—this kind of club scene. I didn't go to places like this before I became a werewolf and started hanging out with people like Rick.

There was a method to the madness of a vampire club. Make it hip and beautiful, and people would swarm, flies to sugar. Why go hunting, when you can set a trap that your prey gladly walks into? The vampires made themselves attractive, and the club gained a reputation as a glorious place to seduce and be seduced. By the time morning rolled around you'd never remember what exactly happened the night before, only that you'd had a great time, even if you did feel a little light-headed, and you wanted to go back.

Psalm 23: the one about walking in the valley of shadows and not fearing evil, that was read at my grandmother's funeral. The previous master of Denver's idea of a joke no doubt. The reminder of the funeral made me sad.

A bouncer stopped me at the front door. Normally, someone wearing jeans and a wrinkled blouse wouldn't be let past the rope, but the bouncers—all of them either vampire minions or human servants of Rick's—knew me. We'd had the argument before.

"I'm here to see Rick," I told the guy, big and burly, wearing sunglasses.

He smiled, showing a bit of fang. "He's not here."

"Yeah, I thought you'd say that. Mind if I head in and look around for myself?"

"I'm telling you, he's not here."

"Is Angelo? Stella? Someone else who can tell me he isn't here, too?"

Scowling, he unhooked the rope and let me in.

Even compared to the nighttime outside, the interior was dark, with mood lighting of various dim colors tucked in aesthetic locations. Couples and small groups sitting at chrome tables around the edges of the dance floor seemed like shadows come to life, flashes of movement between sparks of light. The music was techno, something upbeat and remixed to within an inch of its life. No one was dancing yet.

I let my vision adjust, scanned the room, and found my target sitting in the far corner, on the other side of the bar. Rick's usual spot. Seeing Rick's lieutenant there instead of Rick made my heart trip for a moment. If anything ever happened to Rick, this was what I'd see all the time.

Angelo was young, full of himself, but many vampires were. Nice clothes, perfect hair, and so on. He often served as Rick's doorkeeper—chief minion. Nice enough guy I supposed, for a vampire. But he wasn't Rick, and he didn't look at all pleased to see me when I approached. He sat straight in his chair, studied me up and down, sneered. He fit the atmosphere here better than Rick ever did. The Master of Denver had inherited the place from his predecessor, a very different kind of vampire. One more like Angelo, who played the part and cared about appearances. Who bought into the mystique and made sure to behave as aloof and alluring as all the stories said he should. Unlike Rick, who was just Rick. A few hundred years ago, Rick would have been the kind of nobleman who kept a music room because he liked music, not because it was the stylish thing to do.

Angelo, like most vampires, didn't much like werewolves, and wouldn't deign to speak to me if he didn't have to. Not even to tell me to leave.

"I'm looking for Rick," I said, standing directly in his line of vision so he couldn't ignore me. "I hoped he'd be here."

"He isn't," Angelo said, a dismissive curl to his lips.

"If he's not here, then where is he?"

"That's not any of your concern."

Rick would have offered me a drink by this time. "You think you could pass a message on or something? I really need to talk to him. About this meeting coming up, with the Mistress of Buenos Aires?"

He gave a wave of his hand that might have meant, *consider it done,* or *why must I converse with peons?* It was all posing, and I told myself to be patient.

"If I didn't know better," I said, "I'd say that he was avoiding me and you all are covering for him."

"It does sound like a reasonable explanation, doesn't it?"

"No," I said, "it doesn't. Not with Rick."

"All you need to know is that he isn't here, and if he wished to speak with you, he'd contact you. It's undignified, you chasing after him like this."

"I was never much for dignity." I pointed a thumb over my shoulder. "You mind if I look around a little?"

"I'd prefer you didn't. You're not particularly welcome here."

I grinned. "You just bitter because I can come in here without an invitation but you can't come into my place?"

"I hadn't noticed." He turned away, which left him staring at the next wall over, but never mind.

Glancing around, I let my nose take in the air, catching scents of people, their perfume and deodorant, the thick rush of alcohol, and underlying tint of commercial floor cleaner. And vampires, of course. I wouldn't be able to pick Rick out of the crowd, even if he was here, which he probably wasn't.

"Right. Well. I guess I've taken up enough of your time."

"Yes, you have," he said curtly.

"Angelo—is something wrong? Seriously. You're all acting uptight, even for you guys."

"Nothing is wrong," he said. "Again, lovely to see you, but you really ought to be going."

Dismissed. Got it.

Getting back on the street, in the fresh air and away from the people, felt good. I tipped my nose up and took deep breaths of the city air, studying it as if it could give me answers. I kept coming up with the same one—Rick's Family wasn't having any more luck getting in touch with him than I was.

* * *

I STOPPED off at New Moon, thinking I'd check in with Shaun and whoever else was around that night, drink a soda, and comfort myself with the smells of pack and safety. But I hadn't gotten two steps inside when I spotted Darren and Trey sitting at a back table, deep in conversation over a couple of beers. *My* back table, the one I normally held court at when I came here after shows or met with Rick. Darren was speaking earnestly, Trey was nodding, his expression bright with hope. Darren sat with his back straight, his chin up; Trey was hunched, back curved, gaze downcast—his body language showing submission to the other wolf.

Something inside me—coiled fur and muscle, sharp teeth—wanted to kill Darren right then. But whatever he was telling Trey, he really did look like he was helping the other man.

Deciding I just couldn't face either one of them right now, I turned right back around, left my restaurant, and went home to sleep.

Chapter 11

I HAD TO figure out what to do about Darren. He was causing trouble in the pack. No, if I had to be honest, I was the one having the trouble. He kept rubbing me the wrong way, and I didn't want him here anymore. But was that fair to him? Ben offered to run the guy out of town with the help of his silver bullet–loaded Glock. As much fun as that sounded, I didn't want to admit failure on bringing him into the pack just yet. He wasn't a bad guy, I was sure. He kept challenging our authority without apparently meaning to, and I didn't know how to convince Darren that what he was doing was bad form. If he'd been belligerent, I could have challenged him and run him out like Ben said. But he wasn't being mean; he was just being *rude*.

When Darren called me the next morning to see if I wanted to go out for coffee with him, I was surprised. I'd been thinking of suggesting exactly the same thing. He'd picked up on my favorite method of diplomacy; maybe there was hope for him yet.

We met at a little coffee shop a couple of blocks from the radio station. He bought me a cup and brought it to me at one of the café tables out on the sidewalk.

"The cub learns," I said as he sat across from me.

He actually looked chagrined. "I know I screwed up, and I can tell you don't like me—"

"It's not that," I said, while thinking that yeah, no, I didn't much. I let the white lie stand. "You're very charming. But I'm not sure I understand you. There are times I wonder if you're really a werewolf, or if you're just not used to dealing with authority."

He bit his lip, lowered his gaze. "I was like this even before becoming a werewolf. Arrogant, I think some people call it. Have to be the center of attention. Add that to the werewolf posturing—I either get along with everybody, or nobody. I'm trying, Kitty, I really am. But it's hard for me not to treat it like a game sometimes."

"It's not a game, but you know that," I said. "I've watched people die, trying to get into or out of a pack. Why do you want a pack, really? You must have done just fine as a lone wolf."

"Lone wolf gets lonely. I want friends at my back. I've always imagined meeting someone like Becky—" He blushed at that, and his voice caught. Wetting his lips, he tried again. "I figured if I could fit in with a pack anywhere, it'd be yours." And then with the puppy-dog eyes.

"You're working really hard to sell yourself to me," I said.

"What is it you're always saying? Civilization is worth fighting for. I like civilization, and around here that means a pack."

Smiling in spite of myself, I said, "You listen to the show. Brownie points for you."

"What a relief." I glared, and he had the good sense to drop his gaze, avoiding the barest hint of a challenge. "I really want to make this work, Kitty. Please give me another chance."

God, he was begging. How could I say no? "I'll give you another chance, for Becky's sake. And for her sake, don't fuck it up. All right?"

He agreed, thanking me profusely, then bought me another cup of coffee. I felt like I was being bribed.

I hoped he'd succeed at integrating into the pack more than I believed he would.

CORMAC SLEPT on and off a whole other day, which was good, because it meant we didn't have to argue with him about lying down and keeping his arm still. He woke every couple of hours for soup and painkillers and the bathroom, but that was it. He must have been exhausted. Ben worked at home to keep an eye on him.

It couldn't last.

The next morning, noise woke us half an hour or so before we usually dragged ourselves out of bed. A coat dropping; a hard object scraping on the table.

Ben and I tensed, lifting heads, listening. "What's that?" I whispered.

He thought a minute, then blew out a breath. "It's Cormac sneaking out."

I rolled out of bed, pulled on sweats and a T-shirt. Ben was right behind me. I got to the living room in time to see Cormac struggling to ease his broken arm into its sling, dropping the keys to his Jeep, his jacket tucked under his good arm. I'd never seen him so physically awkward.

"What are you doing?" I said.

"Getting out of your hair. Heading back to my place. I'm fine, I can take care of myself."

He hadn't changed clothes since the hospital; we'd all figured rest was more important. He also hadn't showered, and was starting to smell ripe, of illness and bandages. But if he was having this much trouble getting himself together, how was he actually going to function on his own?

"You can't," I said. "You can't even put your coat on."

"I haven't taken any pills since last night, I want to

get home while I'm still lucid. I'll get back to bed then." And how long would that last?

"How much pain are you in? Don't lie." He didn't answer, and I let out an exasperated sigh. "You're in no shape to be driving *anywhere*! What are you thinking?"

He gave me a look, like he'd be happier if I just kept my mouth shut.

"I'll drive you," Ben said.

"I can drive myself—"

"Stick shift with a broken arm, yeah right," Ben said. He grabbed the Jeep's keys off the table where Cormac had dropped them, then took his jacket from him. With his good hand free, Cormac could finish shrugging on the sling, resting his broken arm more comfortably. How lucid was he, really, if he couldn't figure out how to get his sling on? Pointing that out would have made him more surly than he already was. "Kitty, you want to follow in the car?"

Seemed as good a compromise as any. I was still glaring at Cormac. "Only if you promise to call if you need anything. *Anything*."

"I promise I'll call if I need anything," he said dutifully, to the opposite wall, his shoulders in a defensive slouch.

Not sure I believed him, I continued glaring.

"Amelia will make sure I call if I need anything," he said.

That, I believed. I found my bag and car keys and followed them out of the condo.

Cormac lived in a studio apartment north of town, along the Boulder Turnpike. Not a great neighborhood, but I usually didn't worry. Cormac could take care of himself, and he didn't exactly give off the vibe of someone who could be taken advantage of. But that was when he didn't have a broken arm. Over the last couple of years he'd worked a series of warehouse jobs he'd gotten through his parole officer. Point of pride—he wanted to be self-sufficient. I didn't know how he'd manage work with a broken arm, but he didn't seem bothered.

I parked in front of the building next to the Jeep and helped Ben help Cormac up the stairs. Mostly by hovering. Cormac winced when the arm got jostled, turning a corner and bumping into the wall. For him to show even that much pain meant he was in bad shape. Good thing I'd made sure the bottle of pills was tucked in his jacket pocket. I'd sit on him to get him to take a dose, if I had to.

The apartment's interior belonged to both Cormac and Amelia. The sparse furnishings—table, chair, futon—and bare walls were Cormac's. The books piled everywhere—table, floor, kitchen counter; basket full of dried herbs; skein of yarn; locked and weathered mahogany box; and various maps and diagrams drawn on rolls of paper, held down by candles, statuettes, and other various weighted items—those were Amelia's, the tools of the wizard's trade. I could have pawed through it for hours, looking for meaning.

Ben guided his cousin to bed, while I went to the kitchenette for a glass of water and ice packs. We watched him until he took a painkiller. In the end, I had a suspicion it was Amelia who made him do it.

Pulling a chair near the bed, Ben sat and glanced around the apartment. "I think you've checked out more books in the last year than most people do in a lifetime."

Cormac chuckled. "I guess I like to read. Who knew?"

I'd taken to sending him books during his stint in prison. It started as a joke, but turned earnest. He really seemed to have read everything I'd sent him.

"I think he's reading for two, now," I said, noting some of the titles. Churchill's multivolume history of World War II; Woodward and Bernstein's *All the President's Men;* Betty Friedan's *The Feminine Mystique.* I wondered what Victorian Amelia was making of *that* one.

"Think about it," Cormac said. "If you went to sleep and woke up a hundred years later, what would you do?"

This wasn't a hypothetical question—Amelia really had been out of the world for that long. "I suppose I'd freak out for a little while. Everything I knew would be gone. But then—I'd want to find out what I'd missed. I'd want to explore everything."

He said, "These last couple years—I'm seeing the world in a whole new way. She's never seen anything like it, and all she wants to do is . . . take it all in."

I sat in another chair while we kept watch. Just when we thought he was drifting off, he sat up, propping himself on his good elbow, wincing yet again. He still wasn't used to favoring the hurt arm. He adjusted the pillow he'd propped the cast on, trying to get comfortable. "You get ahold of Rick yet?" he said.

I leaned back. "No. His Family won't admit it, but they don't know where he is, either. He's not at Obsidian, so I'm pretty sure that means he's with Columban."

"At St. Cajetan's?"

"If they haven't already left on some crusade."

"Rick wouldn't leave town without telling you," Ben said.

"I hope he wouldn't," I said, my uncertainty plain.

"I'm going to figure it out," Cormac said.

Ben looked at him. "Figure what out?"

"Those protections he's got up. If we get to the thing that's after him, we can get to him. Can't be that hard."

"Don't worry about it," I said. "Really. Just get some rest."

"You want to know what he's really up to, I'll figure it out." With that, he closed his eyes, snugged down into his pillow, and sighed. In another minute he was asleep.

Ben and I left him to it. I considered taking the keys to the Jeep with us, so he wouldn't be tempted to run off on some epic scheme, but Ben talked me out of it.

"Are you sure he'll be okay?" I said as we got in my car.

"Yeah. I think so. Probably. Seriously, he survived two years in prison, and we're worried about this?"

He had a point.

STILL, I had a feeling. At dusk, on the way home from work, I took a detour to the Auraria campus and swung by St. Cajetan's. Just to see.

I found the Jeep before I found Cormac. Parked on the street at a meter, a block or two away from the church, it was definitely his Jeep, with dried mud on the wheel wells, chips in the windshield, scratches in the paint that might have been normal wear and tear, or might have been, with enough imagination, claw marks. Thing had been around the block a few times. A few dozen times. He'd managed to drive the stick shift, broken arm or no. I parked in a spot nearby and went in search of the man himself, letting my nose guide me. He'd managed a shower sometime during the day, but he still smelled like Cormac, like his leather jacket and the muddy Jeep. He'd left a faint trail through the air he traveled through, and the steps his rough boots tracked on the pavement.

I found him on the church's north side, and Detective Hardin was with him. Her smell was touched with the stale scents of nicotine and breath mint. They stood side by side, looking up at the roofline. His broken arm was held close to his body by the sling; otherwise, he looked normal. He wasn't lighting candles or drawing Greek letters on the sidewalk. I supposed that would have looked suspicious with people still walking around.

"This isn't resting," I said. Hardin glanced over. Neither seemed surprised to see me, and neither said anything. I tried to sound polite, but it came out frustrated. "What are you guys *doing*?"

Hardin wore a satisfied smile. "I think Mr. Bennett is right. My suspect is hiding out here, and I have a warrant for his arrest and extradition. A couple of officers and I scoured the building earlier today and didn't find anything—"

"And you're not going to," Cormac said. "He's a vampire, using magic to hide himself. You could walk right past him and all the holy water in the world isn't going to flush him out."

"Which is why we're here," Hardin said. She was definitely pleased with herself.

"And why are you here?" I said, trying again to make sense out of this.

Cormac said, "Figure the best way to get a reaction out of the guy is to break his protections."

"I've hired Mr. Bennett as an independent contractor," Hardin said. "He's going to help me nail my suspect."

What happened to *hell, no*? "When Ben said you should go into business for yourself, I don't think this is what he meant," I said.

"Yeah, well, he should have thought of that." Cormac pointed along the roof. "The protection spell forms a sphere, not just a circle," he said. "Or maybe a dome. I haven't been able to get into the basement yet, to see if it extends underground."

"Maybe you should check out the dinosaur museum?" I pointed around the corner where I'd seen the door.

"It's closed," he said.

Well then. "This still isn't resting."

"I'll rest better once I've figured this thing out."

"Are you sure that's such a good idea?" I appealed to both of them. "If your information is right, Columban burned buildings fighting this thing in Europe. People *died*."

"And that's why we want him in custody and out of Denver," Hardin said.

Pacing away from us, Cormac muttered under his breath, almost to himself, "I want to know what we're dealing with. What kind of magic. How he made it, what he hopes to accomplish. The nature of his enemy—is it magical or demonic, can it be reasoned with? The shield, it feels different somehow, as if it recognizes me from the last time. Or as if it's waiting for something."

Following him, I narrowed my gaze and said, hushed so Hardin wouldn't hear, "Am I talking to Cormac or Amelia now?"

"Yeah," he murmured, not really paying attention to me.

"Taking this kind of personal, aren't you?"

"Something wrong with that?"

"Well, yeah. You've already broken your arm over it."

"I'll be careful."

"I assume you were being careful when you broke your arm."

"Ms. Norville," Hardin called after us, using her official cop voice. "It might be a good idea for you to leave the area for the time being."

"Yeah, probably." I started at a slow pace, a few steps along the sidewalk between Cormac and the church's pink walls, stepping purposefully across the invisible line he'd marked out the last time I was here. I went all the way to the stucco wall, pressed my hand against it, looked up along its length. I didn't expect firebolts from heaven to strike me, but I thought I might feel something. I didn't, not even a tingle on my skin. But why should I? Hundreds of people walked by here every day, used the auditorium and offices that the church had been converted to, and didn't sense anything wrong. Even now, lights shone through the windows, indicating activity inside.

I turned away and rejoined the pair. "Just for the record, I think this is a bad idea."

"Noted," Hardin said.

Cormac had pulled a length of red yarn from his pocket and began tying knots in it—awkwardly, anchoring with the fingers of his broken arm, manipulating with his good hand. I itched to take the yarn from him and do it myself, in the name of helping. Not that I would have known what I was doing with the knots. It was painful, watching him struggle with the yarn. Sweat dampened the skin along his hairline, either from effort or pain. He had a two-day-old broken arm, he *had* to be in pain, not that he was going to admit it.

Hardin stood politely out of the way—giving her hired expert the space to work. And if that wasn't bizarre—just a few years ago she'd wanted to put him in jail herself. I wondered what Ben was going to say about their partnership.

Dusk fell, which meant the vampires inside—

assuming they were still there—would be waking up any minute now. Fewer and fewer people passed by the church.

"Has anybody tried *asking* the guy to come out?"

"I don't *ask* murder suspects," Hardin said.

We were going to look back on this and realize it was all a big misunderstanding. "How about I just poke my head in," I said and started toward the front steps.

"Kitty—" Hardin said, but I ignored her. Cormac was busy tying knots.

At dusk, after classes and meetings, I figured the front would be locked, but the door I tried opened. Stepping into an unassuming lobby, I almost shouted Rick's name, but a sound stopped me—the voice of a lecturing professor, coming from the next room. Late classes. Right. I poked around as much as I thought I could without drawing too much attention, turning down a couple of side hallways, peeking into a few equipment closets. I didn't even smell much vampire— just a trace of a corpse-like chill, as if one had passed by recently. Too faint of a trail to follow.

I returned to the front of the church and shut the door quietly behind me on my way out. Back outside, Cormac's spell, counterspell, whatever, seemed to be progressing. He was still managing to tie lengths of yarn into patterns. I'd kind of hoped that whatever he was planning really did need two working arms, and he'd get frustrated and give up.

"There are people inside," I said. "Living people, not vampires. You're not going to do anything that'll get anyone hurt, will you?"

He gave me a look, kept tying knots. I heaved a frustrated sigh.

"Don't worry, I'm keeping an eye on things," Hardin said, which didn't give me any more confidence. She had a hungry expression, a hunter on the prowl, waiting for her chance to strike.

Cormac walked clockwise around the church, making his knotted charms and dropping them at the cardinal and ordinal points, eight in all. His plan probably took twice as long as it would have if he'd been able to use both hands to full capacity.

Maybe this wouldn't work.

Both Hardin and I stood with our arms crossed, to keep from reaching to help him.

I tried to make conversation. "You talk to Rick yet?" Not that I thought she had. I would have been offended if she had, that Rick would talk to her and not me.

"He doesn't seem to be answering his phone. You?"

I shrugged, noncommittal.

"So what's his deal?" she said.

"He's five hundred years old," I said. "He doesn't owe us anything."

Rick had spent much of his time as a vampire being nomadic, wandering throughout the West, from Mexico to San Francisco to Albuquerque and who knew where else. People who'd known him for a long time—other vampires—expressed surprise that he'd settled down and become Master of a city. Maybe . . . maybe Rick wasn't cut out for the settled life after all. Maybe he really had left town, taken up his wandering ways again. And why should he tell any of us? We were mortal, we'd be dead soon anyway, from his point of view. I didn't think Rick was like that, but what did I know, really?

If Rick was with Columban, he was here. Maybe in one of those square bell towers, looking down on us from the shadows, suitably mysterious and vampiric. I didn't sense more than a trace of vampire on the air. If they were here, they were keeping themselves inside, and they hadn't left the building in the last few days. Finding food would be easy enough for them to do, after dark on a college campus. Use their powers to draw in prey who'd be none the wiser. They only needed a few sips, and didn't need to kill.

After half an hour or so, Cormac arrived back at his starting point.

We waited. Full twilight had fallen; thin strings of clouds were black against a dark blue sky. Streetlights had come on around us. The pink on the walls of the church had faded, so the building now loomed, a dark, hulking object.

"What is this supposed to do?" I said.

"Just giving the door a kick," he said. "See what happens."

I gave him a look. "And what happens if something actually, you know—kicks back?"

"I've got some backup," he said. Despite the broken arm, despite Hardin standing right there, he seemed to be enjoying himself. His moustache showed his lips pressed in a thin, satisfied smile. Another hunter on the hunt.

"How long until something happens?" Hardin said.

"Just wait."

"If nothing happens, I might think twice about paying you."

He didn't say anything to that.

Cormac was patient. He could stand here all night, waiting for something to happen, sure that something would. The spell that Amelia had woven made sense to him. I couldn't guess what would come next. If nothing else, I stayed to make sure I could talk Hardin out of arresting Cormac for something that might be interpreted as breaking his parole.

About twenty minutes into the vigil, my nose wrinkled, catching a scent before I was entirely aware of what I was smelling. I cocked my head as if listening, focusing on my nose, and the acrid tickling that now caught my attention. A burning, like the ozone that tinged the air during a bad thunderstorm. Lightning was brewing somewhere, but no clouds hung overhead, no thunderheads were blowing in from the mountains like they sometimes did, a late spring storm.

The knotted bits of yarn around the boundary of the church had started glowing. Orange, intense, like the heating elements in a toaster. I squinted against the light, which was searing in the dusk's gloom.

"Cormac," I hissed, not sure why I felt the need to whisper.

He was digging in his jeans pocket for something—a butane lighter, which he nestled in the fingers of his bad arm, then went to his jacket pocket for something else. He'd turned his gaze away from the heated circle now forming around the church.

"Kitty . . ." Hardin stared at the church, at a loss like I was.

Under my rib cage, my gut turned, Wolf wanting out. To leap, claw attack, even though we didn't know *what* to attack, we had no direct enemy. Just this vague, arcane magic. Incomprensible. I curled my lips to snarl. The air smelled of brimstone; I could taste it in the back of my throat.

Sparks started popping from each of the knotted

pieces of yarn, static-like crackles of energy. Then they gathered, forming tendrils, linking to one another. But one of them—the one closest to Cormac—drew the rest of the tendrils to itself, forming a pulsing will-o'-the-wisp. It threw off short, tentative streaks of energy, miniature bolts of lightning—testing, I thought. Seeking out its target.

"Cormac!" I shouted this time.

He saw the gathered lightning storm, glanced at it calmly, and struggled to light his lighter one-handed while holding a smudge stick, a bundle of dried sage bound together with twine. He couldn't get the lighter to strike.

He'd run out of time. The tendrils of lightning were reaching toward him, as if they had sentience and had found the target they sought. Cormac wouldn't back down, but kept struggling with the damned lighter.

I ran at him and shoved. We toppled, and an earth-rumbling crack of thunder ripped over us, along with an atomic pulse of white light. The afterimage of the flare blazed against my shut eyelids, and my ears rang. Someone was yelling, I couldn't hear what.

Wolf got me off the ground; we turned, faced the threat. Another surge of lightning gathered in front of us. I put myself between it and Cormac, crouching in readiness for the next attack. Not that there was anything I could do against a lightning strike. Cormac had kicked the door, and this was what happened—automatic defenses. I didn't know what to do but face it down and hope. I had a werewolf's toughness—it *probably* wouldn't kill me.

The buzzing of voices sounded far away to my still-ringing ears. Hardin had run over to us, kneeling next to Cormac, who was sprawled on the ground, struggling to sit up. He pointed with his good hand and yelled, "Light it! Light it!"

Hardin looked, then picked up the lighter and incense, which had dropped nearby. She needed two tries to strike the lighter to life, then she calmly, efficiently, brought the flame to the bundle of dried herbs. The bundle caught, shone with light, and gave off a tendril of white smoke.

Leaning on me, Cormac lurched toward the detective, who was still crouched on the sidewalk, holding the incense in front of her, staring at it like it might attack her. Its orange light reflected on her staring face. Cormac dropped to the ground next to her, and I stumbled with him, thinking he was falling, trying to support him. But he'd fallen on purpose, to get close to her, to grab hold of her hand that was clutching the incense. He didn't bother taking it from her; he didn't have time.

He raised her hand and the burning herbs in the air and shouted a series of words, a charm or chant. It could have been Latin; it could have been anything, he spoke so quickly and his voice was so rough, urgent. We ducked against the sudden, stabbing light.

The smoke from the incense spread out, flattening from a column to a shield. The piercing light striking from the church reflected off it, making the smoke opaque, easy to see. More smoke, an impossible amount, spread outward, and the purpose became clear—one shield countering the other. The smoke seemed more than opaque, it appeared solid, a thin barrier that the lightning couldn't pierce. Swirling white and gray, the wall of smoke pressed closer, contracting against the sparking boundary shield. The lightning faded, from glowing bolts to static sparks, then to nothing.

The air smelled of smoke, fire, brimstone, sage. I sneezed. I'd somehow come to be kneeling on the ground behind Cormac and Hardin, looming protectively, a hand on each of their shoulders, as if I could have done anything against the light show. The situation had left me chagrined more than once: here I was, big bad werewolf, and how much good was I really? My uses as a real-life monster tended to be narrow: tracking and brute force. But I tried.

Sparks had fallen on some of the foliage around the church's corners; the leaves of a shrub were cackling with flames that spread along the branches. The building itself, and the people inside, were next in line.

Hardin ran, and I shouted after her. She ignored

me. So I dug my phone out of my pocket and called 911 to send a fire truck, while trying to haul Cormac back from what would no doubt become an inferno. *Now,* maybe we could get Rick and Columban's attention.

Then Hardin returned with a handheld fire extinguisher, probably fetched from her car. She had the burning shrub sprayed down in minutes, leaving behind ashes, a chemical burning smell, and a climbing streak of soot marring the pink wall.

When she turned back to us, lugging the spent extinguisher, she was grinning. "This is exactly the M.O. of the arson case in Hungary. Exterior foliage burned and spread to the building. I've got him. That vampire's spell did this—it's reckless endangerment at the very least. Sucker's going down."

At least she was blaming Columban's spell and not Cormac. Small favors.

Sirens blared, growing louder as the fire engine turned the corner and approached. The vehicle growled and lurched to a halt by the curb, and a firefighter in a heavy suit lumbered out. Now, who was going to explain this to him?

Hardin looked. "Who called them?"

I held up my cell phone, and she scowled. "I had everything under control." She marched over to talk to the guy. I didn't even have to ask her to.

Sitting hard on the concrete sidewalk, I forced my-self to calm down, to steady my nerves. Wolf was snarling, and I pulled her back, gasping for breath while trying not to show it. Cormac didn't seem at all bothered. Lips pursed, he cradled his arm and gazed thoughtfully at the church.

"So. Did that do what you wanted it to?"

Straightening, he brushed ashes off his jacket and jeans, wincing as he resettled his broken arm in its sling. The wince turned into a grin. "Didn't manage to knock it down, but I know a little more about it now."

"You seem inordinately pleased." Half a block away, Hardin was showing her badge to the fire-fighter, who had his arms crossed and seemed un-happy.

"Every time it does something, I learn something new. A little more digging and I ought to be able to bust right through that thing."

He didn't even seem interested in the vampires anymore. It was all about the spell.

"The plan didn't work," I said. "Columban and Rick still haven't come out." He glanced at me side-long but didn't answer.

A few minutes later, a classroom-sized group of people came out the front door of the church and trailed down the steps, backpacks over their shoul-ders, talking to each other. Some of them saw the fire engine, and pretty soon they were all staring. But since no alarms were blaring and nothing was actually on fire, the students wandered off.

This could have turned out so badly. I silently thanked whatever might be listening that it hadn't.

The firefighter whom Hardin had talked to and one of his colleagues started walking around the church, investigating—checking for more stray sparks, which seemed wise. Hardin returned to us, extinguisher tucked under one arm. She put her ash-covered hands in front of her, studying them. Some of the white flecks from the firestorm had drifted onto her hair and showed starkly against its dark color.

"You okay?" I asked her.

"I hid behind my badge and managed to convince them the fire was accidental and that we took care of it. I don't want to have to explain the whole story. Mostly because I don't know it." Frowning, she said to Cormac, "I don't see my suspect coming out to check on his spell."

"That's because the spell is still there," he said, cradling his arm and wincing. "I didn't break the protection, just pissed it off."

"So now what?" she demanded.

"Just give me a few more days," Cormac said.

"Maybe I can arrest you for fraud," she muttered. I thought she was joking. Probably. She may have still been bitter that she wasn't the one to put him away.

Maybe she was looking for a second chance. Other than the fried bush and ashy streaks on the wall and sidewalk, no evidence of the conflagration remained. At this point, she didn't have the physical evidence to charge Cormac with anything. But give it time . . .

"You can't arrest him," I said in a rush. Cormac was so close to finishing his parole, didn't he see that? Didn't *she* see it? If he wrecked that chasing down some wild goose that I'd set him on, I'd never forgive myself.

She said, "Did you learn enough about it to try again?"

"Yes," he said. He probably would have said yes no matter what.

"And is this going to get my suspect to come out of there so I can arrest him?"

"Keep knocking at his door hard enough, he'll come out," he said.

She nodded, apparently satisfied.

"Let's get out of here," I said, a hand on Cormac's shoulder to steer him back to the street.

"Hey," Hardin said, stepping into our path, stopping us. "What happened to you in prison?"

"What makes you think anything did?" he said in his usual flat tone.

"Ever since you got out, you've been . . . *weird*. Not crazy, not more crazy at least. In fact I think you've been less crazy."

"*Less* crazy?" he said, with a short laugh, like he thought it was hilarious. As well he might.

"Before, you acted like you didn't have anything to live for. Now, you do."

I looked at him, to see his reaction. Because I thought she was right. Would he tell her the truth?

He bowed his head, smiling wryly. "The system works, detective. I'm rehabilitated."

She maintained an expression of skepticism. Without another word, he stepped around her. I followed. She didn't.

I felt like we'd made a narrow escape. I walked with Cormac to his car. "Rehabilitated?" I said.

"You going to argue?"

I couldn't. He wasn't exactly on the straight and narrow these days, but he was a lot closer to it than he had been. "You really should be more careful around her."

"Naw. I think she meant what she said—she wants to see what happens next."

On second thought, Hardin was wrong. He may have had something to live for now, but he was still crazy. "You don't have to go after this thing anymore," I said. "I'll find another way to talk to Columban and Rick, and Columban can convince Hardin not to arrest him."

He'd opened the driver's side door of the Jeep; I leaned on the hood.

"It doesn't bother you that some vampire is camped in the middle of Denver inside a magical shield, doing who knows what?"

Well, when he put it like that . . . "It's not worth getting hurt over. *More* hurt."

He glanced at his arm in the sling. "I can take care of myself."

"You keep saying that."

Awkwardly, guiding his broken arm so it didn't bang on anything, he climbed into the front seat and slammed the door. He had to reach across with his good hand to do it. When he started the engine, I had to decide if he really intended to drive right over me. He was very likely thinking, I was a werewolf, I could take it. I stepped away from the Jeep as he steered from the curb.

Chapter 12

"DETECTIVE HARDIN hired Cormac?" Ben said, when I finally got home and told him the whole story as we settled in for the night.

"I know, right?"

"That's not exactly what I meant when I said he should go into business for himself," he said, lying on his back and regarding the ceiling thoughtfully.

Lying in the crook of his arm, I drew on his warmth to ease the knots from my muscles. "That's what I told him you'd say."

"And she didn't arrest him?"

"Nope," I said.

"Huh. He could do worse than have a homicide cop owe him a favor."

I propped myself on an elbow. "Are you sure you should be encouraging this?"

"I'm not sure either of us has much of a say in the matter."

My scrunched expression must have looked grouchy. He levered up just far enough to kiss my lips, and I sank back into his arms.

I DIDN'T get much sleep, dreaming about attacks of flaming death. Sparks of spell-laden fire still flashed at the edges of my vision when I closed my eyes, lingering memory of the night before. I wondered if Cormac had gotten any sleep. If I worked more, I could forget about it, so I went to the station early the next day and deleted e-mails for an hour.

My cell phone sitting on the edge of my desk rang, and I grabbed it. "Hello?"

"So, what happened to talking 'tomorrow'?" Cheryl said.

Oh God, what day was it? When had I last talked to her? Days ago. I'd been dealing with Cormac's broken arm and had completely forgotten about Cheryl. I was the worst sister ever.

I planted my elbows on the desk and slouched. "Cheryl, I'm so sorry. You would not *believe* what's been happening. Ben's cousin broke his arm and we had to take care of him, and—"

"Your life is a whirlwind, yes, I know. If you don't want to talk to me could you just say so?"

I glanced at the wall clock. Almost noon. "Are you doing anything for lunch today? I could come over. I'll pick something up, pizza or Chinese or whatever. I'll come over right now." I held my breath, waiting for her answer.

Her sigh was long-suffering. "Yeah, okay. I'm home. You don't have to bring anything, I've got a frozen pizza I can heat up."

"Great. I'm leaving right now, I'll be there in half an hour." I grabbed my bag and left.

Cheryl lived la vida suburbia south of Denver, in Highlands Ranch. As I pulled into her driveway, I thought as I often did, this would have been my life if not for the lycanthropy. Some days, that made me sad. Some days, I felt like I'd escaped something.

Today, I was mostly worried about Cheryl. My big sister Cheryl. Growing up, she'd been bossy and rebellious, and could do absolutely no wrong in my eyes. She wore ripped T-shirts and denim jackets and spiked her hair and stayed out too late going to all-ages shows downtown, and every time she got in trouble felt to me like a blow for freedom. I was enough younger that she never took me along on her adventures, and was always a little cowed by her and her crazy friends. And now she was the one with the house and the two kids and golden retriever in the backyard, and I was the crazy one.

She must have been watching for me, because she

opened the door as soon as I walked up. I met her over the threshold, and we hugged.

Her house was still, silent—except for the golden retriever yodeling in the backyard. Dog and I didn't get along too well—I was a threat to the household, being what I was. Not that I really was, but the thing couldn't tell the difference, and I couldn't reason with it. So he stayed in the backyard when I came to visit. This way, I would never have to explain to my niece and nephew why I beat up their dog.

Cheryl herself was in transition. She'd stayed home when the kids came along. Now that they were older and had started school, she had decisions to make about what to do next. Go back to work, and if so, doing what? Her IT credentials were eight years out of date. I didn't envy her position.

We settled in the kitchen, where I smelled pepperoni pizza baking. I wasn't hungry.

She paced, kneading a damp tissue in her fist. Her footsteps padded on the linoleum.

"Kids in school?" I said. Nicky was eight, and five-year-old Jeffy was in preschool.

"For a couple more weeks."

"Plans for the summer?"

"No idea," she said.

The timer on the oven dinged, and she fussed over it, getting out plates and so on.

"So," I said, growing impatient, my foot tapping

on the linoleum. "What about this party you want to do?"

"You don't really have to help if you don't want to. I just thought it would be nice for you to be involved."

"I want to help. Seriously."

"Don't say it if you don't mean it."

Now I was getting angry. "Cheryl, what has gotten into you?"

She slammed a cupboard door, then stopped herself, closing her eyes and taking a deep breath. "Ever since Grandma's funeral . . . I just keep thinking about what would happen if Mom got sick again."

"Well, she's not sick. Don't worry about it until it happens."

"That's real responsible of you—"

"What is this, I have to help you plan a party to prove I'm responsible?" I flushed. I didn't want to be fighting like this.

"What would you do, if Mom got sick?"

I was out of my depth. She was right—I hadn't thought about it because I didn't want to think about it. I shouldn't *have* to think about it, not until it actually happened. "I don't know. I'll do whatever I need to, just like last time." Like last time, when I'd returned to a territory I'd been banished from on pain of death, that was how far I'd go. Cheryl didn't know about that part.

She continued, glaring at me with a challenge that Wolf couldn't help but respond to, hackles rising.

"They're getting older. They need us—"

"I'm not arguing with that," I said. "But why are we talking about this now, like this?" I felt like I was twelve years old again and getting lectured by my oh-so-older and smugger sister.

Keeping her voice steady she said, "They'll need us to be there for them—"

"And we will be—"

Her patience finally vanished. "But you're never here! You're always off on some weird trip or celebrity adventure. Tell me, how can you help if you're not here? You *never* help—"

"You never ask!"

"I shouldn't have to!"

Something inside me extended claws and growled. I felt a tension, like a leash stretching, then breaking. Snapping, with a satisfying whip crack. And I felt free. So free, all my limbs stretching outward. A prickling, bristling sensation sprouting just under my skin—

I had to go. I had to get out of here.

"Kitty—" Cheryl said, her tone demanding, as I turned and walked out. "Kitty, don't go ignoring me, you can't just walk away from this."

A hand landed on my arm, and I turned, bared my

teeth, made a noise— My sister stumbled away from me. I couldn't guess what she saw.

I had to leave. I went out the front of the house, left the door open behind me, heard my sister call, "Kitty!"

But I didn't hear, not really. I ran, past my car and down the sidewalk.

Wolf was trapped; we had to run, it was the only thing for it. Run, and run. But concrete and asphalt stretched all around us. Rows of houses, a concentrated mass of civilization hemmed us in worse than any chain or bars of a cage. We could run, but where could we go? We tipped our nose to the air and smelled, searching for the wide open spaces and natural shelter that would mean our release, our only release.

Too many people here. Too much prey. Wrong kind of prey. I couldn't stop running, to try to get away from it. To run until exhaustion took me. I'd be running all day.

Then, we found green. A swathe of prairie had been preserved in the middle of this modern suburb, a creek-cut ravine covered with dry grass and cottonwoods. A dry, washed-out, hemmed-in version of nature. But it was open. It smelled clean. I ran, pulling my shirt over my head, dropping it, not caring, and steered toward a stand of cottonwoods. Wanted to hide. Wanted to run.

Wanted to be free, and Wolf slashed my skin with her claws and tore her way out. I hardly cared.

DOESN'T THINK of much of anything but the movement of her body, claws digging into hard earth, wind in her nose. This isn't where she wants to be, but she's trapped on all sides by steel. She will run in circles.

The prey here smells different, wrong, of oil and trash. Prey living trapped by concrete. She is angry, starved for blood. Blood will staunch the anger, so she hunts. So many trails to follow—raccoon, rabbit, fox, even coyote. But the musky, feline scent catches her attention because it is different.

Her target is fast, agile—a challenge. Makes her more fierce. Her blood thunders, her mouth waters, she bares her teeth to the sky. And pounces. It lets out a high-pitched yowl, but only briefly. She devours it, ripping through skin, picking past dense fur. The meat is stringy, there isn't much of it. She finishes it in moments, cracking bones and gnawing them until nothing remains but a smear of blood, fur, and viscera on the ground.

She licks her lips and paws, cleaning herself, then looks at the sky again and howls. No one answers. How lost is she?

Only thing to do is run, her sides heaving and skin quivering.

She runs until exhausted, as the sun drops across the sky. In a hollow under a stand of cottonwoods, she finds shelter, an inadequate den where she lies, panting. Too unhappy, too insecure to sleep.

After minutes or hours or some other vague length of time, a scent crosses her awareness—of home and safety. At the same time, she hears a call.

"Kitty." A low, steady sound. Calming.

She pricks her ears, raises her head high.

"Kitty," the voice says again.

Her mate, his sharp and welcome smell cutting through the noise, stinging in her nose. Without thinking, she stands and runs to him.

He is on two legs, which doesn't seem right. Lowering her head, she paces, uncertain. They should be hunting together. She loops a wide circle around him, waiting for him to join her. But he waits, standing calmly, his gaze turned, his body relaxed.

She is not hunting, she is fleeing. But he smells safe. Maybe she meant to flee toward him. The thought calms her. Her tail and head droop.

"You okay?" he says, and she doesn't know what the words mean. She keeps moving, pacing step by step, waiting for him to react. He only watches.

"We should get home, Kitty. You ready to sleep it off?"

The familiar gentleness of his voice keeps her

from fleeing again. But she isn't ready to come to him.

He walks to a stunted scrub oak and sits, propping his back against it. The urge to curl up against him is strong. But so is the urge to keep running.

Finally, with daylight fading, with the air cooling, she rests, curling up on the prairie ground, tucking in her paws.

Chapter 13

I'D HAD a very bad dream. Funny, because I didn't remember going to sleep. I remembered—not very much, as it turned out. But the evidence around me filled in some of the blanks. I was naked. A bed of dry grass pressed into my skin, crunching under me when I breathed. Ben sat nearby, not touching me, his scent and body heat projecting toward me. He was fully dressed, fully human. I could smell his clothing, hear the rustle of his shirt when he moved. We hadn't been hunting together. Which meant I had Changed and run on my own. My stomach rumbled, my nerves quaked. An awful, tinny taste coated my mouth, a thin film of blood remained on my teeth. I'd caught something, who knew what, but that wasn't what bothered me. The anxiety and fear did.

"Hey," Ben said softly.

"Ben?" I murmured, my voice scratching. As if I couldn't believe he was here, or that I was.

"I'm here."

I opened my eyes. The sky was dark, the glow of the city lighting the horizon. The air was cool, sending a chill of gooseflesh across my back. I hugged myself.

Ben was sitting just out of reach, back against a tree trunk, one knee propped up, an arm resting across it. He'd been watching me, but glanced away when I looked up. A calming gesture.

"I'm not sure what happened," I said finally.

"Not surprised. You must have run off in a hurry."

"How did you know to come after me?" I said, after wetting my lips. I needed a drink of water.

"Cheryl called. Said you looked really upset. I knew it had to be bad, so I checked a map, found the park nearest to her house, came over, and started walking. I knew you wouldn't have gone too far."

"I tried."

"I know."

I imagined how angry I must have been, that Ben had left me alone, that Wolf hadn't curled up next to him, leaning against him so he could brush fingers through her fur. That he had waited rather than reach out to us. Tears stung in my eyes, thinking about it. I propped myself up, stretching awkward kinks out of my muscles, and scooted toward him. He put his arms around me and gathered me close. His embrace was like a blanket, and I flushed at his touch. I could stay here all night.

"You okay?" he murmured after a moment, and I rubbed my eyes dry.

"Cheryl must be really pissed off," I said.

"I think she's worried," he said. "She's not sure what happened."

How could she even guess? The memories came back: the argument, the way everything crashed in my mind at once—too many demands, too many accusations. I had to acknowledge a seed of anger still there, burning.

"I'm sorry," I murmured. Couldn't think of anything else to say. Of course, I'd have to call Cheryl and say the same thing.

"Ready to go home?"

"Yeah."

He moved, revealing a pile of clothes. "Found your clothes. And this." He held up the chain I wore my wedding band on. The gold ring turned, shining silver even in the dark—white gold, Ben's idea of a joke. After almost losing my engagement ring in an unexpected, uncontrolled shape-shifting incident, I wore my wedding ring around my neck so I could take it off in a hurry. It must have fallen to the side with my clothes when I pulled my shirt off. I took it from him and squeezed it in my hand before sliding the chain over my neck. The ring rested on my sternum, right next to my heart. Cheesy, but its weight felt like the pieces of the world coming back into their rightful places.

"Thanks," I said, simply, and he brushed back a lock of my hair.

"I don't know how useful these are actually going to be." He held up my jeans, which had a big rip in the waistband. The shirt had parted along one seam. They were both probably, technically wearable. But I was glad when he also held up his overcoat.

"So," I said. "How many times now have I ended up half-naked in torn-up clothes wearing your overcoat?" I slipped on the shirt—more of a blouse than a pullover now—and started on the jeans.

He grinned. "I think it kinda turns me on."

How could I resist a come-on like that? The flush rolling through my gut helped push away some of my anxiety. I grabbed his collar, pulled myself toward him, and kissed him. His mouth opened to mine, and I leaned in to wrap his warmth around me. There went a little more anxiety.

Pulling away, he donned a thoughtful, puckered expression. He seemed to be licking his lips. "What on earth did you eat?"

The question recalled a memory of dense fur on a lithe, stringy body. "Um. I think I killed somebody's cat."

"Oh geez," he said, and laughed.

I glared. "It's not funny."

"It kind of is. I know, not to whoever's cat it is. But anybody who lets their cat out around here knows about coyotes. It's not exactly safe."

Some cat wasn't coming home tonight and it was my fault. "I feel really bad."

He put his arm around my shoulder and hugged. "That's what makes you a good person. You know that, right?"

Time to get out of here, surely. He helped me slip on the overcoat, then gave me a hand up. He didn't let go, and I happily leaned into the solidity of him. We started hiking across the open field. I recognized where we were—an open swathe of greenway that wound through Highlands Ranch. I was still within a mile of my sister's house. I'd lucked out, losing it this close to a reasonable facsimile of wilderness.

"I remember when you did this for me, I completely lost it, ran off. And you were right there to call me back."

"I should know better," I said. "After all this time, I really ought to know better. I'm the pack alpha—what kind of example is this? I feel so . . . dumb."

"You controlled it enough to stay away from people. You didn't hurt anything, so no harm done, really."

"Except for the cat."

He laughed again. "I'm sorry, it's just . . . you couldn't find anything more appetizing than a cat?"

"You're not helping, dear," I growled.

He'd parked his car by the curb, away from the main road that wound through the neighborhood. I was happy to see it. One step closer to home.

"Oh—we're not telling Cormac about this, right?" I said.

"We are *not* telling Cormac about this," he agreed.

We'd climbed into the car when Ben's phone rang. Ben's, not mine, which was a nice change. I even checked, patting my jeans pocket. The thing somehow managed to stay lodged there through all that mess. The call was probably one of his clients needing to be bailed out or looking for advice—before they did something stupid rather than after, one hoped.

"Hello? Yeah . . . yeah. She's right here. She wasn't answering her phone for a while. Is something wrong?" After a moment of listening, he said, "You'd better talk to her," then handed the phone to me.

Who is it? I mouthed at him, but the voice on the other end of the connection was already talking.

"Ms. Norville? Kitty?"

"Angelo?"

"I can't believe I'm doing this," he said, sounding wheezy, as if forgetting to draw breath in order to speak.

"Do what? What's wrong?" If I didn't know better I'd have said he was in a panic. Vampires didn't panic.

"I need . . . I'm trying . . ." He really was gasping

out the words. I clamped my mouth shut to keep quiet, to let him talk. "I need help," he finally said.

I had to let that sink in. "What?"

"I. Need. Help." He bit the words off.

"No, I heard you, I just didn't believe it. You need *what*?" Oh, this made up for all the times he'd stood at the doorway to Rick's lair telling me I wasn't good enough to speak to the illustrious Master.

"Kitty. Please, I'm being serious."

And he was. The panic was definitely there, in a brittle edge to his voice.

"What is it?" I said.

"Rick is missing."

I turned the words over a couple of times because they didn't make sense. "You mean he still isn't answering calls—"

"I mean none of us have seen him for a week," Angelo said. "He may be eccentric, but he's never been . . . neglectful. I'm fielding calls from the envoy from Buenos Aires and I don't know what to tell him. Rick needs to be here."

If Rick hadn't told his own lieutenants where he was, why would he have told me? I didn't say that. I should have been flattered that Angelo even thought of calling me. How much pride had he swallowed to do that? He was obviously continuing to choke on it.

As for Rick . . . "Yeah, he does."

"He talks to you—you're his friend—"

"And you're not?"

"I know you know where he is. Just tell me."

The thought of tracking Rick down just now made me tired. I needed a shower. And a change of clothes. I looked down at myself, my ratty hair and torn clothes, wrapped up as well as I could be in Ben's coat, and decided this couldn't wait. "I'll call you."

"I want to be there when you talk to him—"

I hung up on him. Ben looked at me. "That'll piss him off."

"I'll deal with him later. *Rick* can deal with him later."

Ben started the car. "Then you know where we're going?"

"Yeah. St. Cajetan's."

"I knew it." The car pulled away from the curb. "What about those protective spells?"

"I just want to talk, we're not going to provoke anyone. We should be fine." Famous last words.

"You sure you don't want to go home first?"

"Let's get this over with."

The drive took almost half an hour. I could have waited, but I called Cheryl instead.

"Hey," I said when she answered.

"Kitty! Oh my God, where are you? Are you okay?"

"I'm fine. Ben found me. Cheryl, I'm sorry I ran off on you." There, I said it. I felt relieved.

"What the hell happened?"

"I lost my temper."

"Oh, is that all," she said, with a thick layer of sarcasm.

"Can it, Cheryl," I said, my exhaustion plain.

"Seriously, Kitty—are you okay?" She actually sounded concerned. Not demanding, not frustrated. She was across town, but I could feel her hugging me.

"I will be," I said, with unexpected honesty. I wasn't okay, obviously. Not completely. "I've just had a lot going on this week. I'm a little on edge."

"And I tipped you over?"

I smiled. "Maybe just a little."

"I'm sorry."

"Me, too."

"Kitty—thanks for calling. You should get some rest, you sound thrashed."

Yeah, I probably did. Too bad I had a couple of chores first. "I'll come pick up my car later."

"Don't worry about it. If we have to move it we will. You dropped your keys."

Of course I did. Just another thing to worry about. "I love you, Cheryl."

"I love you, too."

As I hung up the phone, Ben glanced over. He was smiling. "See? You didn't traumatize her too badly."

"I almost shifted in her kitchen."

"But you didn't. Think positive here."

Yeah, right. "Full moon was just a few days ago. This is supposed to be the easiest time of the month to keep from shifting. But I totally lost it."

"We'll just have to be careful, at least until things let up a little."

I liked that he put the "we" in there. But I didn't like the feeling that I needed to be looked after. Taken care of. Babysat.

By the time we arrived downtown, streetlights were blazing and the sky was full dark. Ben crawled along the street near our destination, looking for a parking spot. Some of the surrounding offices and classroom buildings showed a few lights in the windows, but the church was dark. It loomed like a fortress over its parklike surroundings.

Ben found a spot in the driveway near the church. Between a couple of NO PARKING signs even. I raised a brow at him. "We're not going to be here long, right? Nobody'll know."

The lawyer was saying this?

In the dead of night, with the engine still, the neighborhood's silence pressed in. The streetlights seemed muted, and the air seemed hazy. It gave the place a haunted look. At least, my imagination thought so.

"It's really tough looking for a vampire who doesn't want to be found," I said, stepping out of the car. Ben followed.

"Cormac would say wait until daylight and flush 'em out."

"Cormac says a lot of things."

Craning my neck, I regarded the building, a hulking shadow in the city's nighttime haze. How did I convince Rick that he wanted to be found? I walked around to the front of the church and climbed the wide steps to the front door, to try the only thing I could—the direct approach. This late, I probably wouldn't be disturbing a lecture.

"What are you going to do, knock?" Ben asked, trailing behind.

Glancing at him over my shoulder, I gave a thin smile and knocked on one of the church's wooden front doors.

No one answered. I tried again; the hollow thumping seemed to get swallowed up by the darkness, and by the tall bell towers looming over me. Those towers looked like they might be home to bats; on the other hand, the pale stucco of the church's exterior, still visible even at night, didn't do much for the gothic vampire atmosphere.

I rattled the door latch. Tonight, this late, the thing was locked. The place didn't exactly have a window I could crawl through. Behind me, Ben crossed his arms and frowned. Visions of misdemeanor trespassing passing before his eyes, no doubt.

I trotted down the stairs and walked around the

KITTY ROCKS THE HOUSE 197

building and the rectory next door, looking for a lit window or a door that wasn't bolted tight, but didn't find anything and ended up back by the front steps. I knew Columban and Rick were here, I just knew it. The markings that laid out the protective circle were still here. They may even have been touched up since Cormac's last escapade. This place was still being defended.

Halfway up the front steps, I put my hands around my mouth and called, "Rick! Rick, I need to talk to you! Rick!" I shouted up at those bell towers; their shadowed interiors stared down at me like eyes.

If he was here, he'd heard me. If he didn't come out, he was ignoring me, just like he'd ignored my phone calls, and Angelo's, and everything else. And I couldn't change that.

Ben was at the foot of the steps, not watching me, but the sidewalks around the church. Keeping a look out for me. I worried that I took him for granted. I got in trouble and dragged him with me over and over. It wasn't a good pattern.

Nothing happened.

I descended, my steps landing heavy. What else could I do but call again, leave yet another message? But I could do it from someplace warm and well lit, after a shower and change of clothes. But it felt like giving up.

When I reached the bottom, Ben put his arm around

my shoulders, and together we walked back around the building to the car.

"Maybe he just doesn't want to talk," Ben said.

I scowled. "Maybe he's really not here."

"But if he's not here, and he's not at Obsidian, and the other vampires haven't seen him . . ."

"Maybe he's not here, in Denver."

Rick had spent most of his life being nomadic. If he decided to leave, I couldn't assume that he'd tell me first. I'd been alive for a bare fraction of his years—would only live for a fraction of them. Why should he care about what I thought? I wanted to believe our friendship had meant more than that. Him just leaving—that would mean he didn't consider me a friend at all.

That was still better than thinking he'd been killed, which was an alternative I hadn't voiced. Rick had lived for five hundred years, he couldn't just *die*.

Ben slowed, his arm tugging me to a stop beside him. He nodded toward a back corner of the chapel, where a figure moved, stepping out of shadows from behind a clump of shrubbery. I didn't recognize him at first—he was wearing a T-shirt and trousers, and his dark hair was mussed, flopped around his ears instead of combed back from his face. Without his trench coat, his shape was different.

"Rick?" I said, walking toward him.

He waited for me, lingering by the doorway he'd come out of, as if wanting to stay near shelter. "Kitty."

"Are you okay?"

"Of course. But are you? You look like you've had a rough night of it."

With the overcoat covering them, I'd forgotten my clothes were ripped enough to fall off in a slight breeze. I hugged the coat tighter around me. When I didn't say anything, Rick looked at Ben.

"She lost it," he said. The vampire raised an eyebrow.

"I lost my temper and shifted in the middle of Highlands Ranch."

"She ate somebody's cat," Ben added. I was never going to live that down, was I?

Rick seemed taken aback. "Really? That isn't like you. What's wrong?"

Everything, I almost said. "I'm a little stressed out. And this isn't supposed to be about me, this is about you."

"I'm fine, Kitty. What are you even doing here?"

"Angelo called me. He's worried."

"There's nothing to be worried about," Rick said curtly. "That is, as long as your bounty hunter keeps his distance."

I didn't want to talk about Cormac right now. The protective spell was obviously doing its job; Cormac wasn't a threat. "The Buenos Aires vampires are going to be here in a couple of days, they're bugging Angelo about procedure, and we haven't talked at all about what to say to them."

"I'm sure you can handle it," he said. "There's nothing I can say to them that you can't say perfectly well on your own."

"Besides the fact that I'm a werewolf and they probably won't want to talk to me at all?"

"You'll just have to convince them otherwise."

He was dumping this all on me, all of it. The weight of the world, settling on my shoulders. Even Wolf curled up and whined at the thought.

"What's so important that you can't come out and deal with this?" I said. I pointed at the wall of the church. "What are you and Columban *doing* in there?"

"I'm . . ." He clenched his hands, as if reaching for pockets that weren't there. "I can't discuss it. But yes, it is important. Columban is taking on this battle just as much as we are. I think I can help him."

"But I *know* you can help me."

He started to say one thing, but shook his head. He turned back to the building, changed his mind, and looked back. "Kitty. Ben. I appreciate your concern. But you should go home. Get cleaned up, get some rest. You obviously have enough problems of your own, you don't need to be worried about me." He spoke

with such confidence, in such a decisive, command-
ing tone, how could I argue? I still felt uneasy.

"Ricardo?" an accented voice called from within
the shadows, from an open doorway in the back of
the church.

Ricardo, not Rick. I could see the shape of the
vampire priest's cassock, but not his features. I wanted
to grab him, shake him, demand to know what spell
he'd put on Rick. But I didn't.

"I have to go," the vampire said. I might have
imagined him pressing his lips in an apology as he
turned away and disappeared back through the doorway.

"We've lost him," I said, my voice bleak.

Ben put his arm around me, turned me to the
street. He had to push, urging me, before I could get
my feet to move.

Chapter 14

I CALLED ANGELO to tell him Rick wasn't going to be available for the meeting with the Buenos Aires vampires.

"You talked to him?" he said, astonished.

"Briefly. He wasn't really interested in talking."

"What did he say?"

"I think he's gone sort of Buddhist monk. Can vampires be Buddhist monks?"

"I'm sure I wouldn't know. Kitty—the envoy will be here tonight. He wants to talk to *Rick*. Not *you*."

"Well," I said, feeling hollow. "He's got me. Why don't you send him to New Moon after the show?"

His voice turned arch with disgust. "I can't send him *there*."

"Yes, you can. And make sure he eats something first—somewhere else," I said and hung up the phone.

Either the guy would be there after the show, or he wouldn't.

Friday night again, already. Couldn't be possible, but it was. Ozzie called me around lunchtime, because I hadn't been into work since Thursday morning, and he wanted to know when I was coming in to prep for the show. If there was ever a time I wanted to call in sick, this was it.

Ben insisted on driving me to the station—and coming inside with me, and staying through the show.

"You don't have to do this," I said for the ninth time, as we entered the lobby. The receptionist waved hello, and I made a halfhearted motion in response on our way to the elevator.

"Yes, I do," Ben said. "After your breakdown yesterday? I'm not letting you out of my sight. You might need someone to peel you off the ceiling."

He was worried about me. It was kind of sweet, and I teared up a little even as I argued. "I wouldn't call it a breakdown."

"Then what would you call it?"

Shape-shifting in the middle of the suburbs because of stress? Um, right. I grabbed his hand and squeezed. "Thanks for looking out for me." He smiled back.

We stopped off at my office to pick up materials for the show and were still hand in hand when we walked into the studio. Matt, in position in the booth by the soundboard, waved at me. And Ozzie was sitting in his seat in the corner. Of all the weeks he could pick to play supervisor. I managed not to groan.

Ben leaned in and murmured, "Someone else been keeping an eye on you, I take it?"

"I don't want to talk about it. Have a seat and be good, okay?"

He kissed my forehead and did as I asked. I turned a bright, fake smile on my boss. "Hi, Ozzie."

"Kitty. You haven't been around much this week. I've been worried." He was a good guy, but his worry usually translated as smothering. Made me bristle.

"Yeah, I know. Family stuff came up." In a manner of speaking . . .

"You got something good for tonight?"

"Do I ever. In fact, I'm glad you're here. You'll love it." In fact, I was starting to get an idea . . .

Some weeks, I was on top of things: planning, organizing, recording interviews ahead of time, writing up my rants and speeches to make sure they sounded intelligent and insightful. Other weeks, not so much. I'd tell myself I'd do it tomorrow, for sure. Then I'd wake up, and it'd be Friday, and I'd have a show to do *that day*. This week in particular, Friday seemed to have sneaked up on me. Good thing I always had something to talk about. I kept a folder full of articles, links to online rants requiring responses, and notes of random thoughts. The world never failed to provide shocking, interesting, head-scratching topics for me to discuss.

This week, I literally pulled my topic off the shelf and hit the ground running.

I watched Matt through the booth window, waited for him to cue up my intro with the theme song I'd used since the start: CCR's "Bad Moon Rising." As relevant now as it ever was. The music made the rest of the world disappear, so that nothing existed but me, my microphone, and the show. It felt like flying.

"Good evening, and here we are again. This is Kitty Norville and you're listening to *The Midnight Hour,* where we spend a couple of hours talking about all the things that no one else will. And probably shouldn't. It's a good life, isn't it? I have something very special on deck tonight. Christmas or winter solstice–associated holiday of your choice came to the studio early this year, and I got a present. I don't know who exactly to thank for this, but let me take a moment to express my appreciation to my mysterious benefactor. Thank you, sir or madam. I love it. Now, what is it? Dear listeners, I've been sent a vampire crystal skull."

A month or so ago, I'd received a package in the mail. I got a lot of mail, most of it junk, but this one had intrigued me. The brown paper wrapped box didn't have a return address; the postmark said Texas.

Since the package didn't smell like a bomb or vat full of anthrax, I went ahead and opened it, and there it lay, nestled in a cloud of Styrofoam peanuts. A crystal skull, milky white, a little larger than a grapefruit, rounded and stylized, with deep-set eye sockets and distinctive, sharpened fangs where its eyeteeth should have been. It had been living on a shelf in my office ever since, waiting for the perfect opportunity. Like this one.

I set the skull on the table in the studio right next to my monitor and studied it as I talked. It stared back at me with hollow eyes that reflected and scattered the dim lights in the studio. Was it winking at me? "Is it a gift? A curse? Am I supposed to investigate it? Debunk it? Is it a kitsch object from a Mexican flea market? Or are the stories true, and crystal skulls aren't just the plot device in a couple of unfortunate movies? Are these artifacts the source of some great ancient power possessed by the Mayans, the awesome gift of travelers from the stars, the key to the lost city of Atlantis? Or someone's idea of a joke? Before I tell you what I think, I'm going to open the line up for calls. You've been sent not just any crystal skull, but one with sharpened canines. What do you do?" The lines lit up. Likely, people had called in before I'd even started talking in an effort to get into the queue and didn't have a thing to say about crystal skulls, vampire or otherwise. But someone with an opinion would get through. I checked the monitor, found a likely victim, and pounced. "Hello, you're on the air."

A confused-sounding woman said, "So wait, does that mean that vampires have crystal skeletons?"

I winced. "That's a good one, I hadn't actually thought of that. But no, I don't think so. I think vampires have bones like the rest of us. Just really old bones. Next call, please." I hit the line.

"It's got to be a fake," the male caller said.

Well, yeah, I figured that pretty much went without saying. In the course of my research I'd found crystal skulls for sale in a rock art catalog. But that wasn't the way to keep a show going.

"Why do you say that?" I said, trying to sound genuinely curious.

"Because vampires weren't even in North America until a couple of hundred years ago, so a real Mayan crystal skull couldn't possibly have anything to do with vampires, since the Mayan empire was in decline before then."

"Five hundred, but yes," I said.

"What?"

"European vampires arrived in North America about five hundred years ago, but I see your point."

"How do you even know that?"

"How do you?" My tone was cheerful, which probably confused him.

Flustered now, he said, "I just know it, okay? So it has to be a fake."

"Let me see if I'm understanding you correctly. When you say it's a fake, you're not saying that it's fake because crystal skulls aren't really mystical artifacts, you're saying it's fake because it's the skull of a vampire. And if it wasn't, it would be real?"

"Exactly," he said, pleased with himself.

Well, this ought to be interesting. "Now when you say 'a real crystal skull,' what exactly do you mean?"

He sounded put out. "You don't believe this is real, do you? Why did you even bring it up?"

"Look, someone sent it to me, I'm not the one who brought it up. Well, I am. But I wouldn't have brought it up if someone hadn't sent it to me."

"You're dealing with powers you don't understand!" he said.

"I get that a lot," I said and clicked him off the air. "I did a little research of my own, and here's what I found. Historical records—Mayan, Aztec, or otherwise—show no trace of crystal skulls as part of their worship, and the famous ones that form the center of current mystical belief all seemed to have appeared on the scene in the mid to late nineteenth century. Despite claims to the contrary, they appear to have been manufactured. By plain, nonmystical human beings. Now, I've seen some crazy stuff in my time and I'm willing to entertain the notion that some crystal skull somewhere might have some of the powers its adherents credit to it. But personally, I have to file this one under crop circles. They're just too easy to replicate using nonmystical means. I've got another caller ready to argue with me. Clare, hello."

"Hi, Kitty, thanks for taking my call. I just want to say, there's an alternative that I think your previous caller hasn't considered." She had a light, matter-of-fact voice that made me brace for even more bullshit than usual.

"And what's that alternative?"

"That there are vampires among the aliens."

I had to think about that a moment. "You're right. I hadn't considered that. I mean, generic sci-fi horror movies notwithstanding."

"It makes perfect sense—immortal vampires are the best choice to travel the long distances between the stars. *They're* the ones who would come to visit us here on Earth."

Was it wrong that the concept sort of did make sense? "You seem to have a lot of good ideas on the topic," I said, rather nonplussed. "So I've got this vampire crystal skull. You think it came from outer space?"

"I do," she said.

"I gotta tell you, I'm skeptical. I hold it and it just feels like a big rock. I mean, it's not even a realistic skull. It's kinda small and lumpy. But plenty of people will tell me it's magic. What's it supposed to do? Am I holding it wrong?"

"The skull should give you access to a higher plane of knowledge," she explained. "Place your nose against its nose and stare into its eyes. You should feel your mind *expand*."

I studied the skull where it sat on my desk. Green status lights from my monitor flickered strangely through its depths. Did it seem to be smiling at me? If I tilted my head, looked at it from a certain angle— yeah, it kind of did.

"I'm thinking I should stay right where I am and keep an eye on the microphone. But a little harmless experimentation can't hurt." I looked at Ozzie. "We have a special guest in the studio tonight, my producer, Ozzie," I said, for the benefit of my listeners. "Feel like helping me out tonight?"

He frowned with suspicion, which was probably wise of him. But if he was going to sit in on my show, he could help out. Maybe this was a bad idea, but I'd worry about that later.

"Why?" he said carefully.

"I just want to try something. Please?"

I'd keep nagging until he relented, or tell embarrassing stories about him until he agreed, just to shut me up. He gave a sigh heavy enough to carry over the mike, which made things more dramatic. I loved it.

"Come on over, Ozzie," I said, grinning, and he did. When he reached the table, I handed him the skull. "Okay, hold this. In both hands. Bring it up to your face so your nose touches it."

He held it in one hand, away from himself. "Kitty, I'm not really sure about this."

"It'll be fine, trust me." I'd be a terrible used-car salesman. I glanced at Ben, who had a hand over his mouth to keep himself from laughing. Matt, sitting behind the booth's glass, didn't bother, and was practically vibrating in his seat. Now, if only I was getting the same effect over the air.

Ozzie gripped the skull in both hands and slowly raised it until it was level with his face. "Should I be sitting down?" he said.

Good question. "You're fine," I said, full of confidence, trying to be reassuring. Because nothing was going to happen, right?

He brought the skull close, until his nose touched it. He stared deep into its eyes.

"All right, faithful listeners," I said into the microphone, my voice hushed. "My test subject is now face-to-face with the crystal skull. Everything seems normal. You okay there, Ozzie?"

"I think my eyes are crossed."

"Are you expanding yet?"

"I don't know. It's kind of giving me a headache."

Just as I wished for some kind of funky New Age

flute music to cover up the pauses while we waited for something to happen, Matt pushed a couple of buttons and there it was: "El Condor Pasa" on pan pipes playing faintly in the background. Just perfect. My listeners were at the edges of their seats, I hoped.

"Anything?" I prompted.

Ozzie murmured, "I don't think anything's happening. Can I stop now?"

"Give it an extra few seconds."

"Okay . . ."

Wait for it . . . I had my cell phone in hand, flipped through the setting controls until I found the most annoying ring tone I had, then set it off at high volume. An alarm bell's blaring filled the studio. The sound of cosmic disaster called down by ancient Mayan vampires. Or just the worst that modern technology had to offer. Even I jumped a little and I was expecting it. Ben clapped his hands over his ears and winced.

Ozzie let out a scream, stumbled backward, and dropped the skull. For a heart-stopping moment I watched it fall and almost reached out to catch it lest it shatter. But it bounced on the carpeted floor and rolled to a stop. Upright, facing me. Staring at me. I stared back.

"Kitty, Jesus Christ, what the . . . hell was that?" Ozzie was a radio guy to the core and stopped himself from needing to get bleeped. Good thing, too, because Matt had fallen out of his chair, laughing, and wasn't going to be bleeping anything for a while.

"I'm sorry," I said, sniggering around the words. "I had to do something to get past all that dead air. The skull wasn't doing anything."

"You set me up."

"Kinda, yeah. But it would have been pretty cool if something had happened."

He reached to the floor to retrieve the skull and set it on the desk with a *thunk* that would definitely be audible over the microphone. "Always happy to help," he said flatly. I expected him to walk out of the studio—maybe for good—but he returned to his chair and settled back to keep watching.

"Thanks, Ozzie. You're a trooper," I said, trying not to giggle. "Well, I don't know if we expanded any minds tonight, but we upped some heart rates." The board was still lit up with calls, which comforted me. As long as I had calls, I could pull *something* together for the show.

Meanwhile, the thing was still staring at me. I squinted, and its eyes seemed to flash. Fine, enough of that. I turned it around so it was facing the wall.

"Right, moving on. After the break I'll take some more calls. Anyone out there want to talk some more about vampire aliens or crop circles? Call me."

The ON AIR sign dimmed, and Matt cued up station ID and PSAs. I turned to Ozzie to face the music. He seemed to be stewing, and I wondered if I was still going to have a job at the end of the evening.

Finally, Ben was the one who asked, "You're not going to fire her, are you?"

The producer's stern glare broke into a broad grin. "Are you kidding? Of course not! That was fantastic! That's the kind of thing I'm talking about! Sensationalism! Bread and butter! Good work, Kitty. I'll leave you to it." He came over to me and patted me on the shoulder before walking out of the studio. Leaving me to it.

I looked at Matt through the window, and he blinked, appearing as confused as I was. Ben, likewise.

"Don't question it," he said. "Not if Ozzie leaves you alone from now on."

"You have a minute, Kitty," Matt announced, counting down to the end of the break. The phone lines were lit up. All I had to do was take calls to the end of the show.

I patted the top of the skull. Its work here was done.

WE RUSHED to New Moon after the show.

I'd tried to make myself as presentable as possible, dressing as nicely as I ever did on a Friday night, in slacks and a blouse, and unscuffed pumps even. But after two hours of *The Midnight Hour,* I couldn't hide the fatigue pinching my features or the sweaty perfume I'd acquired. Getting there as quickly as I could was more important than looking nice. Presentable was good enough.

The envoy from Buenos Aires was already at the restaurant when I got there. I'd left tonight's manager—Shaun had the night off—instructions to invite him in and show him to my table in back. The vampire was sitting there now, alert and interested without being tense, elbows propped up and hands steepled before him, gazing over the place with a frown. He wore jeans and a dark blazer over a white T-shirt. His dark hair was cut short, and he had strong, square-jawed Latino features. He gave off an action-hero vibe at odds with the vampire stereotype.

By the warm cast to his olive skin, I guessed that Angelo had offered him some kind of hospitality. I knew the Denver Family didn't kill to eat, but apart from that, I didn't ask for details. Most Families had human servants who willingly donated, or they had hunting grounds that they protected and used sparingly, to avoid drawing attention. All that mattered was the Denver Family didn't draw attention. Angelo himself was nowhere to be found, naturally. Leaving the dirty work to me.

I asked Ben to wait near the front of the restaurant, at the bar, to keep watch. Concern pinched his face, but he didn't argue. If I was going to prove I was strong enough to lead, strong enough to fight, I had to do this on my own.

"Titus," I said when I arrived at the table and sat across from him. "Welcome. Thanks for coming to see me."

His lip curled in what I hoped was amusement. "Indeed."

Oh, this was going to go well . . . "I hope you didn't have any trouble finding the place."

"This setting is a bit . . . common." He glanced around the bar, which was experiencing a late after-theater rush. Raised voices created a flood of noise against the backdrop of the rock music on the stereo system. A few of my pack were here, including Darren, who once again was with Becky. They were sitting at the bar, knee to knee. Not causing trouble, thank goodness. I found myself wishing Shaun was here for backup.

"I kind of like it," I said, smiling fondly.

"Keeps you rooted in the world, does it?"

"Yeah. Rick would say that." I wanted to like this guy. His manner seemed straightforward. I tried to take the measure of him, without meeting his hypnotic gaze, staring instead at the collar of his shirt.

"Are you *certain* Ricardo isn't available?"

"He's following up another lead." My chin was up,

my back was straight, my stance confident. Alpha-like, even. Not inviting argument.

"What am I supposed to tell my Mistress, then?" he said. He had a Spanish-flavored accent, his tone only mildly annoyed, as if he hadn't expected anything different out of this meeting.

"Everything Rick knows, I know."

"Oh, I doubt that."

I gritted my teeth. "All right, *just about* everything Rick knows, at least about the Long Game, I know." Still, with that skeptical lilt to his brow. Flustered now, I said, "I've faced Dux Bellorum twice and survived."

"Really?" He sounded disbelieving rather than impressed. I wasn't going to be able to convince him I had any credibility at all. Was it anti-werewolf prejudice, or was I selling myself badly?

"Yeah. Have *you* ever met the guy?"

"My Mistress has. Many years ago. He offered her power. She walked away. Fled, rather, to the colonies. She opposes him by staying out of his reach."

"How much longer do you think she'll be able to keep that up?"

A trace of anxiety furrowed his brow. "That is why I am here. I had hoped to speak to Ricardo of this."

"I'm telling you what he'd tell you. You have allies.

We've already exposed Roman and a number of his followers. The more of us watching for him, the better chance we have of stopping him. He can be beaten." I *hoped* he could . . .

Another long moment of sizing each other up passed. I had the impression that he could see through me, read my mind even. My skin itched, but through an act of will I didn't fidget.

"I am supposed to tell Mistress Bianca that the Master of Denver has more important business than speaking with her chosen representative?"

Etiquette wasn't my strong suit, and I couldn't help but fail miserably at it where vampires were concerned. I sighed. "I keep forgetting you people have so much time on your hands you have nothing better to do than take offense at everything." He flattened his hands on the table and opened his mouth to speak, but I gestured to stop him. "I know, I know. Sending a werewolf to talk to you is an insult. You'll just have to believe me that Rick is dealing with a serious matter than no one else can handle, and that I really do know what he does about Dux Bellorum."

Titus seemed mollified. "I believe you know enough. This is all so very . . . chaotic."

"Yeah. Tell me about it. We just have to keep paddling along, yeah?" He rewarded me with a thin, amused smile. "Can we contact you if we need to? Will you contact us, if you learn anything?"

He hesitated, and every moment he did my hopes sank a notch. He drew breath and said, "I'm skeptical, I confess. The situation in Denver seems less stable than I was led to believe. Are you and Ricardo truly strong enough to mount an opposition against Roman?"

"We've stood up to him before. Yes," I said, because I had to.

"Then I'll return home and report to my Mistress. She'll send word of her response."

He started to push back from the table, but I rushed out a question while I had the chance. "Before you go, can I ask you something? Do you know anything about vampires working for the Vatican?" Argentina was a Catholic country, right? What could it hurt to ask?

"You're joking, yes?"

"Never mind," I said, sighing.

He stood and walked out without further acknowledgment, without giving me another chance to talk at him. To convince him. Bianca, Mistress of Buenos Aires, was the only vampire Master in South America we were absolutely sure didn't belong to Roman. Not that South America was swarming with vampires, but I didn't much like the feeling of facing an entire continent outside our influence.

I slumped forward and put my head on my arms, just to rest for a moment.

Footsteps approached, and I caught the scent of werewolf before me. Darren. Chin up, shoulders broad, he smiled at me and sat in the chair across from me, the one where Titus had been a moment before. Ben moved toward us in a hurry.

The restaurant had emptied while Titus and I talked. The manager and a couple of staff remained, working to close up. Becky was still here, by the front door, hackles up. The moment seemed frozen—something was happening. I caught Ben's gaze and shook my head, asking him to wait. I wanted to see how this played out. Ben stopped, but almost bounced in place, hands clenched, looking back and forth between Darren and Becky.

Darren ignored him and said, "It's tough, isn't it? Being in charge. Staying in control."

I tried to puzzle out his intention. The obvious condescension in his tone wasn't mean, but wasn't very sympathetic, either. He mostly sounded like he was making a casual observation. Never mind that the words slipped a knife between my ribs.

"I didn't realize I was being graded."

He went on, "You've had to work very hard, haven't you? Leading this pack, putting yourself out there."

Ben leaned in. "You're out of line—"

I held up a hand to stop him. Maybe we could good cop/bad cop this. "I do okay."

Darren's smile cut. "I mean you've had to work

hard to be an alpha. Because you're not, really. You certainly weren't born an alpha. You were happier when you had somebody taking care of you, weren't you?"

I flashed back on those years, bottom of the pack, everyone's baby, everyone's punching bag. Maybe that had been less work, but "happy" certainly wasn't the word I'd use to describe that time. It was never as much work to roll over and show your belly as it was to stand up straight. But standing straight felt so much better.

I grinned, teeth showing. "That's a little Calvinistic, don't you think? Predeterministic? You don't believe in upward mobility?"

"You can't change your basic nature."

A few feet away, Ben was just about trembling with anger. I tried to radiate calm. I didn't want to get blood all over my nice restaurant. "That's the big debate for the ages, isn't it? Nature versus nurture. So you're a nature guy, I take it?"

"All your talk just covers up your fears—you're afraid I'm right."

Talking had worked so far. I leaned back, not breaking eye contact—not giving an inch, not letting him think his challenge was working. I declaimed, "Some are born alpha, some achieve alpha-ness, and some have alpha-ness thrust upon them. You know, that actually has a nice ring to it."

If I was getting to him—discouraging him, making him angry, maybe even amusing him—he didn't reveal it. He would wear me down with impenetrable, paternalistic kindness. He was only trying to help, really. The more I argued, the more I'd prove his point.

Well, it was the only thing I knew how to do, really. "So, what are you doing? You think you can do a better job? You calling me out?"

"You're the one who brought it up, not me."

Ben started to lunge, but I stood and braced against him, stopping him. An aggressive response might have been instinctive, but it showed weakness, showed Darren that he could get to us. Never mind if any of what he said was true. This was all about appearances. This didn't look too good.

I had an urge to attack him myself, really. I imagined the taste of his blood on my tongue, his flesh parting at the touch of my teeth. My heart burned with the thought, but the sound of voices calmed me. The manager in back, talking to the cook who was scraping the grill. This was the human den, the human place, where people sat in chairs, ate with forks, glared at each other across the table and didn't throw punches, no matter how much they wanted to. This wasn't the place for a fight. Not Wolf's kind of fight. Surely I had that much control. I would not start a fight here.

"You can't have Denver," I said, startled at how petulant my voice sounded. I didn't sound strong, but like a whining child, and this all felt like it was happening to someone else. I watched myself glare at him. I radiated challenge. But that was Wolf, not me.

Ben broke away from me, but didn't get any farther than leaning across the table, teeth bared. Darren stood, knocking the chair back to the floor, mirroring the glare and snarl.

"You going to start something?" Darren said, eager.

"There will be no fighting in my restaurant," I said. Not that I could stop them if either one of them decided to cross the table.

"Yeah," Darren said, chuckling. "That's what I thought. You don't have it in you." He walked away, flicking his hand in a way that made me think I was the one being dismissed.

Ben rushed him, and I grabbed his arm, held him back. Somehow, I stopped him. Maybe because I was trembling and close to losing it. My husband curled back to hold me, turning his startled gaze on me, searching for what was wrong. That was what stopped him: I was about to melt, and he paused to take care of me rather than fight the challenger. I leaned into him.

At the front door, Darren paused, waiting for Becky to scramble to his side. She hesitated, looked over her shoulder at me staring back at her—and she didn't turn away. Her gaze, her stance, held determination. Challenge. Then they were gone.

Wolf trembled in my gut. Standing in disbelief, I didn't know which of them I was more angry at. I wanted to murder them both. I almost ran after them, as if murder were not only a viable option, but something I could accomplish. And wouldn't get prosecuted for when I was discovered on the streets of downtown after midnight next to two eviscerated bodies.

Ben lowered me into the chair. I was shaking, trying to hold Wolf in, trying not to howl in fury. If Shaun had been managing tonight, if any of the other werewolves had been here, I might have. They would have understood.

"Kitty," Ben said, kneeling in front of me, holding my face, making me look at him. Bringing me back to myself. I pulled him into an embrace and felt better. He spoke in my ear, "Why didn't you let me murder the bastard?"

"Because we can't fight."

"Of course we can, we're werewolves. We've both fought, we can take him. We can take both of them right now. We have to—"

"I don't know if I can do this anymore, Ben."

His frown made him look suddenly old, furrowed and worried. "What do you mean?"

It was a crossroads. I could walk away from everything. Flee Denver, like I had before. "You're always saying that if I really want kids, if we want to adopt a kid, then I can't keep on with all this, can I? Secret meetings with vampires, battling an international conspiracy, leading a werewolf pack. If I gave it all up, we could have a house, kids, a normal life—"

"You don't mean that."

Oh, but for a moment I did mean it. I could shed it all like a skin. All those people looking to me for answers, me standing tall and declaring that I actually had them. I was tired of it, and the thought of being just Kitty, lowly werewolf making do, made me feel light-headed. Giddy. And the kids thing—I still had hope, though I tried not to think about it. Werewolf physiology—shape-shifting—meant I couldn't have a baby, but I had other options for having children. What would it be like, to explore some of those options, without feeling like I was dragging some poor kid into a war?

Could I really walk away from the life I'd built?

Ben was still talking. "It means leaving Denver. Your family, my family, the restaurant, everything. Is that what you want? If it is, I'll back you."

And if I stayed and fought, he'd back me then as well.

I drew myself close and kissed him. Nice, long, rich, wonderful. He tasted of beer. His muscles relaxed under my hands, and his responding touch gave me strength. I could straighten my back again, and square my shoulders.

Reluctantly, I pulled away, but stayed close enough that my breath brushed him when I spoke. "Darren's making a bid for the pack, and he's got Becky on his side."

"And who knows who else? He's had to have been planning this."

"Yeah," I said. "But I don't think he realizes the job he's taken on. He can't have gotten to everyone. He's assuming he only has to take out us two, then he and Becky step in as alpha pair."

"That's a really big assumption. He takes out us two, he has to deal with Cormac."

I smiled. That was only one of our aces in the hole. "He doesn't know that. He's only thinking about you and me. The thing is, he just might be able to take us out in a fair fight."

He huffed, indignant. "*I* wouldn't make that assumption."

"It's okay. Moot point. Because we're not leaving—and we're not going to fight."

Chapter 15

SATURDAY MORNING, back at the condo, we called everyone. It was an attempt at an end run. Darren had convinced Becky that she could be alpha, that they could be the alpha pair together. But I had a feeling he was working top down. Becky was the strongest, most eligible woman in the pack, and she'd been perfectly willing to be wooed—this was the only way she could move up in the pack, and her wolf must have thought that was a good idea. Darren thought Becky was all he needed to convince everyone else. But if we had a chance to warn people, they'd never stand with him. Becky had to know this.

Never mind what Rick would think of a takeover of the Denver pack. I liked to think he'd side with us and help us keep it from happening, if it weren't for the fact that he was a bit preoccupied at the moment.

Darren had never even talked to Rick, as far as I knew. Either way, I couldn't count on Rick or his Family to pull us out of this fire. We could do that on our own. And if we couldn't, we didn't much deserve to lead the Denver pack, did we?

Darren worked top down. I worked from the bottom up, just like I always had. I called my pack members, told them what was happening, asked them to stand with me. Every single one of them said yes.

Shaun did more than that. "I should have seen this coming. The way he latched onto Becky—"

"I'm not entirely sure what to do about her," I said. She had been with us since the beginning—she was the second wolf after Shaun to leave the old alphas and follow me.

"She wouldn't turn on us, not her." His very decisiveness hinted at his uncertainty.

"I'll find out, one way or another."

"I can take on Darren. Track him down in some dark alley. The problem will just go away." I imagined him making a gesture in the air, a flick of his fingers.

"I appreciate that. But I want to do this in the open, so there isn't any question. I'm trying to build a reputation here."

"You face him down, maybe some of these foreign vampires will take you seriously?"

"I'm that transparent, huh? Darren's a friend of Nasser's. This'll get back to him."

"Whatever you decide to do, I'll back you."

"Good," I said. This was *my* pack, not Darren's, and I'd just proven it.

The hardest call to make was to Trey. All the help I hadn't been giving him, and now here I was, asking for backup. The nerve of me. I thought about not calling him at all—he didn't need to be worrying about me. But he was pack, and leaving him out would be the worst thing I'd done yet.

"Kitty?" he said, answering his phone.

"Hey, Trey? Couple of things. First off, you're right, I haven't been around like I should be, and I'm sorry. You needed help and I wasn't there. I'm going to do better. I'd like to have lunch sometime and talk about Sam, but I'm in the middle of a crisis right now. That's the second thing."

"Kitty," he said. "You're always in the middle of a crisis. But it's okay. Don't worry about it."

"I really haven't forgotten about you, honest."

"I know. But seriously, it's taken care of. Everything's good."

I furrowed my brow, bemused. "It is? Well, that's great. I guess."

"More than great. Sam . . . she said yes. We're engaged." He sounded astonished and giddy.

"Oh my gosh, that's great. See, you don't need my help at all." I might have felt a tiny bit conflicted about that.

"Oh, I wouldn't say that. You know what turned her around?"

"What?" Maybe I could take notes for the next time this came up. God, I hope this never came up again, not like this. But please let him not say talking to Darren is what helped him.

Trey said, "I gave her a copy of your book. The one about being a werewolf."

My first book, a memoir called *Underneath the Skin,* had done pretty well for itself. This was a use for it I hadn't considered. I hesitated, astonished. "Wow. That's . . . that's kind of crazy. But I'm glad."

"She said it helped her see my side of it, and helped her explain to me what was bothering her. We must have talked about it all day." He went on like that, waxing poetic about Sam and how amazing she was, his voice going all dreamy. I heartily approved. I almost forgot about the main reason I'd called.

"She wants to meet you," he said, proudly.

"And I want to meet her, definitely. But I've got another problem right now—Becky and Darren are challenging for leadership of the pack."

He paused a beat. "What?"

Yeah, exactly. I explained, and he said, simply, "I'll kill him. Just point me at him."

That's my pack . . . "I'm hoping that won't be necessary. We've got a plan brewing."

Trey promised to side with me when the time came. We could do this, we really could.

The last person I called was Becky.

Her phone shunted me to voice mail, which I expected. I couldn't imagine what she thought when my name came up on her caller ID. "Hi, Becky," I said in a suitably cheerful voice that probably came out sounding saccharine and evil from her perspective. "This is Kitty. Of course it is. I'd really like to talk to you. You know how it is with me and the talking. No pressure, no strings attached, just talking in a well-lit public place. I'll keep calling until you feel compelled to pick up the phone. Just to warn you."

I called again ten minutes later. Then ten minutes after that. On the sixth call, she answered.

"What?" she'd said, sounding like a kid who'd gotten caught stealing gum.

"Not over the phone. I want you to look me in the eye when you explain to me why you think screwing me over is a good idea."

"I don't have to do that," she said sharply.

"Nope, you sure don't. I just want you to ask yourself how Darren's little coup is likely to succeed when it's you two standing on one side of the fight and me and the rest of the pack standing on the other."

She only hesitated a beat. "He says the others will follow him. When they see how much stronger he is, how much more experienced. Kitty, you know you aren't cut out for this, you never were, and with all the traveling and all this stupid vampire politics—"

"Becky. You know this pack. Who are they really going to listen to, him or me?" She didn't seem to notice that I hadn't actually said Darren was *wrong* on anything he'd said about me. He may have been right. But he'd severely misjudged my response to the situation. He assumed I'd fold. Because I wasn't a "born alpha." To hell with that.

Her voice cracked a little. "If there really is going to be trouble with the vampires, we'll need someone strong, like him."

"And you?"

"I'm strong enough."

"Yes, I know," I said. "Which is why we're going to talk about this."

"Talking isn't going to help—"

"Says you."

"Kitty—"

"Now you're going to tell me I'm being naïve, unrealistic, that I've bitten off more than I can chew, and I'm setting myself up for failure."

She didn't say anything to that. Score a point for me.

"The diner on Sheridan. Can you meet me there in a couple of hours?"

"I'm not sure—"

"Come on, yes or no. You want to come talk to me,

or are you chicken?" I didn't think that would actually work, but it couldn't hurt.

"Fine. I'll be there." Still sounding like a pouting kid. Which meant I was still alpha, at least for now.

I donned the insufferable perkiness of a morning talk show host. "Great! Looking forward to it! I'll see you there!" I clicked off the phone before she could respond.

Ben was watching me from the other end of the sofa. "You got her, but will she listen to you?"

"That, I don't know. I hope so."

"Yeah," he said, unconvinced.

Because if we couldn't talk her out of the coup, we'd have to drive her out of Denver. At the very least.

BECKY WAS already at the diner when Ben and I got there. An attempt to gain the high ground. She occupied a booth and sat facing the door, so she'd see us as soon as we entered. And we'd see her.

Ben and I made our plan before arriving. I went to Becky's booth, and Ben waited by the door, arms crossed, staring at her. She couldn't leave without getting past him. She'd have to sit and talk until I said she could go.

I approached, and she stood. Again, to claim high ground, to avoid having to crane her neck back and look up at me from a weak position. All I had to do was stand and glare. To her credit, she matched my gaze, didn't look away. She really was strong enough to lead the pack, I believed that. I just couldn't let her do it while I was around. I wasn't going to let anyone drive me out of the city again.

"You're not going to change my mind," she said in a rush, another attempt to one-up me by getting in the first word.

I stayed calm. I had all afternoon for this. "Have a seat," I said, nodding at the booth. To press the point, I sat first. Conceding the ground because it didn't matter to me—I was stronger, and I didn't have to prove it.

She sank into the seat opposite me. Looking deeply uncomfortable on the hard plastic, she perched on the very edge, hands folded on the table in front of her, shoulders bunched to her neck, jaw hard and her eyes like ice. Good. This wasn't supposed to be comfortable. Though with both of us sitting like that, staring at each other like we were getting ready to arm wrestle in what was supposed to be a hip happy fun-time coffee joint, we were really out of place. Let people wonder.

"Why are we here?" Becky said, her voice low.

"I want to talk."

"No, I mean why are we *here*?" She gestured at the setting. "Why not New Moon? That's where you usually do your *talking*."

I had a moment of doubt. Becky had been a were-wolf longer than I had; she'd been part of this pack longer than I had. Where did I get off thinking I could boss her around? But I knew the answer to that: she didn't look at the big picture. She wasn't in charge—couldn't be in charge—because she didn't care. She didn't think ahead. Otherwise she would have known the answer to her question.

"Because that's my territory and I wanted to meet on neutral ground," I said. "No, scratch that. Forget about the pack. I want us to have a normal conversation. Two people having coffee. Change of context. Got it?" She didn't let her expression flicker, not a millimeter. I tried again. "I want to hash this out as people. Human beings. Without all the claws and blood."

"If you want to avoid that, you can just leave town. You and Ben both. Nobody has to get hurt."

Oh, she was trying so hard to be brave. Offering me the same deal I'd—me and T. J.—had tried to get from Carl, once upon a time. It hadn't worked then. Didn't Becky remember?

I said, "What do you want, Becky?"

"You know what I want," she said, dodging.

"You think you want to be alpha, right? With Darren? You don't even know him."

"Neither do you."

"I'm not the one sleeping with him."

Her gaze dropped, only for a second before zeroing in on me again. A flash of weakness that made her blush. Wolves didn't blush, that was the human side coming through. "He's right, Kitty. You shouldn't be alpha if you can't even be here to lead."

They were going to keep beating me up with that, just like Cheryl did. But only if I let them, ha. "That's a different issue entirely. One we can deal with separately. Right now I'm talking about *you*."

"I'm strong enough to be the alpha. Darren and me both."

"I never said you weren't." My smile felt absolutely rigid. Titanium hard. "I just want you to understand something. If we can't work this out here, we have to fight. You and me, Darren and Ben. Same shitty cycle over again. I'm not going to leave, and it sounds like you're not going to leave. If we can't decide not to fight, then we'll fight. But let me warn you: if I have to fight, I will win, because I'm fighting for me, Ben, my job, my family, my home. My whole philosophy and outlook on life. I'm fighting for everything I believe in—everything I've fought for up to this point. And what will you be fighting for? A guy you met a month ago? He's cute, he's got charm, and maybe he's a great lay—and what else? Who do you think's going to win that fight, Becky?"

When she looked away, turning her gaze to the tabletop, I knew I'd won. Without lifting a claw. I didn't say anything, didn't gloat. Just waited for her to answer my question, to tell me what she wanted to do next, so we could finish our coffee and move on.

Her head bowed, her hair fell across her cheeks, and her now-slouching shoulders began to tremble. She made a sharp noise, half-gasp, half-whine.

I leaned forward. "Wait—are you laughing or crying?"

When she looked up, her cheeks shone with the stripes of tears, but she was smiling. Both, then.

"I'm trying to imagine having a talk like this with Meg." The laughter won out, and she wiped her eyes. "I'm just not seeing it. She would never have done anything like this."

"That's kind of the point," I said. I traced the ring of moisture my cup left on the table. "I still have nightmares about her sometimes. Both of them. You know their old place is for sale?"

She went wide-eyed. "You're not thinking of—"

"God no," I said. "Never. Getting a place in the woods is one thing, but their place? No." I shook my head to emphasize the point, then drank a long sip of now-lukewarm coffee. Didn't matter, the stuff had only been a prop anyway.

Becky took a deep breath. "I'm sorry."

If I'd asked her for what, I'm not sure she would have said the thing I thought she should be sorry for. For her ambition? For the near-betrayal? For her infatuation with Darren? All of the above? It didn't matter, none of it did. Just as long as we could walk out of here on speaking terms and not on the verge of war. So I didn't ask. Just accepted and moved on.

"Don't let it happen again."

"There's something else," she said, and I raised an interested brow. "I don't think he came here for any job, like he told you. I don't think there's even a cousin."

"Really?" I said flatly, wheels in my mind turning.

"The apartment he got is really posh, and he never actually seems to go to work. At least, he's always right there when I call him. I think he might have come to Denver just to check out the pack."

"Well, then," I said. "I'm going to have to think about that."

"Yeah," she answered, sounding tired.

Ben took the opportunity to saunter over, slouching into the booth beside me in a mostly unassuming manner. He directed his gaze toward Becky instead of at her.

"We good here?" he said.

"Are you two going to pay a little more attention to the pack? If you don't want guys like Darren waltzing in here and playing games, you have to actually *be* here."

"Yeah. We'll talk."

We flagged the server for another round of coffee. And we talked.

Chapter 16

O N SUNDAY, my mother called, as she always did, to ask how things were going, was I doing okay, so on and so forth. As usual, I couldn't give details, like how I was in the middle of dealing with a coup attempt on my leadership of the Denver werewolves, helping to organize an international supernatural conspiracy, hanging onto my job, trying to stay sane—

So I deflected, and brought up the problem I *could* talk about. "I'm worried about Cheryl. I think I really pissed her off this time."

"Don't worry too much about that," she answered, sounding amused. "You two have been pissing each other off since you were little."

That was true. But it seemed like as kids we could forget about the grudges more quickly. Fight at lunch, friends again by supper. "Do you think I'm neglecting you all? Because I'm always running around trying to do too much?"

"Kitty, I know if we really need you you'd be here in a heartbeat. You were at Grandma Norville's funeral, weren't you? Of course I'd like to see you more often, we all would. But you have your own life to live."

"If you say so. But Cheryl—"

"She's going through a rough stretch right now, but she'll be fine, eventually. You might call her every now and then, take her out for lunch or dinner. Let her know you haven't forgotten about her."

"I can do that." It wouldn't even be difficult. And just like that, life got a little brighter. "Thanks, Mom."

PART OF the talking Becky and I did at the diner over third and fourth cups of coffee was make a plan. Darren had a plan. Becky was part of it, and she hadn't told him the plan was off. So that was how we'd face him. Follow his plan, right up until we didn't.

Their plan was for Becky to call me that evening and say that Darren was hurting her, and could we please come help. They'd be out by the full moon den, a remote space where we could have a proper showdown. Darren also picked the spot to be symbolic—this was the place the wolves called home, he wanted to prove he could control it. Becky would call, Ben and I would ride to the rescue. Trap sprung.

The hardest part of the new plan was going to be Becky convincing Darren she wasn't lying when she told him that the old plan was still on. He'd be able to smell the deception on her. On the other hand, he'd only known her a few weeks. He didn't know any of us, really, any more than we knew him. Maybe he'd think her strangeness was nerves.

She went home and showered to get the smell of the diner, and Ben and me, off her. Then, we went home and waited.

"We should call Cormac, let him know what's happening," Ben said, pacing across the living room.

"And have him ride to the rescue with his gun and silver bullets? No," I said. We could do this without him.

Wincing, Ben scratched his head, ruffling his hair even more than usual. "You're right. God, I hate this."

Finally, Becky's call came. "All right," she said. "Time for you to rescue me."

Darren must not have been within hearing range. She didn't sound scared, or even like she was faking being scared. Nervous, yes. But also determined. I expected nothing else from her.

"We'll be there soon," I answered. "Just hold on."

"Yeah," she said and hung up.

I looked at Ben, and he kissed me.

"What was that for?" I said.

He shrugged. "I felt like it."

"You want to maybe do it again?"

He did, arms closing around me, lips soft against mine. Well, I felt better.

"Ready?" he said, after his next breath.

"Ready."

THE SUN had set by the time we reached the mountains and turned onto the side road in the national forest where we spent most of our full moons. The air was gray, the trees lost in shadow. Not the best time of day to be fighting.

We had troops in reserve: Shaun, Tom, and Wes, the toughest males in the pack. They followed us in a second car. Darren hadn't talked to anybody else in the pack. He recruited Becky and expected the two of them to be persuasive enough to convince everyone else to drive us out. He was old-school, monarchical. All he had to do was prove he was stronger, and everyone else would fall in line.

Shaun parked, and Ben pulled our car up beside his, my passenger window next to his driver's window.

"He'll smell you as soon as you get close," I said. "So hang back. Ben'll call you. Keep your phone on and you'll be able to hear everything. Maybe this'll just blow over."

He grinned. "You just keep thinking that. The rest of us will be ready to pounce." He gestured to his companions, who glared with lupine glints in their eyes. Yeah, I was glad they were on my side. "We'll stay downwind," he added.

And so the general marshals her forces.

"Worried?" I asked Ben, as he guided the car along the last hundred yards of dirt lane to the meeting point.

"Naw, not really," he said, though the hint of sweat on his skin put the lie to that. "I probably ought to be. But I have the confidence of the righteous. It's like a trial—I can't walk into a courtroom expecting to lose or I've already lost."

He kept his handgun in the glove compartment, just in case.

Around the next curve in the road sat a car I didn't recognize. Darren's, I assumed. We parked behind it. Under my rib cage, Wolf kicked. The triggers were here—the place, the time, the smells. Ben at my side, moving carefully, keeping a strict control of himself. It was time to run. Everything said so. But no, not now. Maybe later. Next full moon for sure. That was how this worked.

We stepped out of the car. "Shall we?" Ben offered his elbow, an elegant gesture.

Smiling, I wrapped my arm around his and we continued on, as if heading to a fancy dinner or the symphony. Hmm, there was an idea, for after we got through this. Assuming we got through this . . .

Ben dialed Shaun's number on his phone, exchanged a short greeting, then put the phone in his pocket. "There. We're bugged."

Twenty more paces brought us into the clearing, a meadow bounded by pines on one side and lichen-covered boulders on the other. Nice, open ground, all of it shadowed in the twilight. Nowhere to hide. Darren and Becky stood in the middle, waiting.

"Hi," I said, super cheerful, arm raised in a wave. "We're here to rescue Becky. That's what's on the script, isn't it?"

"I wasn't sure you'd show up," Darren said.

"What, was there a schedule? Are we late?" I said, looking at Ben.

"Hmm, my watch must be slow," he drawled.

"You can't lead this pack," Darren said, hands in fists, teeth bared in anger. "You haven't been leading it for a long time. You should admit it. Step aside. It's best for everyone."

I clicked my tongue. "Wow, about that. We have different ideas of what's best. You put on a good show, but you strike me as being one of those alphas who thinks all they have to do is beat people up and that makes them strong. Did Becky tell you, we had a couple of those alphas in charge before I took over? Nobody liked it much."

"And you were stronger than them, to be able to take over. You're stronger than you look. I get it."

"No, not really. Meg was stronger than me in a straight-up fight. So I shot her. Silver bullet. Worked great."

Taking a reflexive step back, he was unable to suppress the flash of panic in his eyes. But I didn't draw, and neither did Ben. This wasn't the case of blind rage and desperation that that previous confrontation had been, so we'd left the gun in the car. Darren figured that out after a few deep, testing breaths, his nose flaring. But the damage was done; he'd shown that sliver of weakness.

"Becky?" Darren said. "Tell her."

Becky stood to his right, a step or two behind, waiting for a cue. His or ours. She was tense, hands clenched, arms at her sides, shoulders bunched. Schooling her expression to calmness.

"Becky?" he said again, when she didn't come forward.

She licked her lips. "I can't do it, Darren." Her voice was steady. Mine probably would have cracked.

"Yes, you can."

"Then I *won't* do it."

"We talked about this. I thought you agreed with me—"

"I said I wanted to be alpha of the pack. I wasn't thinking about . . . what the consequences would be.

But Kitty's right. Things have been so much better since she got rid of Carl and Meg. She's earned a little loyalty."

"It's too late for that," Darren said. "There needs to be a change. We all know what's coming, the vampires, werewolves, all of us. Someone *strong* needs to lead that fight. Someone physically able to fight, who doesn't have any doubts at all."

"Yeah," I murmured. "History is full of people who didn't have any doubts."

He stalked forward. His voice growled, "I'll take you down, I can fight you both."

I was very careful to stand rooted. I couldn't afford to be scared; the stakes were too high. I said, "By any chance do you know what happened to Carl? The other half of the old alpha pair?"

He pulled up. "I'm guessing you shot him, too."

"No," I said. "The rest of the pack tore him to pieces."

They came when I called, as I'd had no doubt they would, stalking through the trees and into the clearing. Shaun went shirtless, displaying lean strength in his arms and chest, his gaze locked on Darren. Tom and Wes had shifted and trotted on either side of him, each of them two-hundred-plus pounds of wolf, lips curled back, ears pinned.

I smiled, showing teeth. "So?"

Darren laughed. "So what? You know what that

tells me? You're not strong without them. You can't be alpha without your pack backing you up."

"That's the whole point."

Shaun and the others kept moving, fanning out around the clearing, keeping Darren in the middle.

Darren wasn't backing down. The challenge had faltered, but he was still focused, radiating aggression. No wonder—we'd cornered him. He'd fight us all if he had to. Even if he had to know he couldn't stop us all.

"Hold up there, guys," I called. Shaun and the wolves stopped pacing, though my four-legged henchpeople padded in place, heads low, circling, anxious. "Darren, you're not a bad guy. I really do think we're all on the same side, and we need all the people we can get to face off against Roman and his army. I don't want to hurt you—"

"You can't hurt me."

I waved him off. "—but I want to know something. Did Nasser send you here to take the pack from me? Because he doesn't think I can handle it?"

When he didn't answer, I knew.

Ben huffed. "How do you like that? Guy comes here looking for allies and thinks he can do better?"

I said, "Yeah, I'm kind of used to people not taking me seriously. You want to go back and tell Nasser that we're doing just fine?"

I'd hoped to give him an out. He could just walk

away. Or he could talk back, engage in an actual conversation, tell me more about Nasser, find a way to work with me and mine. Convince me we really were all on the same side. He was a cornered wolf, but a smart one. But I misjudged.

He turned and lunged at Becky.

She scrambled back, but his arms were around her, one hand at her throat. Shaun let out a snarl and charged, along with the wolves, who reached them in a handful of long strides. Ben and I also lunged without thinking, ready to pounce on him to tear him apart before our claws had time to sprout.

But Darren shouted, "I'll rip her head off!" He held her head in a lock and swung her around as a shield, while she hung on to his arm. His hands were thickening, the nails of his fingers sharpening into claws that pressed at the skin of her neck.

We all stopped.

A werewolf could survive a lot of damage. He could slash her throat, and she'd live, if she could get enough air to keep breathing. If she didn't lose all her blood. We healed fast. We just had to live long enough for the healing to catch up with the injuries. Silver poisoning, take the head or heart—those were the ways to kill a werewolf. He knew what he was doing, of course he did.

Good thing Becky wasn't going to wait around for him to do the deed. Instead, she started shifting.

Her back arched, bucking against his hold, her muscles contracting and straining as they bent into another shape, rough and wolfish. Her face stretched; her teeth sharpened, and her clawed hands slashed bloody ribbons down his arm. He roared at her, but couldn't hold her thrashing form. She slipped straight down out of his grip.

Shaun and the others pounced. The human-shaped Shaun grabbed Darren's arm and twisted it back, the wolves locked their jaws on throat and thigh. Darren screamed; the noise roughened into a snarl. His teeth became fangs, and his body stretched and morphed. The fight became a tangle of fur and blood.

Ben and I ran to Becky, who was full wolf now and caught up in her clothing, denim jeans ripping, shirt in rags. She twisted back on herself like a fish flopping on land.

"Shh, hold on a sec," I hissed at her, tearing fabric away as best I could. I thought she might snap at me, but she only bared her teeth and pinned her ears.

The noise of the fight rattled through the clearing. Ben stood guard between us and them. When Becky tore free of her clothes, she lunged back toward the others. The tang of blood was thick in my nose, and my own Wolf reached through me, wanting to join in.

Darren was holding his own. I couldn't believe it. His hands slashed in different directions, while his fanged jaws took a swipe at Shaun. He kicked Wes away, then swooped around to punch Tom. When they shook themselves off and piled back on him, he did the same, moving fast, never seeming to tire. He held himself to his form, part wolf, part human, standing upright, but roughened with the sheen of fur, his eyes gleaming amber. I'd never seen anything like it. He really was stronger; but then, I'd never thought he wasn't.

Again, he swatted and turned, throwing them all off him and away. Shaun bounced and rolled. Someone yipped in pain. Darren paused, looked over my shoulder, and those wolfish eyes widened. His back arched, and he let out a half-cry, half-howl of frustration. His control slipped, and his body lost its humanoid shape. Finally wolf, he dropped to all fours and fled, shaking off clothing as he went. The gray-brown beast ran with strides so long he seemed to fly across the grass and into the trees.

My two wolves shot after him. Shaun trotted a few paces then stopped, muscles knotted along his back, hands in fists, holding back, staying human. Becky circled back to me and Ben. She had blood on her mouth, and more streaking from a cut on her neck.

I hollered after Wes and Tom, my cry almost a howl. The wolves hesitated, slowed, loped back around. They listened to me. And Darren said I couldn't lead.

"Let him go," I said as they returned. "We can wait." I sat next to Becky, leaning into her, and she licked my chin. I hugged her.

Even if he hadn't been winning the fight, he hadn't been losing, and if four of my wolves couldn't drive him off . . . I looked over my shoulder.

Rick stood at the edge of the clearing, in a white T-shirt and jeans, his hair mussed, his body in a stance that made him look like he'd been running. Since he wasn't breathing heavily—or at all—I couldn't tell if he had been.

I could smell him, now that I was paying attention. Skin chilled and unnatural.

"Are you all right?" he said finally.

"I think so," Ben said. Me, I was speechless. Becky trembled against my arms, suspicion charging her anxiety. The other two wolves stared at Rick, their gray and tawny coats bristling. Shaun's gaze had a lupine cast to it. "So, what brings you out here, if you don't mind my asking?"

"I went to New Moon at dusk to find you. One of your wolves, Trey, was there and when I asked after you, he told me where you'd gone. Said you'd been challenged, that you were in trouble. I came as fast as I could." He ducked his gaze and looked almost sheepish, just for a moment. "I wondered if my not being available had contributed to the issue. I suppose

Denver's looked like a city without a Master for the last couple of weeks."

"Yeah," I said. "It kind of has."

"But I see you have everything well in hand, here," he said.

I laughed, though the sound was strained. "Rick, it's so good to see you."

Tension broken, the three wolves gathered close, rubbing their bodies against me, heads and tails drooping, gazes downcast. I brushed my hands through their coats, rubbed my face against theirs, took in their scent and gave them mine. Ben reached to me, and I took his hand and pulled him down to sit with me. My pack, half-human, half-wolf, piled together, calming each others' nerves. We'd won.

"Thank you," I said, sighing a breath. "Thank you all so much."

Shaun slumped tiredly to the ground. Tom sidled up to him, bumped his shoulder, and reached up to lick his face. My lieutenant had a claw slash running down one cheek. Smiling, he rested his face against Tom's ruff.

"You okay?" I asked.

"Yeah. Becky?"

She pricked her ears at him, licked her lips. She had cuts and wounds as well, but nothing serious. We were all a little battered, but not broken. Thank God.

Rick stood aside, looking off into the trees—avoiding intruding on what must have seemed like a private domestic lovefest. I gave the wolves one more face rub each, squeezed Shaun's shoulder, kissed Ben, and extricated myself from the pile. The air seemed cold after being surrounded by so much fur and affection.

"Did he really think you'd just roll over for him?" Rick said to me as I joined him, brushing off my jeans.

"I don't know," I said. "I think he made some assumptions. And he didn't really think I'd be able to talk my way out of things." Becky made a soft whine and tucked in her tail, and I smiled at her. She'd almost been convinced; she and Darren could have taken us by force, if it had come to that.

"Then he doesn't know you very well."

"No, not at all," I said.

"You really think he's one of Nasser's?" Rick asked.

"I don't know that he *belongs* to him, servant or employee or whatever the hell that means," I said. "But they're working together. Probably a lot like we are."

"I suppose it's too much to hope that he just keeps running and we never see him again," Ben said.

I didn't know what Darren would do. He was here

on a mission from Nasser—the mission had failed. Would he try again? Try to take us out and convince the pack to follow him after the fact? Or would he acknowledge that if we were strong enough to face him, we could stand against Roman? With or without Rick's help? God, this was making me tired.

"We probably ought to track him," I said. "Figure out where he's going and make sure he doesn't cause any more trouble."

"I'm on it," Shaun said, pulling away from the group hug.

"Take Tom and Wes with you. You have your phone?" I asked. The wolves perked their ears at me.

"Yeah, I'll call when I find out anything." Waving, he stalked off into the woods. The two male wolves trotted along with him. Strength in numbers.

Otherwise, it was quite a nice night. The daytime heat wasn't able to drive away a chill in the air once darkness fell. Pine trees creaked under their own weight, and a nocturnal critter shuffed through detritus on the forest floor. A first-quarter moon shone in the west.

"I suppose we ought to think about heading back," Ben said.

Becky had curled up, half-sprawling on Ben's lap after circling in place a couple of times. Looking for the right spot, the right position before committing, a familiar ritual.

"We should wait until she's awake and human," I said, nodding at her. "I think the stress of the last couple of days did her in." I returned to them, settling on the ground beside her. Ben leaned up against me.

"Mind if I join you?" Rick said, indicating the ground a pace or two away.

Wolf wasn't sure she liked him out here in our territory, where he hadn't been invited. We had our meeting places, and we kept our dens separate. But I nodded. He settled himself gracefully onto the ground, crossing his legs, looking as at home and in control here as he did everywhere. As comfortable here as he was in the basement of Obsidian.

He said, "It looks like I need to write a sternly worded letter to Nasser. Something about how 'allied' does not mean 'invited to interfere.'"

"If you think it would help," I said. "Hey, does this mean you're back? Still Master of Denver and not haring off on some crusade?"

He gazed at the sky, or the treetops, or at some far-off thought. No lines of anxiety creased his features—but when was he ever anything but calm? I couldn't know what he was thinking.

He shook his head, and my heart sank.

"I wish I could make you understand how much Columban has helped me," he said. "To be alone, doubting myself for hundreds of years—"

"You were never alone," but as soon as I said it I

knew I had no idea what I was talking about. Other vampires I'd met had known Rick, I'd picked up bits and pieces of his history and they usually involved other people. But that wasn't the same as not being alone. I didn't know anything about him.

His answering smile was wry. "And when could I ever say that I still believed in God, after everything that's happened? A Catholic vampire—you had that response yourself. Now, to find that there are others, that I'm not alone—if only I have the courage to reach out to them. Maybe it's time I go on a pilgrimage."

It was all I could do not to panic. "Am I being selfish, wanting you to stay?"

"I'm grateful for your . . . faith in me. But you know I never wanted to be Master of Denver."

"That's why you're such a good one."

"You're speaking in clichés, now."

I slumped. Becky slept peacefully. Absently, I smoothed the fur along her flank; her ribs moved with steady breathing.

"Angelo can be Master of Denver," Rick said.

"He doesn't want it, either. Did you know that?"

He stood, brushing off his jeans. "I should be getting back. I'd only meant to talk to you about how your meeting went, and I didn't tell Father Columban I was going."

My nose wrinkled. "Do you need his permission?"

"I'm . . . not really sure. But this was important, so I came."

I felt a lecture coming on. "Rick—" Ben squeezed my arm. A reminder that some tact might be in order. "I understand that Columban showed you something, or offered you something that you've been looking for, that you need. If it'll make you happy—I can't ask you to walk away from that."

He said, "If I had never left Spain, if I had been made a vampire in Europe, where Saint Lazarus of the Shadows has been established for centuries, I might have joined them from the start. My life would have been very different. Not better or worse, just different. As it was, in Mexico, cut off from the European vampires . . . how was I to know?"

"You don't need a religious order to be a crusader—"

"My religion is what's guided me all this time. It's the thing that made me believe I could do good, *be* good, no matter what demons might take hold of me."

"But do you need someone with rank and title telling you that?"

"Kitty, when I leave Denver, I'll tell you. I promise." He turned and walked away.

I watched him for a long time, until Ben squeezed my shoulder and brought me back to myself.

"He won't do it," Ben said. "Not really. We both know how much he likes Denver."

When I spoke, my voice cracked with stifled tears. "He didn't say *if.* He said *when.*"

Chapter 17

EN AND I sat with Becky until after midnight while she shifted back. Her fur thinned, vanished; her limbs stretched, and contracted. The metamorphosis was painful to watch, in that it called up a throbbing in my own limbs, a memory of my own episodes of waking up, aching, piecing together how I had arrived at this new place. I thought sometimes that this was why we slept through our shifting back to human—feeling our bodies break and reform once during the Change was plenty. We couldn't take any more than that.

She slept for another hour, appearing vulnerable, which I knew she wasn't. But we watched over her, Becky's head on my lap, my head on Ben's, as I napped for a few minutes. Becky started awake in a heartbeat, pushing herself up, alert in an instant. The move sent all our hearts racing in communal panic.

"Shh, it's okay," I murmured, hands on her shoulders, hoping to transmit calm. "He's gone, everything's fine."

Groaning, she covered her face with her hands. "I feel like crap."

"You got a little beat up," I said. Her wounds had healed; the cuts appeared as raised pink scars that would vanish by dawn.

"I suppose that went well, considering."

"I kind of hoped he'd just walk away," I said.

"No. He thought he was right. Where'd he go?"

"He ran. Shaun and the others are tracking him."

She nodded and pursed her lips.

Ben looked across the clearing. "You two ready to get out of here?"

We were.

WE'D GOTTEN Becky—wrapped in Ben's ubiquitous coat, since her clothes were a shredded mess— safely back to her apartment and had just arrived back at the condo when I got a call from Shaun. The sky was growing pale, the murky gray of predawn, when I couldn't tell if the day was going to be overcast, sunny, bright, or dim. My mind felt equally muzzy, as if I couldn't see my next step clearly. What day was it again?

We waited in the car for Shaun to explain. "We tracked down Darren. He's asleep. His wolf bedded down in a park in Golden." Then he wasn't planning on leaving town. If he had been, he'd have just kept running, or stayed in the hills and circled back to his car. "Can you show me where he is?"

"Yeah. You sure that's such a great idea?"

"He's sticking around because he wants to talk."

"Or he's sticking around because he wants another shot at you."

Also a possibility, I had to admit. "We'll find out, I suppose."

"All right, then." He gave me a spot to meet him at and hung up.

I looked at Ben.

"I think it's a bad idea," he said.

"He's still a strange wolf in our territory. If we let him alone he'll think he's getting away with something."

Ben couldn't argue with that. He started up the car, and we headed back out.

By the time we reached the park and found Shaun, the sun tipped over the horizon. The day was going to be clear and warm. Following Darren's wolf, Shaun had come all this way on foot, and he was exhausted.

Werewolves were stronger, could run faster and farther, even in human form. But he'd really gone above and beyond. He'd sent Wes and Tom back to the den to sleep off their wolves and bring the car back.

"Get in the backseat," I told him, nodding at the car. "Get some sleep."

"You going to be okay?"

As if he'd be any good in a fight after the night he'd had. "I don't think he'll try anything. Not after last night."

He didn't need any further convincing. I owed him a steak dinner after all this.

This close, I could track Darren's scent myself. He'd found a stand of trees in a gully, safe and hidden. As an afterthought, I grabbed a blanket from the trunk of the car.

"You want to hang back some?" I asked Ben.

"What, insult him by showing him you don't think he's a threat?"

"Proving a point," I said, lip curling.

Ben slowed his pace, letting me move ahead alone.

I found Darren sprawled under a low-hanging pine branch. Naked, he lay with his arms and legs bent, clenched, fingers digging into the ground like claws, as if he had collapsed where he stood instead of settling. Even in sleep, his brow was creased, worried. I could almost be sympathetic. Sitting upwind, a dozen feet away, I waited for him to catch my scent.

Didn't take long. His eyes opened, focused on me. Then he froze, waiting. Probably wondering which way to jump. I'd cornered him, and that felt pretty good.

When I didn't move, he took a moment to glance around, his nose working to catch smells, to see who else was stalking him. He had to smell Ben, but I was the only one in sight, and his gaze turned back to me.

I smiled nicely. "Good morning." He didn't answer, but I didn't expect him to. "I'm just here to point out that I could have killed you, and I didn't."

"Don't do me any favors," he said. His voice scratched, a symptom of a night of growling and running.

"I'm all about favors," I said. "It's how I get things done. So, I didn't kill you. Now what I'd like you to do for me is to leave Denver. You can go back and get your car, and I'll give you a couple of days to get your things together."

He pushed himself up to sitting, broad shoulders flexing. Guy was pretty ripped. But I focused on his eyes. He was glaring back, not showing an inch of submission.

"I came here to *help*," he said.

"Maybe you should have asked first," I said. My own fatigue was catching up with me. I wanted to walk away, get naked myself and curl up with my mate. Sleep for a week. "Look, Darren, I'm not going to turn down help because you're right, we need all the help we can get against Roman. But not like this. We need allies. Go back to Nasser and be an ally." I handed him the blanket.

After a moment, he lowered his gaze and took the peace offering. I kept my face a blank, but inside I sighed with relief.

Wrapping the blanket around him, he said, "I wasn't really going to hurt Becky."

My smile turned wry. "No, not physically. But you were going to use her for your own ends. That's so not cool."

His own lip turned up in acknowledgment. "How about I go back to Nasser and tell him that you're stronger than you look?"

"Remind him that Marid called me Regina Luporum."

He bowed his head at that.

I continued. "You need a ride anywhere? Change of clothes?"

"No. I'll get out of your hair just as soon as I can."

"Appreciate it," I said.

Hauling himself to his feet, he gave me one last flash of his beefy body—on purpose I was sure—then tipped a salute at me, another one off to the edge of the park where Ben was waiting, and walked away. He looked odd, a well-built guy walking across the scrubby grass with a blanket over his shoulders and clasped around his middle. If any cops spotted him, he'd get picked up for sure. On the other hand, he'd probably avoid getting spotted by anyone.

I walked back to the car, and Ben met me halfway.

"*Now* can we go home and get some sleep?" he asked.

"After we drop off Shaun."

"I don't think anyone can accuse you of being an inattentive alpha after all this."

That wasn't really the main point of all this, but I'd take it.

Back at the condo, I was too hyped up to sleep, but Ben coaxed me into bed. Not that he had to coax too much, offering his warm body to cuddle with. His safe, familiar scent in my nose, his warm naked skin against mine, made the world a better place. A few minutes of contact was worth an hour of sleep. For a short time, I didn't think about Darren, worry about Rick or my sister, or Roman, or anything. I even slept, for a little while. That was enough, at least for now.

I had to wait until nightfall anyway, before I could talk to Rick, at least one more time.

Chapter 18

BEN DIDN'T trust Darren to just leave, and I agreed. The guy had acted defeated enough this morning, but he might have some other plan cooked up. Ben offered to drive past the apartment where Darren had been living to check. Even if it meant leaving me alone.

I grinned. "Aw, does that mean you're not worried about me spontaneously shape-shifting anymore?"

"I'll always worry. But after last night, I think you'll be fine."

That left me to go talk with Rick. It was Ben who suggested Rick might be more forthcoming if I showed up by myself. I hadn't considered that. The theory was sound, might as well give it a try.

I arrived at St. Cajetan before dusk, early enough that the main doors were still open, and I got inside.

What used to be the church's main hall had been

converted into an auditorium, but signs of what the space used to be were evident. A wide, domed ceiling in back would have arced over an altar. Simple stained glass filled the windows along the walls on either side. Any religious symbols had been removed. No crosses, no statuary. Folding chairs and tables had been set up as if for a meeting, and two people, one of them with a clipboard, were discussing a schedule. They glanced at me, and I gave a quick smile and left to explore the rest of the building. Stairs led up to a choir loft, which seemed to be used as a storage area for folding tables and cardboard boxes.

The halls and stairways I moved through smelled simple, bureaucratic. Carpets, fresh paint, lots of bodies moving back and forth. The smell of vampire pervaded, but faintly. They could have been anywhere. Stairs led down. The basement held offices for the geology and paleontology departments. A room had been converted to a museum with hundreds of dinosaur-track fossils and casts of fossils. The vampires weren't here, either. Their hiding place, where they spent their days asleep, was very well hidden. So, I had to wait.

Time passed, the light outside the windows faded. People left the building, locked up after themselves. Nobody checked for strays, so I was able to stay. If I couldn't convince Rick to stay in Denver, maybe I could convince Father Columban that he was needed here. Then maybe Columban would convince him to stay, since he was the one Rick seemed to be listening to now.

I made another circuit of the building, upstairs and through offices, calling as I went. "Rick? Father Columban? We need to talk."

Even if they were here, if they didn't want to talk to me, they didn't have to. At least I tried.

I returned to the auditorium one more time before heading out, and there they were. Two figures straight out of a gothic novel, the brooding hero in his fitted T-shirt and jeans, the priest in his dark cassock, side by side, standing under the arched roof, watching me. I approached, feeling a bit like I was on trial.

"Hi," I said, my echoing voice making me even more uncomfortable. "I just want to talk. Rick, I don't know if there's anything I can say to convince you how much you're needed here, that would convince you to stay—"

"If something happened to me, you'd all carry on without me, one way or another," he said.

"Yeah, I suppose you could say that about pretty much anyone. I'm talking ideals here. Father Columban—can't Rick join your order and still stay here?"

"He has a mission," Columban said. "You would not understand."

Not helpful. I ignored him, returning my attention

to Rick. "I know I'm being selfish, wanting you to stay. If you really want to be a priest and go have a crusade, I know I should be happy for you. But you need to know how much you'll be missed." If he still insisted that he had to do a wild pilgrimage, I wasn't above crying and begging.

Columban began to lecture. "This is just one city. For a thousand years, through the Crusades, the Inquisition, through centuries of warfare that engulfed the whole of Europe, when the enemies of light would lay waste to civilization, the Order of Saint Lazarus of the Shadows has stood against the darkness because we *understand* it. Because who else could oppose it as we have? Rick understands. He was born for this, and he came into this life for this."

Destiny? Was that what this came down to? "Don't you think Rick should decide that?"

"He'll choose the path of righteousness."

"Yeah, and who gets to define righteousness?"

Not the thing to say to a Catholic priest, vampire or otherwise. He actually pointed at me as he drew breath to launch into another spiel.

Rick had been standing to one side. Now, he stepped between us. "Father, Kitty, please. I know all the arguments already. I must make this decision on my own." My stomach dropped, and I held my breath. Then he turned to Father Columban. "Father, I'm sorry. I'm going to stay."

I was sure I had heard him wrong, but no.

The priest stared at him, expression slack. "What are you saying?"

"You've gotten along well without me all this time," Rick said. "You and the order will still be here for centuries. But I've only been Master of this city for a few years, and I'm not ready to give it up just yet."

He was staying. I almost jumped up and down, cheering.

The priest looked at Rick, apparently unable to speak. Rick went on, "I'm grateful to you. I've been alone with my faith for so long, and now I feel like I have a family again. Not just my own Family. But I'm not a priest. I'm not a crusader. I never have been. I can hold to my faith without joining your order. I hope you'll understand."

"I do *not* understand. You turn your back on God—"

"No, of course not. But I think my calling is here."

Columban folded his hands so they were hidden in his sleeves and regarded his wayward student. "I suppose I should be grateful that you feel you *have* a calling."

"I always have. And now I can even believe I'm not crazy."

"You will change your mind someday, when you see what it truly is that we face."

"Something I've learned about our condition,

Father—we usually have time to change course if we've made a mistake. So maybe you're right. I hope you'll let me keep in touch with you."

Columban nodded in acknowledgment. "Ricardo, will you pray with me? One more time?"

Rick said to me, "Kitty, I'll join you outside in a moment."

"Okay. I'll be there."

I went outside, carefully closing the door behind me so it wouldn't make any noise.

According to some people, vampires were supposed to be servants of Satan, minions of hell. That was what some of the stories—urban legends, really—said, and it was a belief that many people clung to. Some people said the same thing about werewolves, and I had a ready answer for them: if I was a minion of Satan don't you think I'd know about it? Prayers were supposed to be poison to vampires, and maybe they were, to some of them. But obviously not to Father Columban. Or Rick, who'd probably been praying by himself for five hundred years. To me, it was proof that vampires and hell had nothing to do with each other. But the stories about hell—what a great way to mark a group of people that you wanted to keep at a distance.

I supposed a lot of vampires found it easier to match the expectations of those stories. Werewolves, too—and yeah, some days I wanted nothing more than to run to the wilderness and be an agent of chaos. But civilization was worth fighting for. Worth a prayer or two, if you believed in prayer.

I sat on a step about halfway down the staircase and waited for Rick.

Fifteen minutes later, Cormac, arm in a sling, came walking around from the west side of the church.

He was sprinkling something on the ground, from a pouch nestled in his sling. Creating a circle, for some nefarious purpose. He even looked sinister, in his leather jacket, wearing sunglasses at night, no matter that they must have wreaked havoc on his vision.

"Hey," I called, holding back offended annoyance.

He stopped and looked. "What are you doing here?"

"I could ask you that."

"If I told you it'd be a good idea for you to get out of here, I don't suppose you'd leave," he said.

Oh, now I was *very* curious. "Not a chance. You're not trying again, are you?"

"Yeah." He continued on, sprinkling as he went. Smelled like sage, with something else, an herb I couldn't identify.

I trotted down the steps. "What makes you think it'll work this time?" Stepping along with him, I followed him around the building, to the east, where he'd started his circle.

He paused before joining the two ends of the circle together. "You want to do me a favor and step outside?" He pointed to the obvious doorway he'd left.

"What if I say no?"

"Kitty. Please."

I wasn't sure I'd ever heard him say the word *please* before. At least, he didn't use it often. He sounded urgent, out of patience. Cormac was the most patient guy I knew—he could go hunting, waiting in a blind for days for his prey to come along. Now, whatever he was doing, he didn't have time to argue. I stepped out of the circle; he closed it behind me, brushing crumbs off his good hand on his jeans.

"Cormac, what are you doing?" I said, hoping to match his seriousness.

"I'm still working for Detective Hardin, and she's still got a warrant for that vampire. I just want to see what's so badass it needs a spell like this to protect against. I think I've got it this time. We'll scare the guy out."

"You *think*? And what are you going to do once you get a reaction out of him?"

"She says she can arrest the priest, I'm not going to argue with her."

Hardin had gone up against vampires before, and she claimed arresting one as her lifelong ambition. Columban wouldn't wait quietly for her to put handcuffs on him, no matter what anti-vampire weapons she threatened him with, no matter if Cormac managed to break his spell.

Cormac was prepared. He had a whole bundle of stakes hanging in a makeshift quiver off his belt, along with a spray bottle, probably filled with holy water, dangling alongside it. A large gold cross hung on a chain around his neck. All of it, including the sunglasses, protection against vampires.

This was going to get messy.

"I don't suppose I could talk you out of it?"

He shook his head, expressing exactly what he thought of that idea. "Tell you what, you stay out of my way, I'll stay out of yours."

Hardin found us glaring at each other, beside the shrubbery between the church and the rectory.

"What are you doing here?" she said to me.

"The evening's most popular question," I said. "Just taking a walk, officer."

She huffed in disbelief.

Cormac shoved the pouch of herbs back in his jacket pocket and drew a piece of chalk out. "I need you two to not interrupt me during this. You think you can do that?"

"Sure," Hardin said, and I didn't say anything.

He knelt and started drawing on the sidewalk, the usual indecipherable arcane marks that went along with this sort of thing.

Pointing at the scribble, I said, "You going to let him get away with vandalism like that?"

She aimed a long-suffering glare at me. "Kitty . . ."

I crossed my arms. "I don't think you can arrest a vampire." Kill, maybe . . .

"I'm sure going to try. I've got two patrol cars for backup on the driveway." She rested a hand on the radio hooked to her belt. Next to it was a handheld crossbow, loaded.

By this time I thought I'd be numb to the sense of foreboding welling up in my gut. I felt it so often. "Just . . . Rick's my friend. You'll leave him out of it?"

"I tried calling him, but if he won't talk to anyone there's not a lot I can do."

I wondered what would happen if I crossed the circle to beat on the front door, to warn them? I had no idea if it would simply ruin the spell, or do something more nefarious, like zap me with lightning or fire. That was why, in the end, I didn't do it. The vampires must have known already that something was happening.

Cormac progressed clockwise around the circle, drawing symbols. The letters weren't really glowing, I told myself. The yellow chalk just showed up oddly under the streetlights.

He completed the circuit around the building, then started on a third, dripping wax from a red candle.

The process no doubt made sense to him; to me, it seemed random, confusing.

"Tell me—why'd you hire him? You used to want to arrest him," I said to Hardin.

"What can I say? Guy seems to know what he's doing."

"What do Denver PD regulations say about hiring magical consultants?"

"I followed the same regs I would for hiring any other consultant. Captain signed off on it and everything." Her grin was smug. "I'm following your advice."

My advice, that supernatural law enforcement ought to follow the same rules and procedures as any other law enforcement. If people like me—lycanthropes, vampires—wanted to be out in the open and treated like everyone else, then we had to be part of the same system. I'd run headlong into some barriers regarding that belief. Problems that the existing system just couldn't handle. Problems like Roman, for example. Nonetheless, I admired Hardin's effort in spite of myself.

Cormac completed the third circuit of the building, where the protective boundary had been laid. I had to press my lips tightly together to keep from asking him what came next.

Chanting, it turned out. Might have been Latin. He spoke too quickly and softly for me to hear, almost breathing the words rather than speaking them. This was Amelia. She was working this piece of the spell; maybe she'd been in control for a while. If I called Cormac's name right now, he wouldn't turn around; but if I called hers, she would. They traced the circle again, his good hand stretched over it as if they could wipe it away.

Doors slammed open—the sound came from the front of the church. Cormac had moved around to the back, he wouldn't have heard it. I ran to the front in time to see Father Columban pounding down the front stops. "Stop! Stop this!" he cried out. "You have no idea what you're doing!"

"Ha, it's working," Hardin said, coming up behind me. To the stairs she called, "Columban, I have a warrant for your arrest for arson and murder."

"You probably shouldn't have given him any warning," I murmured.

Columban made an impatient brush with his hand, dismissing her. On her radio now, Hardin muttered instructions to her officers while unhooking the wooden-bolt-loaded crossbow from her belt. When Columban reached the base of the stairs and strode past her, she raised the weapon to aim at him.

"I need you to stop and come with me," she declared.

Ignoring her, the vampire reached toward Cormac, who'd almost returned to his starting point at the north side of the church. He hadn't yet crossed the spell's circle. "No! You must stop!"

But Cormac finished chanting and lowered his arm to his sides.

"Kitty, what's happening?" Rick said, trotting down the stairs toward me.

I just stared, because this wasn't playing out at all like I thought it would. With the spell cast, I expected fire, screaming, the smell of brimstone. At least a flash of light, a scent in the air to tell me something had changed. But I didn't sense anything. We all waited. The smallest noise would have made us jump.

"Do you have any idea what you've done?" Columban said, stark despair pulling at his features. Stepping back, Cormac grabbed the spray bottle from its hook on his belt, set it in the crook formed by his sling, and reached for a stake, which he held toward the vampire. But Columban didn't move.

"I will not harm you," the priest said. "I will not have to."

He turned away, his cassock billowing out, and marched back to the stairs.

"You are in danger," he said, pointing at me as he passed by. My shoulders stiffened, and Wolf bristled. He turned to Rick next. "As are you. Both of you, come with me."

"What?" I said, more than a little startled. "No."

Rick had joined him, walking back toward the steps. "Kitty, don't argue."

"Tell me what's going on—why are the three of us in danger but not them?" The three of us, the vampires and the werewolf, not the uninfected human beings. Cormac was haunted, not infected. My skin prickled all over—Columban was terrified of something that could hurt the near-immortal, invincible creatures. What on earth—

Columban stopped at the base of the stairs, glancing up and around. "It's too late."

The fire and brimstone happened right now, it turned out.

A black wind flew up from the ground, a collection of dust and debris coalescing into a funnel cloud, roaring with fury. A couple of uniformed cops ran up from the road, but fell back as the wind buffeted them. I ducked away from it, raising my arm to shelter my face as dirt pelted me. The others were doing likewise. Except for Columban, who held his hand over his eyes for protection and glared at the tornado, his sharp canines bared.

The swirling wind made a jet-engine roar. The storm cloud grew until it was as tall as the building, writhing with smoke and oil, growing with mass that came from the air itself, because nothing was actually flowing *into* the vortex. The smell of it was . . .

fire and grease, sewer and sadness. Like how I imagined oil-drenched wildlife must smell when I saw the pictures from an offshore spill. The wind was polluted, and it was alive.

It didn't have eyes, but I felt it looking at me.

"Fuck, what is that thing?" Hardin yelled.

Wasn't it obvious? It was the thing Father Columban had cast his protective circle to defend against.

Chapter 19

THE OILY vortex had expanded to include most of the church and sidewalk around it. The boundary markers of Cormac's spell had vanished and no longer had meaning.

Cormac had gotten himself out of the way by running toward us. He dug in his pockets, but the yarn and sprigs of herbs he pulled out flew from his hand, caught in the gusts. He tried holding his broken arm up, using the sling as a shield, but the wind pinned him down to the sidewalk. Hide or cast a spell, but not both.

Leaning all my weight against the wind in order to move, I went to Hardin. Every step was an effort. The detective held her gun in one hand and minicrossbow in the other; her head was bent away from flying debris, and her ponytail lay smashed against her cheek.

"We have to help him!" I shouted at her ear and pointed at Cormac, who was bent to the ground in the shelter of a lamppost.

Huddling together, we lurched toward him. At least, we tried. She made it. On the other hand, I fell back, crashing to the sidewalk and rolling away from the others. I didn't lose my balance, I didn't trip or stumble. In fact, I would have sworn that someone grabbed my shoulders and yanked me to the ground. I could feel the start of bruises where the fingers had dug in.

Then Rick was kneeling beside me, helping me up. I clung to him. A sharp smacking noise came from the next gust that struck us, and Rick's head whipped to the side—punched, hard. He didn't hesitate, but sprang up, cocking back to strike whatever had chosen to do battle with us. He was a blur, moving so quickly I couldn't see him, his vampiric speed and strength at the fore.

But the tendril of wind that had struck us was gone.

My heaving breaths came out as growls. I braced on all fours, Wolf ready, but no enemy presented itself, I had nothing to attack.

Hardin abandoned the crossbow and pointed her gun at us, bracing it before her with both hands. Not at us, rather, but at whatever had attacked us. She couldn't see it, either, and swung her aim away from us. Her jaw was set.

A voice rang out, even over the blasts of wind.

Father Columban, speaking from the church steps, a booming chant cast against the storm, definitely in Latin. He was praying, arms raised before him. His gaze focused on something close to us, though I couldn't make out any details amid the swarming dust and smoke. There might have been a million insects attacking us and I wouldn't have been able to tell. Rick, arm bent before his face, watched Columban and inched toward the staircase. He was murmuring—I couldn't hear very well, but he seemed to be matching Columban's words, adding to the prayer.

Whatever they were saying didn't seem to be helping.

Hands closed around my neck.

Again, I could feel the action, make out the pressure of fingers on my throat, note the strength of the arms that hauled me backward. I thrashed, fighting against it, ignoring the fact that it had cut off my air. Didn't need air, just had to get free. Claws wouldn't do me any good—I had nothing to slash. When I reached back, my hands passed through nothing.

But I heard a voice near my ear, soft, a murmur under the wind. "My bounty is for the priest, but you'll do." Indistinct, impossible, like the whisper of a tornado.

I struggled harder, but how did you escape a storm when you couldn't run? Especially one that seemed to be speaking to you?

Rick flew. Or seemed to. His leap had sent him into the wind, and he sailed above the space between me and the steps.

He couldn't see our opponent any more than I could, so he grabbed onto me, wrenching me down as he dropped back to the ground. My captor kept its grip and would rip my head off, I thought. I wouldn't survive that, and I twisted to try to keep whole. My muscle and bone seemed to crack. Suddenly, it let go, and I fell along with Rick.

Visible above me, I finally saw something clearly: a weapon—a long staff with a sharpened point reaching out of the black wind. A wooden staff, expressly designed for killing vampires. *My bounty is for the priest . . .*

The spear aimed at Rick.

I lunged at it, hoping to shove it away, maybe even take the strike meant for him. I'd survive it, even if it struck my heart. It was only wood. But the spear withdrew, looped around me, and thrust again. Rick dodged, of course he did. Impossibly, though, the staff anticipated his movement. As fast as the vampire was, the spear tracked him, moving just as fast. He couldn't escape.

Columban shouted. "No!" He leapt from the stairs, toward the battle.

Rick fell away from the spear; Columban pushed him. And the spear went into Columban.

The priest fell, gripping the wooden shaft that protruded from his chest.

Columban was old, and in seconds his body returned to the state it would have been, buried in the ground all this time: rotting, blackened skin crumbling to ash, revealing muscle and bone that also crumbled to ash, his cassock decaying along with the flesh. Rick stumbled, staring at the disintegrating body with shock-widened eyes. The dust scattered, dispersing into the wind, leaving nothing behind. Columban might never have existed.

Rick stayed frozen at the spot where the vampire priest had been. I could have knocked him over myself. I paced around him, back and forth, manically trying to keep myself between him and the spear, which had pulled back into the whirling smoke. The point of it still tracked us. Since Rick wasn't paying attention, I had to defend him. It might strike at any moment.

Now Cormac was chanting, and it wasn't Latin.

He might have been at it for a while, and I hadn't noticed. Hardin was beside him, holding something—an extra hand to make up for Cormac's broken one. In his good hand, Cormac held a lighter, though getting it to work in the tempest would be a trick. They pressed toward us, opposing the gusts of wind. Hardin cupped both hands together, protecting whatever she held.

Rick looked up at Cormac, and his expression darkened into rage.

"Rick," I muttered, my voice rasping, dried out from the wind and full of repressed growling. That spear still lurked, and I prepared to leap at it, an attack of desperation.

Cormac's chanting increased in speed and volume, doing battle with the blasting of the wind until it reached a climax, a series of shouted, individual words. Then he flicked the lighter, using his body as a windbreak. Amazingly—magically, even—the flame came to life, flaring yellow. At the same moment, Hardin threw her handful into the air. Bits of dried herbs, shredded paper, who knew what else. The potpourri passed over the lighter flame and caught fire.

The burning debris rocketed toward us, propelled by the wind, by the spell, by Cormac's chanting. I ducked, pulling a still-stunned Rick down with me.

The spear had been moving toward Rick, ready to strike—but the cloud of fiery debris hit it. And vanished.

So did the smoke, wind, swirling dust, and oily vortex that had engulfed the church for what seemed like hours, but had probably only been a minute or two. The world fell still, and I could see the sky again, its dark arc and haze of reflected city lights. I gave a deep sigh—I'd been holding my breath. The air smelled burned.

A figure stood nearby, holding the spear. A woman. And she was bound. Flickering yellow ribbons, like fire given solid form, wrapped around the wooden shaft of her spear; around her arms, pulling them from her body so that she couldn't move; and around her legs and torso, anchoring her in place. Color and light slid along the bindings, giving the illusion of movement. But the figure remained immobilized.

She seemed tall—hard to tell how tall, because I was on the ground at her feet, looking up. From my vantage, she seemed to fill the sky. Muscular, she wore a close-fitting jacket, thick leather pants, tall boots. A biker's armor. Her dark hair was short, spiky. Straps fitting across her chest and around her waist held weapons. More wooden spears, along with blades, whips, a sword across her back, a nightstick at her hip. Nothing with moving parts, no guns, nothing apparently explosive, but lethal in so many ways all the same. She also wore tinted goggles strapped to her head, sealed tightly to her face, making her eyes seem huge, stark, against her pale skin. I couldn't tell if she was looking back at us. Her chest worked, taking in deep breaths, as if she were exhausted. A lingering cloud of black fog roiled in a layer at her feet.

Her mouth twisting, she lunged against ribbons that bound her. They didn't budge, and she threw herself forward again. The bindings only tightened. She didn't waste her energy struggling for long, and after the second attempt, she simply stared. At least, she seemed to. Who could tell with those goggles? Her lips pressed into a thin line. She might have been admitting defeat.

"Cormac . . ." I murmured.

"Huh," he said, as if surprised how this had turned out. "Hoped we'd catch something."

He *hoped*?

"Who the fuck are you?" Hardin said, gasping to recover her breath as much as the rest of us. All of us except Rick, at least.

The woman tipped up her chin in stoic refusal, like a prisoner of war.

"Do you have any idea who she is? Do you?" Hardin demanded of Cormac and Rick in turn.

Rick murmured, "I might have some ideas."

At the same time Cormac nodded, "Yeah, I think I do."

"I want to see her eyes," I said vaguely, frustrated at the dark lenses that made her expression blank. The face turned to me, and I flinched. I couldn't see her eyes, but I could feel her attention.

"The light hurts her eyes," Rick said. "It's dark where she comes from."

"But it's night," I said. "There isn't any light."

"It's *very* dark, where she comes from."

She let a smile flash. Just a tilting of her lips. One

gloved hand flexed on the spear; the other closed into a fist. I hoped Cormac's spell held.

Moments passed. The scene froze, the area around the church remaining incongruously quiet. Hardin's backup officers stood a ways off, guns at their sides, but they didn't know what to do next any more than the rest of us.

"Now that we've got her, what do we do with her?" I asked. What *was* she? Demon, I was guessing. But that covered so much ground and didn't tell me anything.

"Can I arrest her?" Hardin said. She was probably put out that she didn't get Columban after all.

Father Columban, who'd known what was coming all along. This demon had been hunting him, maybe for centuries. And now he was gone.

The first thing to do when you wanted information was to ask. Nicely, if possible. I stood and faced her. "You said you had a bounty on the priest, but that 'I'd do.' Father Columban said that all three of us were in danger." I gestured to include Rick, and asked, "Why?"

She actually answered, in clipped words. I couldn't place her accent. "He was a traitor. Like him. Like you."

"A traitor?" I said, indignant. "I'm not a traitor, I haven't betrayed anyone—"

"A bounty," Rick said, interrupting. "Placed by whom? Whom do you serve?"

She bared her teeth—straight, white, normal. I expected them to be sharpened, vicious. She gave the impression of laughing at us and said nothing.

"Did Roman send you?" I asked. "Dux Bellorum, Gaius Albinus?" He probably had a dozen other names I didn't know.

Now she did laugh, a short and mirthless sound. "Idiots."

"If not him, then who?" I said. Pleading.

"You know so little," she said, showing her teeth again.

"Then tell me. *Educate* me. What are we up against here?"

She said, "I was sent by the one who commands Dux Bellorum."

I tilted my head, as if that would help me hear better, though I'd heard her perfectly well. "And who is that?" I said.

Rick answered me: "Dux Bellorum is the general. The one who leads the army. Not the one who rules the nation. That would be Caesar."

I stared at Rick. I had never considered such a proposition, and now it rattled in my brain like bells. Church bells, sonorous, tolling doom.

Hardin was getting frustrated. "You still haven't said if I can arrest her or not."

"No," Cormac said. "I don't think you can."

"Well, I can't condone killing her if that's your other option."

"You don't kill something like this," Cormac said. "You banish it."

"Then you know what she is?" I said, my ears still ringing. *Who was Caesar?*

"Demon," Cormac said, which I'd already known—

I heard the wind before I felt it, a sucking noise, a single, powerful blast of air. The oily vortex reappeared. Narrow this time, it focused on a point—on the woman in leather. She braced against her bindings and tilted her head back.

Dust and debris smacked my face, but I didn't want to turn away. The tornado shrank, closing the demon in its circle, sucking black smoke into the ground. She opened her mouth, and I couldn't tell if she was laughing or screaming. The vortex collapsed, taking her with it, wind, dust, smoke, and demon, all of it falling into the ground, to nothing. The firelit ribbons that had bound her fell to the sidewalk, then turned to ash and scattered.

The air fell still, dust and smoke vanished. She was gone. My nose itched with the smell of soot.

Hardin spoke first. "What happened?" She looked around, not questioning anyone in particular.

I looked at Cormac. "What did you do?"

"I didn't do anything," Cormac said.

"Yes you did, something happened—"

"That wasn't me. Something yanked her back before I could do anything."

"Yanked her back? What? To where?" I asked.

"To wherever she came from. I don't know." Turning away, he rubbed his forehead, like he had a headache. I know I did.

Beside me, Rick looked lost for a moment, glancing around him, returning again and again to the spot where Columban had been. His expression was stark, eyes unblinking. I wanted to reach out to him— anyone else I would have hugged, tried to comfort. Tried to share the grief. But I couldn't touch him. I reached out my hand, then drew it back.

"Rick," I said softly.

Rick's gaze came to rest on Cormac. "You might as well have killed him yourself."

The vampire closed on him in a second, almost invisible with speed. Cormac had a stake in hand just as the vampire reached him. The tip of the stake rested on Rick's chest, but Rick's hands gripped Cormac's neck and squeezed. Cormac choked, but his hold on the stake didn't waver. Both were ready to deliver killing blows. Rick bared his teeth, showing prominent fangs. He was usually so good at keeping them hidden.

Shouting, I ran, the strength of my Wolf carrying me in a couple of long strides, and crashed between them. "Stop it!"

They fell back. Cormac held the stake at the ready; Rick was braced to fight. But they waited. Really, they didn't have to listen to me. But they did. I held out my arms, keeping a space between them.

Rick spat his words past me. "You knew what would happen when you broke his protections. You knew *something* would attack."

"Question is, did you?" Cormac appeared calm, but he was sweating with nerves. "Did he tell you what was after you both?"

"Both of you shut up," I said, the words growling, my teeth bared.

They looked at me, and might have shown some concern for my state of mind. I felt fur prickling just under the skin, and wished Ben were here, because all he'd have to do was touch my arm and I'd calm down. But hell, if me threatening to shift uncontrollably got them to stand down, so be it.

Rick lowered his arms, but Cormac wasn't moving that stake an inch. If I had to stay here all night, I would. I wasn't going to let them near each other.

Hardin had been at the curb along the street, talking to the uniformed officers she'd brought. They'd walked off, probably searching the area for any evidence, or random destruction, or whatever. I doubted they'd find anything. Seeing the three of us in a standoff, she put her hand on her holster and walked over.

"There a problem?"

I wasn't going to say anything—let one of them back down. When none of us answered, she continued. "Right, then who's going to explain to me what the *hell* just happened?"

Good question. I wanted someone to do the same for me. But Cormac and Rick kept glaring daggers at each other.

Maybe if I started thinking out loud. "Columban knew he was being hunted. I'm betting that fire in Hungary was part of it. He knew how to protect himself, but when the shield was destroyed—"

"I got all that," she said. "What about you and him? All that stuff she said at the end about being traitors? And Dux Bellorum? That's Roman, right? That megalomaniac vampire freak who came through a couple years ago? And where did she *go*?"

Right to the heart of it. How big was this really? Was this a backstreet scuffle, or a battle in an ongoing war? I knew where I was putting my money.

"You don't really want to know," I said weakly.

"Oh, yes I do." Her expression blazed.

"The Long Game," I said, swallowing to get control of my voice, to pull Wolf back to her cage.

"I've heard you both talk about that before. It's got something to do with Roman?"

"He's worse than you think, detective," I said.

"Kitty," Rick said. "You don't have to explain to her. You don't have to bring her into this."

On the contrary, I thought it was long past time we explained everything to her. I said to him, "We're looking for allies. I consider her an ally."

He nodded at Cormac. "You consider him an ally, too, and look what happened."

"Rick—" I begged.

The vampire glared at Cormac, who might very well have turned to a flaming crisp if he hadn't been wearing sunglasses to protect him from meeting Rick's gaze.

"I do not ever want to see you again," Rick said. "Be grateful I'm not forcing you to leave my city."

"What makes you think you could?"

"Don't push me."

For a moment, I thought Rick was going to try, right then and there. A demonstration, because however brash Cormac acted, Rick could get around that stake and overcome him. But I kept myself between them. I even caught Rick's gaze. Looked him in his blue eyes. He could have used his hypnotic power, commanded me to step aside, brought me under his control. But he didn't. *Please,* I tried to tell him, even though he wasn't telepathic. I was pretty sure he wasn't telepathic.

Rick turned and stalked off. In three strides, he'd vanished into the church's shadow. If I ran after him, he'd be gone. Again, he was gone.

"A little uptight, isn't he?" Cormac said. Humor

covering nerves. He was still holding the stake in a white-knuckled grip.

"Lay off him." My lip curled in a snarl.

He glanced at Hardin, back at me. Frowned. "You want to know where that demon came from, I've got some research to do." He stalked away, to the street and his Jeep.

"Cormac—"

He ignored me, just like I expected him to.

Where did that leave me? I looked around. The place didn't look any different than it had a week ago. The confrontation hadn't left any evidence behind. Not so much as a streak of soot on the concrete. Even the air smelled normal, full of people and cars, brick and asphalt, with a hint of distant mountains. A fire engine siren echoed somewhere.

Columban's markings, the ones that drew out the boundary of his protective circle, were gone.

"Are you okay?" Hardin asked. She'd put her gun away and stood, arms crossed.

"I don't know," I said. "I guess I will be."

"Can I take you out for a cup of coffee?"

That sounded like a marvelous idea to me.

We ended up at a twenty-four-hour diner a few blocks away, on Colfax. The waitstaff recognized Hardin and sat us in a booth in back, in relative quiet and privacy.

I called Ben.

"Hey," he said. "I was just going to call you. Shaun and I tracked Darren. He's out of here. Loaded up his car and drove. I don't think we have to worry."

"Okay," I said, my voice flat. "Good."

"Kitty—what's wrong?"

My breath shuddered out of me. I didn't know where to start. "We had a bit of a showdown at the church. It . . . didn't go well."

"Are you okay? Where are you? I'll come get you—"

"I'm fine, I'm with Detective Hardin."

"You're not under arrest, are you?" He didn't sound like he'd be surprised if I were, which made me smile.

"No. We're having coffee and talking. I'll come home straight after, probably in an hour or so."

"You're sure?"

"It makes me really happy that you'd rush over here to get me, you know that?" Even after a thirty-second conversation with him, I felt better.

"Good, I guess. But I don't think I'll be happy until you get home. So hurry."

"I will." I clicked off the phone.

The coffee arrived, and Hardin looked at me. "I don't want to hold you up too long, but I really need to know what happened, and what I'm supposed to tell my Interpol guy about Columban."

I took a long drink. What was it about hot caffeine

that made everything better? Even Wolf settled. My skin stopped itching with prickling fur.

"I don't have all the answers. I can only tell you my side of it."

"Well then, why don't you get started?"

I told her about the Long Game, or what I knew of it. That there were networks of vampires, some of who were gathering power, others who opposed them. Roman, his followers, the coins they possessed. They were trying to take our cities from us, and we had to try to hold the line. No matter how much I learned, there was always more I didn't know. I peeled back layers of the onion, and I always found more underneath. But this was all coming to a head. The two sides would clash. We had to be ready.

"What?" Hardin said, staring at me like I was crazy; or worse, worried that I was right. "Like a literal war? Some kind of battle?"

"I don't know. Something. Roman's gathering allies, and they're everywhere. We've been trying to collect allies of our own, but it all seems to go wrong. Columban was supposed to be an ally." My lips turned in a wince.

"He was wanted for murder."

"Or was he defending himself against that demon? Did he start the fire, or did that demon, when she tried to attack him?"

Turning thoughtful, she looked away. "I thought I was starting to get a handle on this shit."

"I don't think it's possible." You thought you knew, and then the universe opened a vortex and dropped a bounty-hunting demon in your lap. What a world. "I wouldn't be surprised if your Interpol contact has some wind of the Long Game. Maybe even of Roman or some of his allies. Maybe they have some mashed-up coins in evidence."

She ran a hand through her hair, which was coming loose from its ponytail. "I've got enough to worry about just looking after Denver. I don't know if I can take on any more."

I said, "If there's any way you guys can pool information, set up some kind of database, compare cases—"

"You think we'll find patterns."

"Yeah, I think you will. I don't know if it'll help, but it couldn't hurt."

After a moment of thought, she gave a fatalistic nod. "All right. I'm in."

I HAD to see Rick. Somehow. The next night, I went to Obsidian and knocked on the basement door. I brought him a present, wrapped in a brown paper bag.

Angelo answered. Instead of his usual smirk and

put-down, he stared at me with stark desperation, silently, as if he couldn't find words. He smelled frightened, sweaty. What had happened to him? The hairs on my neck stood up, but I tried to act neutral. Normal.

"Is he in?" I asked, gesturing hopefully to the back hallway. "In and willing to talk to me, I mean?"

Gripping the door frame, he glanced over his shoulder, turned an anxious gaze back to me. "You have to talk some sense into him, please. He won't listen to any of us."

"What are you talking about?"

"He's packing to leave." That was the expression he was showing me, I realized: that of a person whose spouse was walking out, and he couldn't do anything about it.

There had to be a mistake. "But—he told me last night he'd decided to stay—"

"That was before. Please, talk to him." He grabbed my sleeve and pulled me through the doorway.

Baring my teeth, I snarled and shoved him off, backing into the hallway, away from him. What the hell was going on here?

"Please, Kitty, talk to him!"

"I can't believe he'd just abandon all his ties here," I said, but the argument didn't sound persuasive.

"Rick doesn't *have* any ties here," Angelo said.

"But you're his Family, you all are connected, surely he'll listen—"

"None of us are Rick's progeny. Not directly. Most of us were Arturo's, and we became connected to Rick through him when Rick took his blood. As far as I know, from everything I've heard, Rick has never created another vampire."

That sounded impossible. "At all? Ever? In five hundred years of existence?"

"Not one," Angelo said.

The Master vampires gained power by creating minions and maintaining control over their progeny. Rick—he'd traveled through his five hundred years alone. All his power was his own.

"You have to talk to him," Angelo said. "You're the only one he listens to."

"You're giving me way too much credit."

"Please, try," he said, and pointed down the hallway to the closed door of Rick's office and living room.

My nerves were on fire as I walked the last few paces to that door. Angelo stayed where he was, slumped against the wall, hugging himself, anguished.

I knocked on the door and called, "Rick? Can I talk to you for a minute?" Tried to sound casual and nonthreatening. The paper bag crinkled in my grip.

Time ticked on. After what happened last night, I wouldn't blame Rick if he decided never to speak to me again. But finally the door opened, and there he was. I looked up, earnest and hopeful, probably close to the sad little puppy I felt like.

He appeared much as he had at the church, though the jeans and T-shirt were fresh. His dark hair was ruffled, as if he'd been pulling at it. The suave aristocrat in the silk shirt he usually showed to the world was gone.

After regarding me blank-faced for a moment, he turned away, leaving the door open. I took that as an invitation. He didn't say anything, didn't look at me, just went straight back to his desk at one end of the room. Its drawers were open, and he was putting items into a black canvas duffel bag. Packing, as Angelo had said.

"I brought you a present," I said, holding up the bag.

"I'm sorry, I'll probably have to leave it behind. I'm traveling light."

My throat tightened, and I had to work to talk like nothing was wrong. "Where are you going?"

"Italy," he said. "Vatican City." He moved a pair of small, ancient-looking leather-bound books into the bag, then wrapped a chipped clay cup in a scarf and packed it away.

"I thought you said you were going to stay," I said, pleading.

"I have to tell them what happened to Father Columban."

"Can't you call? Write a letter?"

Pausing, he leaned on the desk a moment. A living human would have taken a deep breath, but he gathered his thoughts silently. "I thought it best that I tell them in person."

"You think you have to replace him in the Order of Saint Lazarus of the Shadows."

He bowed his head. His hands, resting on the desk, clenched into fists. "I—I would like to meet the other members of the order. It's important to me."

"But you'll be back?"

The pursed lips, the glance away, were something of an answer.

"Would you like to sit?" He gestured to the sofa on the other side of the room, and he joined me there. I perched on the edge of the cushion, wondering what I could possibly say to change his mind. Surely I could say something.

I just couldn't think of what.

He radiated the chill of his bloodless, undead vampire nature. It should have felt unnatural, making me nervous, but he was just Rick. He'd always been like that. No heartbeat, no breath. But still human, somehow. He studied his hands, resting on his lap.

He said, "Father Columban told me a very strange thing—the order knew about Fray Juan, the vampire who made me. He used to be one of them, but turned apostate and fled. They assumed he had been destroyed during the Inquisition. Many vampires were. But they never imagined he'd fled to the colonies to start his own empire. Columban actually thanked me for destroying him and preventing that. Because Columban didn't just know Fray Juan—he was the one who made him a vampire. So Columban was my grand-progenitor. I could have learned so much from him."

"You and Columban were shut up in there for days. Is that what you did all that time? Talk about history, where you came from?"

"Isn't it enough?" he said. "We talked, told stories, prayed. Confessed. A lot of sins to confess, after five hundred years. Many acts of contrition to say. It was . . . good. To feel some sort of absolution."

"A Catholic vampire. Well then."

"So you understand why I must go, to tell them what happened. To learn whatever I can, to help them."

"I *don't* understand." Except that I did. He'd had a glimpse of something he thought he'd lost. He wanted more. I shook my head. "I'm sorry about what happened. If I hadn't set Cormac on the trail—"

"Blame doesn't solve anything. Only forgiveness. You did what you thought was right. So did Cormac and Detective Hardin for that matter."

"That woman—the demon—she would have killed us, if Cormac hadn't stopped her. I'm pretty sure a few of her knives were silver."

"Yes. Father Columban knew that the three of us were in danger," he said. "She was after *us*, the vampires and lycanthropes."

"Why?"

"Because of what we are. Is there another reason?"

I pondered that. As if I didn't have enough to worry about. "Is she gone for good, or will she be back?"

"I don't know. We have enemies, we already knew that. The details hardly matter."

Unless the details told us how to kick their asses. I imagined Rick was taking the long view here, as usual.

"Do you remember when we first met?" I asked.

"I do," he said, a smile playing on his lips. "I think you'd been a werewolf for all of six months. Everything terrified you."

"Can you blame me?" I had almost forgotten those days myself. Repressed them. I had no idea what it must have looked like from the outside. But Rick would remember.

"Not at all," he said. "Around all those hardened wolves you were so . . ."

"So what?"

"Unworn. Fresh. It's an odd piece of fate that threw you among Carl's folk. Trial by fire."

"Wasn't so bad," I said, but the words felt false. I only said that because I knew now, after meeting dozens of other werewolves and seeing other packs, how much worse it could have been. Or I honestly didn't remember how bad it *had* been. Just as well, probably. Darren was more right about me and how I started out than he knew. "But that wasn't what I expected you to say. More like inexperienced. Naïve."

"It's a matter of perspective, I think. Others saw you as weak. I thought you had a lot of promise. You were a survivor."

I looked at my hands twisted together, because my eyes had started stinging. I didn't want to cry, not here. "The first time we met, you were the only one in that crowd, all the werewolves and vampires jockeying for status and position, who treated me like a person. You didn't care if I was weak or strong, you didn't expect me to behave a certain way. You asked how I was doing. And then you listened. I don't even remember what I said, I think I rambled for a long time about nothing in particular."

"You said you were doing all right, but you weren't. You were sad and nervous and confused, but couldn't say it so you talked around it."

"And then you backed me up when I started doing the show. Everyone else wanted me to quit."

"That was about the time you stopped being so confused."

"I'm still confused."

"But not about who you are. Not like you were then."

"Is that because I'm more comfortable with the werewolf thing, or because I've gotten older?"

"Yes," he said, his smile turning lopsided.

"I guess you would know about getting older."

"I would."

Rick had become one of my favorite people in the world. Bloodsucking vampire and all. How had that happened?

I bit my lip. "Angelo told me you've never made another vampire. You may be Master of the city but you don't have vampires of your own. Is that true?"

"Angelo must be smitten with you, to start telling you my secrets."

I chuckled. "I don't know about that. So, is it true?"

"It's true. It's simple, really. Why would I inflict on anyone else what happened to me? It would bring me power. But no. I wouldn't put that burden on my soul."

"You're a good person, you know that?"

"I've at least come to believe that I'm not entirely damned."

There wasn't going to be a good moment for this, but I'd dragged the thing all this way so I might as well go through with it.

"I brought you a present," I said, retrieving the paper bag and handing it to him.

"And it's not even my birthday," he said. Peeling back the opening, he reached for the object within and drew it out to the open.

It was the vampire crystal skull. Rick held it before

him, staring at it eye to eye. In the muted lamplight, the thing glowed golden. The little crystal fangs glinted.

"Alas, poor Yorick?" Rick said at last.

"I was hoping you'd say that," I said, grinning.

"Well, happy to oblige. I expect it'll make a nice bookend. Unless there's some ancient Mayan curse on this I should know about?"

"Naw," I said, turning it over to point at the base. "It has MADE IN INDIA etched on the bottom. I just didn't mention that part on the show."

"Thank you. I think." He stood and went to the bookshelves on the wall, where he found a niche for it. But then he returned to the duffel bag and zipped it closed. "Angelo will look after the city while I'm gone," he said.

Like I thought a kitsch item, however lovingly given, would convince him to stay.

"Angelo doesn't want the job," I said, standing, begging. "He's a wreck out there. I thought he was going to cry."

"He'll grow into the part."

I had my doubts about that. "As soon as they hear you're gone, Roman's minions will be all over the city," I said.

"I don't think they will," he said. "They know you're here, after all."

"Rick—"

"Kitty. I have to go." He came around the desk to stand in front of me. He seemed so calm. At peace, even. He ought to be on the edge of tears and shouting, like me.

When he stepped forward, arms open, I fell into his hug. We stood like that for a good long moment, me gripping his shoulders, him holding me.

"Take care of yourself, all right?" he ordered, as we pulled apart.

I nodded, unable to say a word.

AND THEN I left.

Angelo was still sulking by the outside door. He glanced up when I approached. "Well?"

"He's leaving," I said. "I'm sorry."

"He's an idiot," he muttered. The anguish from before seemed to have fallen away. Now, he just seemed tired, slumped against the wall, frowning deeply.

I was going to have to deal with this guy on a regular basis. All that posturing, when he was a minion who got off on treating me like a stupid werewolf— we'd have to leave that behind. Water under the bridge. We had a city to protect.

"He's a man with a mission. For what it's worth, he seems to think you'll do just fine as Master of Denver."

The man's chuckle was bitter. "It's not being Master of the city I'm worried about. I can handle that. I can even work with you, if I have to. But I'm not sure I can stand up against Dux Bellorum the way you and Rick have."

That was where the fear came from, then. He wasn't even wrong to be afraid, even without knowing the whole story. My smile might have been a little stiff, thinking of the goggle-eyed demon and a theoretical Caesar.

"Oh, it's not Dux Bellorum we have to worry about," I said.

He stared at me as I walked past him and into the night.

Epilogue

Wasn't it nice, having a literal pack of supernaturally strong guys to call on to help us move?

We did the whole thing in a day—loaded the truck, hauled it across town, unloaded it into the house we'd finally settled on. Southwest of Denver, closer to the mountains, but still with reasonable access to the city. The place wasn't huge, but it was on a full acre of land, adjoining county open space. Like Carl and Meg's place had been, but not *just* like. A more modern house, with an open layout, big kitchen, and high ceilings. I walked in and breathed easier. I'd been living in dorm and apartment-sized spaces since college. This was going to be an adjustment.

The pack finished, and I fed them like a good alpha should, with mountains of barbeque, sodas, and beer. I could throw parties in a place like this. I could have the family over, even. Cheryl's kids could play in the backyard.

After everyone left, Ben and I sat on the patio in the quiet backyard, regarding our view of the sunset over the mountains. Clouds streaked orange and pink against a fading blue sky. Scrub oak marked the boundaries of the property, and wild grasses replaced the lawn. The yard needed a little work after a winter of neglect. I looked forward to it. This was *ours*.

"We did it," I said, sounding more than a little startled. "I can't believe we did it. Look at us, house in the suburbs."

"Well, we still have to clean and rent out the old place, get the mail transferred, do something about this yard, finish the basement—"

"Details," I said. "It's all details." I leaned over and kissed his cheek, and he smiled.

My senses stretched out. I smelled deer, rabbits, coyotes, fox, and a dozen other creatures on the wind. A feast, right on our doorstep. In my gut, Wolf stretched. She wanted out, to run through this space and mark it as her own.

Not now, I told her. Time enough for that later. Now, we were human beings with a house and a bed and all was well.

Ben's hand closed around mine. "You're feeling it, too?"

Our Wolves spoke to each other, smelling the need

on each other's bodies, feeling the tension in the other's muscles.

"Next full moon," I said. "It'll come soon enough."

I WAS as nervous as I had been meeting my own in-laws. Well, in-law. Ben's mother was sweet and welcoming, if a bit sad. Ben's father was still in prison on a decade-old weapons conviction. Not only was I not sure I wanted to meet him, I wasn't sure Ben wanted me to meet him. They'd had a falling out, when Ben refused to represent him in court. He hardly ever talked about him.

Family was such a fraught thing. However tangled and difficult it was, pack was family. Trey was bringing his fiancée, Sam, to New Moon to meet us.

"This is weird," I muttered at Ben. "They're not looking for some kind of approval, are they? Because that shouldn't matter, if they love each other that's it, right?"

He was smiling at me, amused by my discomfort as he often was. Like I was this social science experiment playing out in front of him. Thank goodness one of us was laid back. More likely, I had a feeling he just hid his nerves better than I did. I had to *talk* about everything.

"It's a version of that thing that happens when two

different groups of friends collide," he said. "You just want everyone to get along. Imagine how nervous Trey probably is right now."

Yeah, no doubt. Bringing the love of your life to meet the parents, or wolf parents, or whatever.

The front door opened, and I stood. There he was, and I swore I saw his tail wagging. He held the door and guided her in, fussing, hovering near her shoulder, almost trembling with enthusiasm as he gazed longingly at her. I wondered if she recognized the body language and understood how much devotion he was showing her.

She was cute, with short, dark hair, and a round face. Dressed for business in a skirt and blouse, pumps with low heels. No jewelry or makeup, just her own beaming smile. Sensible, friendly. She clasped his hand as Trey led her across the dining room. I decided I liked her.

They reached our table, Trey made introductions, and there was an awkward shuffle while everyone sat. We ordered drinks, and finally we had to get past the small talk to the issue at hand.

"It's really good meeting you, Sam. Trey hasn't talked about anything but you for a month."

Blushing, she smiled at him. Yeah, I liked her.

She pulled a familiar-looking book from her purse. "I'm almost embarrassed to ask, I'm sure you get this all the time—would you sign this for me?"

I did, happy to. "Trey said it answered some of your questions?"

"I don't know if it answered them . . . but it did make me feel better. Like maybe this isn't so weird after all. I have to be honest, I'm not sure what I should think about you all. This pack thing," Sam said, wincing. "Trey tried to explain it, that you were sort of like family, but not really, or maybe a little like AA, but not really—I'm a little confused."

Werewolf pack as group therapy? There's a thought. I considered for a moment and said, "Think of us as a really weird set of in-laws you might have to deal with every now and then."

A spark of understanding lit her eyes. I asked about her job, their plans, and then let them talk. Under the table, I held Ben's hand.

I CALLED my brother-in-law Mark and made him promise to watch the kids on Saturday night, so I could kidnap Cheryl. She complained—10 P.M. was way past her bedtime. Whatever. She only agreed to it when *Mark* told her she needed to get out and have some fun. She hadn't smiled in months, it seemed like. Maybe I could help.

"Wear something punk," I said when I called to tell her I was picking her up.

"Punk? I don't think I have anything punk, not anymore. Not that'll actually fit."

"I've seen you wear that ratty Ramones T-shirt you've had since high school. That and your grossest pair of jeans." Which I'd also seen. They were pretty gross, covered in paint streaks and missing both knees. She kept them specifically for housework.

"Since when do you get to tell me what's punk?"

"I'll see you in an hour," I said in my most chipper voice.

She did a pretty good job with the punk thing, in exactly the jeans and Ramones T-shirt I'd told her to wear, with her hair in a ponytail and black eyeliner marking her eyes. Especially considering I didn't think she'd been out to a club or concert in a dozen years. Well, we were going to change that.

I drove us downtown, wove my way into the night-life traffic on Broadway, and sprang the cash for the convenient parking rather than trying to hunt for free parking ten blocks away.

"Why can't you just tell me where you're taking me?"

"A guy at KNOB told me about this club that does a pretty rocking eighties' night. I wanted to check it out and thought you might like it." Also, the only vampires likely to hang out there were any who were made in the eighties, and I didn't think the Denver Family had any of those. Either way, they weren't likely to give me trouble.

"This is going to be weird," Cheryl said, not sounding at all convinced that it would also be *fun*.

"We don't have to stay long," I said. "I'll put a couple of drinks in you, we'll listen to the music, and you can not think about kids or getting a job or anything for an hour. Okay?"

She gave a decisive nod. "Okay."

I followed Matt's directions to find the club, in the basement of a much hipper bar. We entered through a door in the back. I paid our cover, we got our hands stamped, and I dragged Cheryl inside.

The DJ had just put on "99 Luftballons." I couldn't have timed our entrance better for pure emotional nostalgic hit than if I'd done it on a Hollywood soundstage.

"Oh my God," Cheryl said, stopping at the edge of the room, a cramped dance floor ringed by white vinyl booths, with a well-stocked bar at the far end. Candy-colored lights broke the darkness. "It's tenth grade all over again."

Except we were old enough to drink without fake IDs, now. "Rum and Coke?" I asked.

"Yeah. Sure." Her mouth was open, astonished, like she really had traveled through time back to high school. I guided her to an empty booth and made her sit.

For the most part, the music was a few years before my time. But it hit Cheryl's adolescent sweet

spot exactly. In hindsight, she might have indirectly
set me on my path. We were far enough apart in age
that she hadn't wanted much to do with me when she
hit her teen years, but I thought she was a goddess
and tried to follow in her footsteps. Mostly by listening to her music, which led to me listening to *my*
music, then to deejaying at the college radio station,
then to KNOB. And, well, everything else.

Yeah, the music here was a little like time travel.

I got her a drink, me a plain Coke, and headed
back to the booth.

Matt must have known I'd like the place, the min-
imalist design in monochrome, white-and-black
checks painted on the walls, just a couple of lighting
effects in play. The crowd here was a mix of a dozen
different cliques that I could spot right off, and nobody hassled anybody. Goths in black vinyl, some
bachelorette party in cocktail dresses and feather
boas, young kids laughing at the theme, middle-aged
former punks who'd been dancing to this music for
twenty-five years. And plenty just like me and
Cheryl, in jeans and T-shirts, looking for a good
night out.

Everyone here but me was human, as far as I could
tell. The smells were all normal—sweat, alcohol, dry-
wall that needed repairs, a floor that needed to be
cleaned. No fur under the skin, no chilled blood on

the air, no weird magic. I hadn't felt this mainstream in years.

I could watch people all night, leaning back in the booth and sipping my soda, Wolf resting contentedly for once. Half the people on the floor were dancing and texting at the same time, which made for a pretty neat trick. More songs followed, and it didn't seem possible but each seemed more iconic and nostalgia-inducing than the one before it. Pet Shop Boys, Erasure, Blondie . . .

Next to me, Cheryl wiped at her cheek and sniffed. More tears followed.

"Hey," I said, leaning in.

Her face grimaced in a vain attempt at a smile. "This is making me maudlin."

I hadn't meant to make her cry. I just wanted to get her out of the house. "We can go—"

She kept talking. "You know I think it's been twenty years since I heard this song? How did that happen? What have I been doing all this time?"

"Living?"

"It seems like I should have done . . . *more*."

I put my arm across her shoulders and pulled her close. We sat like that through the next dozen songs, until around midnight, when the music starting turning harsher, more industrial and less New Wave, and Cheryl was ready to go home.

* * *

A COUPLE of weeks later, Cormac called and said he'd found something.

The first time he came over to the new house, he never really said whether he liked it. He looked around at the spacious living room, out the sliding glass door to the great outdoors, and said, "Awfully domestic of you."

"I thought that was the point," I said. Cormac had never been very domestic, and I couldn't imagine him ever choosing a house in the suburbs. I felt a little bit of a pang at that thought, at the long lost might-have-beens. We'd traveled a long way since then.

"And next time you break your arm, we have a guest room for you," Ben said.

"I hope I never break a damn thing again."

By this visit, his arm was out of the cast and sling and in a neoprene brace. He still kept it close, favoring it. He was supposed to be going to physical therapy to get it back to its former strength and usefulness. I bugged him about it, asking if he was actually going, and he never gave me a straight answer. I hoped that Amelia was making him go. It was her arm, too, in a way.

Times like these, it was almost like they were married, which was an odd thought. I didn't dwell on it.

We sat on stools around the island counter in the

kitchen and ate pizza. That had been another consideration in choosing this house—wilderness was nice and all, but we had to be in range of pizza delivery. After eating and small talk, Cormac pulled a book from a jacket pocket—a thick hardcover with a fraying cloth binding. I couldn't see a title.

"I've been reading up on that thing that attacked the church. What I have isn't real satisfying," he said. He looked down, watched his fingers tap the edges of the cover. "It's a demon, but that's a catchall term. Lots of supernatural beings get called demons if people don't know what else to call them, or the name is untranslatable. This one didn't do much to identify herself—she might even have been a human magician if it weren't for the smoke, and the way she escaped—"

"Wait, she escaped? She's not . . . gone?" I didn't say *dead,* which might not have meant much, depending on her origin.

"She got pulled back to wherever she came from," he said.

Ben asked, "So what is she?"

Cormac pursed his lips like he didn't want to answer. Then he said, "Amelia thinks she was one of the fallen."

"Fallen what?" I said.

"Fallen angels."

We stared at him, absorbing that little tidbit.

"You're serious," Ben said finally.

Cormac opened the book to a page he'd marked and started reading, following the line with a finger. "'Such place Eternal Justice had prepared for those rebellious, here their prison ordained in utter darkness . . .'"

The tinted goggles she wore, because even the nighttime glow was too bright for her. Disbelieving, I said, "That's *Paradise Lost*. Milton."

"It's just an idea," he said.

"She was from hell? Actual, real, capital H hell?"

He said, "You like to talk about how a lot of the stories are real, or at least have a seed of truth that inspired them. Maybe it was something like her and wherever she came from that started the stories. Not sure it really matters. Whoever summoned the demon to go after the vampire priest—some brand of ceremonial magician most likely—is probably the one holding Roman's leash. That's your Caesar."

The rabbit hole got a little deeper. "And who is that?"

"I did some hunting around at the church. Didn't find anything."

"You hire an assassin so no one can trace you," Ben said.

"Yeah," Cormac said. "I'd have assumed it was Roman who'd summoned her, if she hadn't said anything."

"There's really nothing we can do but keep on keeping on, is there?"

"You can be damn careful is what you can do," Cormac said. "Amelia'll put up protections around the house, your cars, the restaurant, the radio station."

"I'll let Angelo know—his places will need protecting, too."

"Angelo," Cormac said. "Then Rick really did leave?"

I looked down, studying abandoned pizza crusts left in the cardboard box. From the outside, nothing in Denver would look like it had changed. But the vampires I talked to, Angelo and his minions, were subdued. Wounded, almost. From their perspectives, they'd been abandoned. It didn't matter if Rick had a mission. Me, I just missed my friend. I assumed he'd arrived in Italy all right, but I hadn't heard from him yet. I wasn't sure I would.

Taking the silence as his answer, Cormac shrugged, ultimately unconcerned. "See if this guy wants my help first. What are the odds?"

Angelo probably wouldn't want Cormac's help any more than Cormac wanted to give it. "So much for the great alliance," I muttered and took a long drink of beer.

Cormac said, "I'm not sorry for what I did."

"I'm not expecting you to be," I said.

"Does anyone want another beer?" Ben said, getting

up and heading to the fridge. A diplomatic interruption.

Cormac leaned back and picked at the seam on his wrist brace, turning inward as he often did—having a discussion with his resident spirit, most likely. Maybe she could talk some sense into him. I had a thought: if I asked her what he was really thinking, would she tell me? At least he didn't walk out. He would have, not so long ago. Back when he thought he didn't have anything to lose.

That may have been the most terrifying part of this war I insisted that we all fight: we had so much to lose. Would it be worth it? Would I ever know?

Ben returned from the fridge, and after popping bottlecaps and distributing the goods, held up his bottle. "Here's to achieving victory by the seat of our pants."

"And kicking ass," Cormac said, clinking bottles.

I considered them. For now, the moment was quiet. I had to let the future take care of itself. Smiling, I raised my own bottle.

"Here's to family."

A little more Kitty is never a bad thing....

Kitty in the Underworld

NEW YORK TIMES BESTSELLING AUTHOR

CARRIE VAUGHN

AS DENVER ADJUSTS TO A NEW MASTER VAMPIRE,
Kitty gets word of an intruder in the Denver werewolf pack's
territory and investigates the challenge to her authority...
only to be lured into a trap, tranquilized, and captured.

Kitty awakes in a defunct silver mine: the perfect cage for
a werewolf. Her captors are a cult seeking to induct her
into their ranks in a ritual they hope will put an end to Dux
Bellorum. Whatever she decides, they expect Kitty to join them
in their plot...willingly or otherwise.

★**"ENTERTAINMENT EXEMPLIFIED!"**
—*RT Book Reviews*, 4 ½ stars,
on *Kitty's Big Trouble*

TOR

Award-winning authors
Compelling stories

Please join us at the website
below for more information
about this author and other great
Tor selections, and to sign up for
our monthly newsletter!